ROYAL ELITE BOOK FIVE

VICIOUS
PRINCE

ROYAL ELITE
SCHOOL

RINA KENT

This novel is entirely a work of fiction. The names, characters and incidents portrayed in it are the work of the author's imagination. Any resemblance to actual persons, living or dead, events or localities is entirely coincidental.

To the ones who wear a smile like a loaded gun.

AUTHOR NOTE

Hello reader friend,

I usually dream of my plots and characters. However, *Vicious Prince* is a book that spoke to me instead. Ronan and Teal lived in me for a long time after I finished writing. There are scenes that were so raw and visceral, but I forged on anyway because I owe those two that much.

If you haven't read my books before, you might not know this, but I write darker stories that can be upsetting and disturbing. My books and main characters aren't for the faint of heart.

This book deals with molestation. I trust you know your triggers before you proceed.

To remain true to the characters, the vocabulary, grammar, and spelling of *Vicious Prince* is written in British English.

Vicious Prince can be read on its own, but for better understanding of Royal Elite world, it's recommended to read the previous books in the series first.

Royal Elite Series:
#0 *Cruel King*
#1 *Deviant King*
#2 *Steel Princess*
#3 *Twisted Kingdom*
#4 *Black Knight*
#5 *Vicious Prince*
#6 *Ruthless Empire*

Don't forget to Sign up to Rina Kent's Newsletter at www.subscribepage.com/rinakent for news about future releases and an exclusive gift.

He's prince charming. Just not hers.

I have a secret.

I stole a heart, or rather a marriage contract.

It wasn't mine to own, to look at or to even consider.

But it was there for the taking so I took it.

Huge mistake.

Ronan Astor is a nobility in this world.

Arrogant player.

Heartless bastard.

Vicious prince.

Now, he's out to destroy me.

What he doesn't know is that I'm out to destroy him too.

My name is Teal Van Doren, and I'm where princes go to die.

PLAYLIST

Worst In Me—Unlike Pluto

Nightmare—Halsey

Dying In A Hot Tub—Palaye Royale

The Last Of The Real Ones—Fall Out Boy

Alone—I Prevail

What A Man Gotta Do—Jonas Brothers

Bad Liar—Imagine Dragons

To Tell You The Truth—Written by Wolves

Doctor Doctor—YUNGBLUD

Popular Monster—Falling In Reverse

Imaginary Illness—Call Me Karizma

Old Me—5 Seconds of Summer

I'm Gonna Show You Crazy—Bebe Rexha

Play with Fire—Sam Tinnesz & Yacht Money

Everything Black—Unlike Pluto & Mike Taylor

Circles—Post Malone

Sick of Me—GARZI & Travis Barker

Leach—Bones UK

ROYAL ELITE BOOK FIVE

VICIOUS PRINCE

ONE

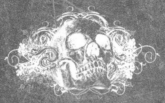

Teal

The beginning is the end.

The beginning is when you decide how the finale will be.

For some people, the ending is a mystery and the greatest discovery of all.

Not for me.

I'd already decided the end before I'd even started. It's all in folders, tucked in neat boxes and waiting to be unleashed on the world.

Like Pandora's box.

I've come so far. I dreamt of this—or rather had nightmares about it. This scenario has existed in every night terror, in every sleep paralysis where he sat on my chest like a fucking grim reaper.

He stole my breath, my life, my damn existence.

And now, I'll steal his.

My name is Teal Van Doren, and I'm a thief.

The type who's not interested in pieces of jewellery or goods, but the type who's after lives.

His life.

"Teal?"

At the sound of the soft voice from my right, I lift my

head from my phone, shifting my focus from the article about Napoleon's war tactics.

My foster sister, Elsa, watches me with a slight furrow between her brows. Her golden blonde hair is tucked into a long ponytail that covers her slender back. The look in her electric blue eyes is filled with concern and…something else I can't identify.

The only reason I figured out the concern is because of the twisting of her lips, the furrow of her brows, and the way she's clutching the strap of her backpack. It's some sort of a tell with her, which makes it easier to figure out her emotions.

At least this one. Usually, she maintains a resting bitch face that's hard to decipher.

Or it's probably because I'm bad at this human interaction business.

Some are born for peopling; I was born for anything that doesn't include that.

Elsa is the definition of angelic beauty with her pale skin and slim figure. However, I've never once felt non-existent beside her, even with my short black hair in a blunt lob and my generally grim makeup. When people started calling me adorable with snow-like beauty in my youth, I smothered it.

What others find beautiful escapes me, so when I first met her, I thought she was the bitch heiress to Dad's fortune. She proved me wrong by the way she acts—like right now.

As if she took lessons from my brother, she always makes sure I'm not too lost in my head.

We're walking to the first class of the day. The grand hall of Royal Elite School, or RES, nearly swallows us. It's one of those schools the privileged have direct access to, the type of school the greatest names in the UK attend, Dad included. The feeling that I'm continuing in Dad's footsteps is one of the reasons why I tolerated the idea of leaving Birmingham to come all the way to London.

And *him*.

The one who'll soon go down.

Other than that, nothing interests me here. Not the high towers, the prestigious education, or the students with millions in their trust funds.

They look at me like I'm a freak, and I don't acknowledge them at all.

Why?

Because I was never interested in fitting in.

You can't covet something you never actually wanted or even thought about.

I have my world, and no one is welcome in.

Sometimes, like now, their faces blur until their features blend into each other, leaving stark lines behind.

Wrenching my attention from them, I focus on Elsa. "Yes?"

"I heard about your deal with Dad." She retrieves a bar of dark chocolate.

I don't hesitate when I take it from her and have a bite, savouring the rich taste. Elsa acts like an older sister even though she's only a few weeks older than me.

"You don't have to do that, Teal." Her voice softens.

"Don't have to do what?" I steal another look at the Napoleon article.

"You know." She clutches me by the elbow of my uniform's jacket, which is my cue to pay attention.

"It's not rocket science, Elsa. Dad needs help, so I stepped up."

She traps her lower lip under her teeth, and I'm not sure if it's some sort of seduction tactic or her way of reining something in. I've seen her do that with her boyfriend, and I still can't figure it out.

I'll go with the need to suppress something because I doubt she'd want to seduce me. That would be, eh, awkward, especially since I'm almost certain she's kind of figured out who my crush is.

"Dad would never make you do something you don't want, Teal. Remember how he acted when I refused the arranged marriage?"

That's because you're his biological daughter and his pride.

Not that Dad doesn't like me and my twin brother. He's taken care of us since that day he found us curled up in balls, bleeding and starved to death.

But the fact remains: we're only his foster children. Elsa is his real daughter.

"I volunteered," I say.

Elsa stops in the middle of the hall, drawing some attention from onlookers. "What?"

I lift a shoulder. "I told Dad I'd do it."

"But the other time you asked me if this was what I wanted to do. I thought you were against arranged marriages."

"I was asking if you wanted to do it, and if you didn't, I would step up. Someone has to help Dad after you chose not to."

"Ouch." She grimaces.

"Eh, sorry, I guess." Since I started to somehow grasp human nature, I've learnt they get offended when the truth is shoved in their faces. My twin brother Knox says I'm too direct and that I sound like a bitch.

"It's okay. I know your mind is only thinking about getting the point across."

My lips part as her mouth pulls into a smile. She…knows. All this time, only Knox and Dad understood the way my brain works. I never thought Elsa would catch on this soon.

"Thank you." My voice is barely above a murmur, and I take another bite of the chocolate to fill the silence.

"Teal." She clutches my shoulders and meets my gaze. "It's not that I didn't want to help Dad. It's that I couldn't marry someone else since I'm in love with Aiden. That's not how it works."

In love.

Not how it works.

I allow my brain to pause on those words and their foreign meanings. Elsa keeps saying these things, and I crash into them every time as if they're a metal wall.

Sure, I know the dictionary definition of love, but that's only theoretical. The real world is the practical field, and there's no such thing as love.

There are hormones, neurotransmitters, and endorphins—chemical reactions.

I wonder when Elsa will finally figure that out. She's smart in everything except for this.

"Sure," I say instead. There's something else I've learnt about human interactions: if you agree with them, they drop it, which means less headaches and more peace of mind.

"Besides, Dad will join forces with Aiden's father, so there's no need for more allies."

"Of course there is. Dad returned from a nine-year coma, during which he was cut off from the world. He needs all the allies he can get. Aiden's father, that Jonathan King bloke, isn't trustworthy. Do you really think he'll play nice with Dad after the grudge he held for ten years? He holds Dad responsible for the death of his wife, and that doesn't just disappear."

She drops her hands from me and bites her lower lip again. This time, I'm almost sure it's because she's contemplating something.

"You're right." She sighs. "But I believe Jonathan and Dad will fix their problems over time. You don't need to sacrifice yourself."

My brows furrow. "Sacrifice?"

"Well, you already have...you know, a love interest. Marrying someone else is a sacrifice."

"A sacrifice means slaughtering an animal or a person as an offering to a deity. In other words, it means giving up

something valued for other considerations. I'm doing neither."
I allow a small smile to curve my lips. "If anything, I'm gaining
something valuable."

She releases a breath, which means she doesn't understand
my logic. It's fine, I guess. It's true Elsa understands some of my
thinking, but she won't get everything so fast.

Besides, no one actually knows me—or at least not the way
they think.

They don't see the constant shadow over my shoulder or the
tears trapped in the middle of nowhere.

Only I do.

"What does Knox think about this?" she asks.

"He—" I'm cut off when a strong hand wraps around my
shoulder. It's so sudden, I stiffen and lift my elbow.

A dark figure is grabbing me, his fingers are on me, his smell,
his damn —

"Did I hear my name?" An awfully cheerful voice cuts into the
usual vicious cycle of thoughts.

My brother. Knox. It's only Knox.

Usually, I'm okay with someone touching me when I see it
coming, like when Elsa clutched my shoulders earlier. I saw her
before I felt her and that was fine, but a sudden attack always
triggers this stony state.

"Sorry," Knox whispers, and he loosens his hold.

He of all people knows how it feels. That darkness, feeling
without seeing—all of it.

I lift a shoulder, pretending I wasn't on the verge of an episode.
He masks his apology with a grin as he plants himself between me
and Elsa, clutching each of us by a shoulder.

Knox and I are fraternal twins, but we barely look like siblings.
Where my hair is black, his is chestnut. All his features are like
those of models—or gigolos; I can't actually tell the difference.
It's a serious issue—don't judge. I don't think it's okay to compare
your brother to a gigolo, but he is one in some ways. For one, he's

charming with a happy-go-lucky personality he only uses to get things done.

And he talks a lot, like a fucking *lot*. It gives me headaches.

"So what's with me?" He nudges us both. "Is this some conspiracy, *Game of Thrones*-style? Because I watched all the seasons—I can tell."

Elsa laughs. "I was just asking Teal what you think about her new decision."

He retrieves a packet of crisps and throws two into his mouth then offers the rest to us. We both refuse—Elsa because it's forbidden to eat food outside the cafeteria and she follows the rules a lot, and me because I don't eat that junk food. I picked my poison, and it's dark chocolate.

"More for me." He grins, swallowing a handful.

I nudge him so he'll give me some space. He's crunching in my ear, the sound heightened with his proximity, and that's another way for the triggers to seep in.

Knox releases me, now only holding on to Elsa.

"So, what do you think?" she insists.

"Me?" He feigns innocence. "I don't care."

Liar.

"Really?" Elsa grabs him by the elbow.

"I'm T's brother, not her father. She gets to do what she wants. Do you know how freaked out I was when she said she had something to tell me? I thought she was going to say she's pregnant and was planning a party to mourn my youth." He points at me with his bag of crisps. "I forgive anything except making me an uncle this young."

"Anything?" I smirk.

His grin falters for a second. "You're a pain in the arse, T."

"Compliments first thing in the morning?" I feign a gasp. "What have I done to deserve you?"

"You kind of stole my egg."

"Your egg?" Elsa asks.

"Ellie, you know how twins are formed, right? Like once upon a time, I was swimming in my whore mother's womb and I fought all the other fuckers who wanted to go into the egg. I won, by the way. So there I was, happy in the egg and shit, and then T here sneaks in and shares my egg."

Elsa bursts out laughing as I just give him my signature blank stare.

"What are you laughing at?" Knox squeezes Elsa's shoulder. "That's really how twins are formed."

"Identical," she says.

"Huh?"

"That's how identical twins are formed. You and Teal are fraternal. She didn't steal your egg—there were already two."

"How do you know that?" He narrows his eyes on her. "Were you there?"

"God no."

"Then we'll go with my story."

He's so daft, my brother, and I have no words to describe how much I appreciate him for it.

I wouldn't have come this far if I didn't have him.

When the darkness swallows me and I have nowhere to go, he's there, telling me without words that we have each other.

We always have, since our whore mother's womb.

We had each other even when that same whore wanted to make us like her.

When we thought we were going to die in that hollow, dark place while we almost bled out.

I retrieve my phone, ready to go back to my article about Napoleon. There's something interesting about war, not the mass destruction or the casualties, but the ways they've started.

They ways they've been finished.

In between, there's chaos, but chaos doesn't come randomly.

I'm at the beginning phase, where the smallest action can trigger a bloody battle.

The first of many.

As I'm about to get lost in the words, in the debauchery of the human mind, another presence steals my interest.

He walks towards us with an arm around Aiden's shoulder. The latter—Elsa's boyfriend—is the tall, dark, and handsome type, and he's playing the role with that scowl that says *Come close and I'll slaughter your family tree.* It's why the onlooking students admire him from afar, not daring to get in his way. For Aiden, only one person exists in the female population—or the entire population, actually—and it's my foster sister.

Aiden King is one of a group known as the four horsemen of this school's football team, something stupid about the damage they do to their opponents' defences. Aiden is Conquest, and true to his name, he's already conquered Elsa.

While he ignores everyone, his attention falls solely on her, as if he can cut the distance and magically appear beside her.

The one by his side is doing the opposite of ignoring his surroundings.

He winks at one girl, high-fives another, and tells a random freshman to call him with a huge grin that nearly splits his face open. They all eat it up, nearly tripping over their feet in front of him.

Ronan Astor.

An earl's son with a Prince Charming complex.

Nicknamed Death for his position on the team.

He doesn't know that death isn't a title. Death is the beginning of every war, and I've already started mine.

I stole his will, his future, and soon enough, his life will follow.

I have a secret, I'm a thief.

Ronan Astor is my next target.

As well as my future husband.

TWO

Teal

Beauty is subjective.

    I read that once, and since then, I've had this weird feeling that it spoke to me.

Beauty is a strange concept for me. Black is beautiful, and dark chocolate with nuts can also be considered beautiful.

But other than that, what's human beauty? Gigolos—sorry, I mean guys with model-like looks such as Knox's—are considered beautiful. Aiden, Elsa's boyfriend, is handsome, too.

There's a different type of beauty that's darker, a bit sinister, hiding under the surface rather than pushing to the top.

I guess that's beauty for me. It's not about the physical aspect but rather about what the exterior hides. You can feel it when someone possesses no beauty by societal standards but their charisma speaks to you in one way or another. You can't see it, but it's there.

Ronan, however, has no beauty at all.

His is the shallow type like gigolos. If he were a woman, he would be labelled a slut, but in his case, he's called a playboy.

From the outside, he has a well-proportioned face, and it's symmetrical, actually. It's the same on either side of his proud straight nose, from the eyes to the cheeks to the sharp jaw and even to the ears.

It's a symmetry like I've never seen in my entire life. Some people, like actors, have what resembles symmetry, but never actually a perfect one.

He does.

His face is too symmetrical, as if it were sculpted by a Greek god. People's eyes usually have a slight asymmetry—not his. Even as the outside sun shines on them, they both glow in a rich identical brown colour.

I guess it's part of his filthy aristocratic blood, a heritage he claims by being the whatever generation of the world's nobility.

His beauty makes no sense at all for two reasons. A, he's too aware of it; it's cringy. B, and most importantly, there's no depth behind it.

At least in Knox's case, he uses the plastic easy-going personality as a defence mechanism to get what he wants. I know all too well what he's hiding beneath all the laughs and grins.

In the few weeks I've watched Ronan, he's never shown another facet of the sickly, cheerful personality. He's always smiling, laughing, grinning, throwing parties, fucking, and fucking, and more fucking.

It's…boring.

And yes, I have watched him. After all, he's part of my plan.

He just doesn't know it yet.

Soon, though. So very soon.

"Drop your arm, Van Doren." Aiden stops in front of us. He's smiling, but there's no warmth behind it.

That.

The depth.

The human desolation.

It's what makes him beautiful, not as a man, but as someone who stands out from the crowd of normal.

Aiden is anything but. He's all darkness with little light that he only shows to Elsa.

"Come on, King." My brother grins. "She's my sis."

"You share no blood. Actually..." He pauses. "Even if you did, I'd tell you to drop your arm."

Elsa suppresses laughter by biting her lower lip as Aiden tugs her to his side by her other wrist. I tilt my head as she snuggles to him, wrapping her arm around his waist while he holds her with a hand at the small of her back.

It's like they can't get close enough or touch each other long enough.

Why would they do that?

Human touch is overrated. I've tried it, and it didn't really matter. At least not in the way I wanted.

Knox and Aiden go into some sort of argument that doesn't really register. It's like they're speaking in outer space— no idea if I'm the one blocking it out or if it just doesn't exist for me anymore.

As I slide my attention back to my phone, a harsh glare registers in my peripheral vision. When I lift my head and my eyes collide with that infuriatingly symmetrical gaze, a grin greets me, all perfect and put together and worthy of an earl's son.

I could swear someone was glaring at me just now, but he's the only one in sight. Someone with his reputation and shallowness doesn't even know how to glare. Ronan is all about laughs and having a good time to the point that negativity is considered below him. I've never seen him angry or displeased. Even when Elsa was taken to the emergency room, he came by filled with laughs and jokes, trying to cheer her up.

"*Bonjour, ma belle,*" he tells me, his tone light, welcoming, and I think there's some flirting in there, too, but I'm not sure.

Ma belle.

My beautiful.

I don't know why he calls me that when he's never once thought I'm pretty. I heard him talking to Kimberly—Elsa's best friend—the other day, and when she told him I'm pretty, he said, "There's pretty and there's creepy, and she falls in the latter category. Mmmkay?"

It was the first time someone said those words. Creepy? Sure. I've felt it during my limited interactions with humans, but no one has said it out loud, or maybe no one has said it out loud for me to hear it. They usually think I'm crazy, abnormal... mad.

I'm curious to see how he feels now that he's forced to marry a creep, but I have neither the mind nor the patience to pursue it.

Curiosity can be beneficial, but its outcome is usually disastrous, and I have no time for that in my life.

Focusing back on my phone, I turn around.

They're all so busy talking and throwing shade, so I doubt anyone will notice I'm gone.

Knox nudges me, a sly grin on his lips.

Okay, anyone but my brother.

I ignore him and walk down the hall. I'll have to take the longer route to get to the classroom.

I don't mind as long as it gets me away from that circle.

Lacking a talkative nature can be a disadvantage when surrounded by people who won't shut up. Sometimes, Elsa and Aiden's group of friends throw remarks my way, and I usually figure it out too late. I hate that.

It's not my fault I'm not so witty like all of them seem to be.

I pass by the faceless students and try focusing on one of them, squinting to form an image. How hard could it be? Two eyes, a nose, and a mouth. It's that easy.

Only it's not.

I need a lot of focus to form faces, a familiarity of sorts, but I still don't have that with RES's students. The one I concentrate on barely has eyes; they're washed out, and the person quickly strides past me, shattering any focus I had.

I shake my head and rekindle the connection with my phone.

Maybe one day after the war finishes, I'll stand in a public place and recognise every face and every person. I'll be normal.

Though, what's normal? I never lived it, never experienced it, so how come I want it so much?

I'm a human, after all, like my therapist says. I can deny it all I want, but I keep snapping back to what's considered normal even without my permission.

Stupid anatomy.

"A word, *ma belle*," a low voice whispers in my ear from behind.

I startle and my hands shake, nearly dropping the phone on the ground.

Something jerks in my chest, as if invisible hands are rummaging through my organs.

It takes me a second too long to regain control over my breathing.

Refusing to show Ronan a reaction, I continue walking as if he didn't just set off my second trigger for the day. First Knox, and now him.

I'm usually more aware of my surroundings for this exact reason, but I spent all night searching for and watching videos of my opponent, making sure I know him better than he knows himself.

I guess a lack of sleep can cause a deficiency in attention.

"Did you hear me?" He speaks with that smile plastered on his face as he falls in step beside me.

"Yes, and my silence was the answer, just like how I left to stop being in your immediate vicinity."

"You're getting it all wrong, but I'm generous so I'll fix your misconception. Silence is a sign of affirmation."

"For me, it's a sign of denial." I stride faster than I usually walk, but it's useless. He's way taller than me and his legs eat up the distance, keeping pace with me without any extra effort.

"That's lovely." He smiles, but I don't think he believes what he said—the part where he thinks this is lovely, I mean.

No, it can't be.

He's as readable as it gets. Even with my weird relationship with feelings, I can figure him out. I watched him for weeks on end before I took this step. He can't possibly be hiding anything up his sleeve.

"Do you mind?" I stop, motioning at him to go ahead. Ronan and I often throw jabs at each other. What? I'm allergic to his over-positivity, and I can't stay quiet about it. He always retaliates and we soon drop it.

But that's only when someone else is around.

I never spend alone time with Ronan, and it's for a reason. He's always surrounded by people; it feels suffocating just watching from afar.

"I do, actually." He smiles again, adding a wink, but it's not at me—it's at a girl passing us by. "Party at my place, Nicky!"

She nods several times like an overeager kid on Christmas morning then blushes when he winks at her again.

I sidestep him and continue on my way. After all, I don't want to hinder his man-whorish ways.

I make a beeline to the library to return the book *A Military History and Atlas of the Napoleonic Wars*. I read the whole thing last night, so I might as well take another one.

I'm in front of a shelf when a strong hand grabs me by the arm from behind.

Third and final trigger.

My heart nearly stops beating as I shriek. The sound is so loud my ears pop.

Only no sound comes out.

A hand wraps tightly around my mouth, killing any protest I could form.

I stare up at Ronan's symmetrical eyes. There is no laughter in there, no winks or anything familiar. It's a bit blank, a bit too...empty.

It's almost as if I'm staring at a different person.

The change disappears in a second as a grin breaks out on his face, and just like that, the shallow version returns.

Was it even there? Maybe the change was a play of my imagination because of the trigger I just experienced.

My ears still ring from the effect of it, so it can't be far off.

Still, my chest rises and falls so heavily it's like a war has already started in my heart and is now about to take me over.

Ronan lowers his hand as if he didn't just muffle my scream and trigger my damn episode.

"What the hell do you think you're doing?" I snap.

"Shh." He places his forefinger in front of his mouth, motioning at Mrs Abbot, the librarian. "We're at the library."

"And what are you doing here?" I whisper.

"Told you." He gives me back my personal space as if he didn't confiscate it a second ago. "I want a word with you."

"And I told you no." I turn on my heels, breathing heavily and trying to subdue the shadow on my shoulder, trying to keep it from pouncing at me.

I need to get the fuck out of here and take a pill to calm down. Otherwise, I'll be jittery all damn day.

My episodes have that effect on me.

An arm shoots out in front of my face, and I push back, jolting as it clutches a shelf, blocking my exit.

Damn him.

I can already feel the usual shortness of breath and trembling of my toes. If he keeps doing this, I'll really have no way to stop whatever's brewing in the distance.

Might as well get this over with.

"Fine." I breathe out, meeting his gaze. "What do you want?"

"I'm happy you changed your mind." He tilts his head with a smile.

Changed my mind? More like was coerced into it.

The fucker.

I still can't pinpoint if he did it on purpose or if it was a lucky hit. Please let it be the latter, because if it's the former, I'm in trouble.

The best thing about laying plans is to follow through with them. Everything is a domino; once one falls, the others soon follow.

I'm the only one who can push that first domino. No one will do it for me.

I tap my foot on the ground and whisper due to the library's strict policies. "I'm waiting, in case you haven't noticed."

"Oh, I did notice. Doesn't mean I care. This is about me, not you, *ma belle*, remember?"

Arrogant prick.

"If there's a point, you should have reached it by now." I pretend to stare at my watch. The numbers are there, but for some reason, I can't seem to read the time. Shit. This one is worse than any of my recent episodes.

"Here's the thing, *ma belle*. My father told me I'm getting a fiancée. At first, I was fine since it was Elsa, but apparently, there's been an internal sister swap as if we're in medieval times. I know I'm part of old-school aristocracy, but this behaviour is insolent—imagine that in the queen's tone. Anyway, point is, I don't want a fiancée. I just turned eighteen and I have this brilliant plan that starts with me staying single for the next fifteen years and shagging exotic girls all around the world. It's not me, it's you. Now, do me a favour and fucking disappear, mmkay?" He grins.

"Why would I do that?" I don't even pause.

"What?"

"Why would I do you any favours? Last time I checked, I owe you nothing."

He chuckles, the sound low and discreet in the silence of the library. "Is that what you want? To owe me something?"

"That's beside the point. What I meant is that I have no obligation to do something for you. Not now, not ever."

"*Ma belle, ma belle…*" He's still smiling as he muses. "I call you *ma belle*, but you keep missing the point entirely."

His words give me pause. What is that supposed to mean? I resist the urge to ask him just that, and I have a problem with not being direct. It's as if the words will suffocate me if I don't speak them. If he meant to rattle me, he's going to be disappointed, because he won't be getting a reaction.

He reaches a hand to my lips, the touch soft, almost like a feather. Just when I'm about to push free, he presses on the tender skin and smears my purple lipstick onto my cheek, making my jaw move with the motion. "I think you missed the memo about makeup. It's supposed to make you prettier, not uglier."

I'm caught off guard by his brutal touch, and I barely register the softly spoken words. There are so many contradictions in his touch, how he started gently then ended it brutally, how he spoke softly yet lined it with a mean edge.

I snap my head away from his immediate vicinity. His lips curve in a smirk before he quickly masks it with his usual easy-going smile.

What. The. Fuck.

"So, here's the thing. During tomorrow's dinner, I want you to sit down like a good little girl and tell everyone you don't accept this engagement, and then I'll gift you a new set of purple makeup shit. Deal? Glad to do business with you."

"If you're so against marrying me, why don't you speak up yourself?" I know why, but me getting on his nerves is only fair after the way he not only triggered my anxiety attack, but also gave me the foreboding sensation he's able to ruin my domino castle.

Ronan Astor is the sole heir of an earl, and he has no way to refuse his father's wishes. He's the perfect puppet, someone used for his symmetrical face and playful nature.

He was always meant to have an arranged marriage, and he has no way to refuse it. That would mean disgracing the great

Edric Astor's name, which is something that man will never allow.

Instead of the anger, or at least annoyance, I expected, his grin widens further. "Why would I speak up when I have you to do the dirty work, *ma belle?*"

I'll be doing more than your dirty work.

Instead of saying so, I give him a smile that mimics his, but I'm bad at faking this, so I doubt it comes out as anything but a grimace. "And if I say no, your lordship?"

"I'll give you one piece of advice, just because you're Elsa and Knox's sister."

I don't get a warning before he grabs me by my nape. His hand covers the tiny space, shocking my skin as it wraps around my neck from behind.

The scent of something spicy fills my nostrils as he leans in to whisper against the lobe of my ear. "Run, *ma belle.*"

THREE

Ronan

B eing me is easy.

There are a few recipes for success.

One, always smile.

And that's it. You don't need anything else. There's some philosopher who said that people lose their fight, their anger, and even feel humiliated when you counter their maliciousness with a smile.

Though I suspect he meant it as in, *Try to be good people, kids.* I must've missed that part somehow in my philosophical journey, which is basically listening to Cole spout nonsense about the latest book he's read.

Why waste your life reading books when you can live it? When you can breathe it into your lungs and exhale it back to the world?

While nerds like Cole drown in books, I'm giving authors inspiration and writing material. My life is the best form of storytelling to ever exist.

Don't thank me yet.

I yawn as I stumble from the bed and to a robotic standing position. The first weird thing I notice is the absence of meat. I mean, girls. You know, their limbs are usually draped around me in pairs of three or four—I don't have a limit.

Today, no one is in my bed.

Surely I didn't smoke enough weed to imagine an entire fun night, right? Fuck, if I did, I need more of that shit the Liverpudlian sold me.

I stagger to the bathroom and have a quick shower. That's not enough to wake me up, so I stand at the sink and splash water on my face. When I lift my head, my expression greets me in the mirror.

They say you know how you feel about yourself by the way you react to the reflection of your face. If you scowl, you're not happy. If you grimace, you have confidence issues.

My face moves into an automatic smile. Fucking liars. There are other types of people, like me. *Try finding a category for me, fuckers.*

I brush my teeth and pay a morning tribute to Ron Astor the Second. Yes, that's my dick's name, and yes, I always need to give him the morning routine. Usually, there's a girl's mouth willing to ease him into the day, but today he had to restart his affair with my hand.

Seriously, though. Was last night real, or do I need more weed?

I step back into my room to find Lars smoothing my pressed uniform on the made-up bed. I swear he has supersonic speed. When the hell did he even make the bed?

The room is all bright and shiny and smells of some lavender shit. We're only missing unicorns for the picture-perfect period drama.

"Morning, Lars." I head to my closet. "Today, we have dinner. No uniform."

"You said to remind you to wear the uniform so his lordship and her ladyship don't suspect you skipped school." He speaks in a professional old BBC-like tone. He watches *Downton Abbey* a lot and takes this whole thing way too seriously. I even suspect he has a little black book with notes tucked somewhere.

Lars is in his late forties with a tall, slim build. He's wearing a black butler's tux with the bowtie and the white gloves. Since he's the head butler, he makes everyone dress like him, and he's a Nazi about it.

His blue eyes might appear polite, but he'll judge you with them all the way to infinity if you don't stick out your pinkie while drinking the tea he brings.

I snap my fingers at him. "Thank you for reminding me of my genius thoughts, Lars."

"Any time, sir."

"Father and Mother aren't here—forget the sir."

"Yes, young lord."

"You're not funny, Lars."

His face remains stoic—snobbish, actually, which is his default. You never know if he's judging or teasing, like he did just now.

I pull the trousers up my legs then my memory filters back in.

Fuck.

Mum and Dad are returning today. That's why the girls disappeared and…

The party.

"Is everything in order?" I ask Lars, looking at him out of the corner of my eye.

"Just like this room."

"Perfect. You're the best, Lars." Not only because he covers up for me, but because he does a brilliant job at it too.

He doesn't want my parents to be disappointed in me, so he and I struck a deal as soon as I took a special interest in partying.

"I know I am," he says with a cool expression.

"I'm taking it back."

"With all due respect, you cannot take a compliment back."

"Watch me. There. It's taken back."

I button my shirt and then my jacket in record time. Being late is kind of my thing. I even dress in the car sometimes.

"If you'll excuse me." Lars approaches me and smooths my jacket with a few professional tugs. "Now, please do something about your hair."

"Are you saying my hair is a mess?"

"Your words, not mine, sir." His tone doesn't change.

"Screw you, Lars, mmmkay? If you knew what my hair witnessed yesterday, you wouldn't be saying those things."

"I assume you washed it?"

"I'm curious, Lars. Are you still a virgin? Because if you are, I can plan an orgy for you."

His expression remains the same. "You cannot even plan your day."

"Planning my day isn't my specialty. Orgies are."

"And I should be impressed?"

"Fuck right, you should."

"Pass."

"Lars!"

"Yes, young lord?"

"I'm the best at what I do."

"I'll take your word for it."

Lars leaves and I follow behind him, enumerating my qualities so he'd agree. Since I was a kid, it's always been this way with him. After all, I spend more time with him than my own parents. It's cooler, too, since he's the best party planner in the whole of London.

We go out of my room and take the marble stairs. Our mansion—no, the Astor family mansion—has stood here for centuries, since the time of Henry V.

There are two sweeping stairs that split the entrance hall. Portraits of my dead ancestors stare back at me with snobbish haughty expressions. We all share the nose, which is Dad's pride and the reason he knew I'm without a doubt his son.

His words, not mine.

I smile at them, too. What? Just because they're dead doesn't mean they don't deserve some love.

As Lars said, everything is in place. The kitchen staff buzz around the dining room carrying utensils and whatnot. The whole house smells of jasmine, of Mother, of her spring presence and all that jazz. It's the only scent I don't resent too much.

Aside from weed.

John runs in the entrance, catching his breath. He's Lars' assistant, and yes, Lars is prim and proper and needs assistants and calendars and order.

"His lordship is here," John shouts, like in some play.

And just like a play, the scene shifts with a shuffling of feet, and everyone stands in a line, like they're in the military or something.

I plaster a smile on as the double doors open and in comes my father in all his lordship glory.

Okay, that's a lie—there's no glory, just the title. And okay, maybe the glory follows the title.

He was right to say I'm his son; it shows. We're about the same height, but I'm a bit leaner. His face has gained a lethal edge over the years, giving him an older masculine look, nothing like some of the boyishness still scattered on mine.

We share the eyes and the proud Astor nose, as he calls it. I'm a replica, a carbon copy.

The future of the witch coven. Sorry, I mean the clan.

A tiny woman has her frail arm in his, seeming so little in comparison to his otherworldly existence, but the expression on her face is anything but little.

She's listening to something he's saying, and her face shines with compassion, affection…love.

Fuck how much she loves that tyrant. How much she went through just to be with him, leaving not only her country but also her family to be by his side.

Lord Astor's face remains blank as he talks to her, no expression, no smile, no nothing. We agree that Dad is a robot, and by we, I mean Lars and me.

Fine, Lars just listened with a judgmental expression while I informed him of that fact.

The staff bows upon my parents' entrance. It's been…what? A few months since they graced me with their presence?

They've been doing this a lot lately, disappearing to go to conferences, or more like my father dragging my mother with him to the other ends of the world like India and fucking Australia.

They used to do that when I was a kid, but I thought it was over around middle school. Nope, they're back at it like a druggies searching for their high.

Not that I'm complaining. After all, I get to throw all the parties I want in this mansion every night. Win-win.

The moment Mother's eyes fall on me, they brighten and soften. I almost imagine she appears too weak and thin, or is it only her pale complexion? She releases my father and runs towards me, ignoring her long dress.

"*Mon chou!*"

Both Dad and I reach out for her when she trips, but she catches herself at the last second and squeezes me in a tight embrace. I have to lean down so she can rest her cheek on my shoulder. She smells of jasmine, of warmth.

Safety.

"I missed you so much." She speaks with a slight French accent that she hasn't been able to lose even after living in England for twenty-three years.

"Missed you, too, Mother." And I mean it. Maybe I missed her more than I'll ever admit.

Her absence triggered something I don't even like to think about.

There was no safety or jasmine—just like that time.

"Mon petit ange." She pulls back to cradle my cheeks with her frail hands. "Although you're not little anymore. I should start calling you *mon grand*."

"That's right. Have you seen these muscles?" I grin, and this time it's not automatic or forced.

"Oh, I have. You've grown so much, and I wasn't there." A sob tears from her throat.

"Mother...?"

"Charlotte." My father is by her side in a second, wrapping a hand around her shoulder. It's his way to control her, to have her act the way he likes.

As if he pushed a button, she straightens, wiping under her eye with her thumb. "It must be exhaustion from the flight."

Or your husband's controlling fucking nature.

"I'll freshen up before we receive the guests. I'm so happy you decided to do this." She rises up on her tiptoes and kisses my cheek, her lips trembling before she pulls away. "I won't leave this time, *mon chou*, I promise."

"Charlotte." Father warns her in his usual *Do it my way or I'll throw you in the highway* tone.

"I'll be right back, *mon amour*." She kisses him on the cheek, too, before heading to the stairs.

Father motions for Lars to follow her, and he does so with a nod. The rest of the staff scatter like ants with another motion of his finger.

Mon amour.

That word leaves a sour taste in my mouth. How can he be her love? He's her tyrant.

The Tyrant of the Estate.

I've been trying to convince Cole to write that book. I'll let you know how it goes.

Dad continues watching my mother until she disappears up the stairs. When he finally focuses on me, his blank expression is back.

I smile. "Hey, Father."

That's what's expected of me: a smile, stellar behaviour, and to shut the fuck up.

Silence remains for a few seconds. My smile doesn't falter or even flinch. I'm a pro, after all.

"I heard you know your fiancée from school." He jumps straight to the heart of it in Edric's typical direct style.

"Which one are we talking about? There have been a few."

His expression remains the same. "Teal Van Doren."

"That one. Hmm, I'm sure you know she's not Ethan's real daughter, right? With him having Steel as his last name and her being a Van Doren and all that? Are we even sure she's not from the family of that German Nazi who killed my great-grandfather in World War II?" I motion behind him then make a cross, speaking in a dramatic tone. "Rest in peace. You served our country well."

"That's my great-grandfather, not yours, and he died at seventy from pneumonia."

"Oh, then maybe it's the one behind me?"

"How about you stop beating around the bush. Do you have something to say to me, Ronan?"

"No?" That wasn't supposed to come out as a question.

Lars, you fucking fool.

If he mentioned anything about the partying, I'm spiking his precious tea with cheap stuff from the grocery store that his snobby side hates so much. Let's see how he reacts when I ruin his stash.

"No objections about the engagement?" My father presents it as a question but is, in fact, making it clear that he'll take no bloody objections.

Not that I would make any.

I know what's expected of me. When the fish is caught in the net, the smart ones don't move; if they do, they exhaust what remains of their energy and die faster.

Now, if I store that energy, I get to bargain for greater things. I learnt that by myself, by the way; I didn't need Cole's philosophy books.

The moment I was born and my parents decided there was no need for a second child—fuck you, unborn second child, by the way—I was raised to know my duties as the sole heir.

I can do this the easy way, or I can clash with my father and cause my mother pain.

I would never do that—be the source of Mum's pain, I mean. She's one of the few reasons why I stay afloat, and I can't make things ugly for her.

Marriage of convenience is first on the list of mandatory shit to do. I'll do it one day, as expected of me.

Only that day isn't today, or even fifteen years from now.

That's why my little toy will play her part and say no during tonight's dinner.

I've already sent her an instigation she'd be a fool to refuse.

Teal isn't the first I've secretly convinced to refuse the arranged marriage on my behalf. Let's just say Dad has been trying to set me up with his associates' daughters for years.

I told Lars Dad is like one of those bored housewives with nothing better to do than play matchmaker. Lars wasn't amused—not that he ever is.

Teal will bow down like all of them.

My grin widens, and he frowns. I wonder if he knows the type of fuckery my smile hides.

"Not at all, Father. Everything will be perfect."

FOUR

Teal

"**W**e can turn around and leave this instant, Teal." Dad clutches me by the elbow, causing me to stop in front of the double golden doors of the Astor mansion.

Elsa, Knox, and Agnus stop, too. My brother takes the chance to smooth his denim jacket and hair. Elsa gives me a pleading look, silently begging me to think about this.

Agnus, Dad's right-hand man, is forty-three and so well-built he gives the younger generation a run for their money, and now he is watching me with a neutral expression. Knox and I lived with him for many years, and I know that neutrality means he cares—to an extent. He just doesn't show it.

Like me.

Perhaps that's why I look up at him, expecting something, anything to come out of his mouth.

He says nothing.

It's Dad who grips me gently by the elbow and stands in front of me. Dad is also broad and well-built, not like Agnus, but Dad has an aristocratic face. He's warm but hard. Noble but old-fashioned in a way.

His chestnut hair is styled like a proper gentleman, and his suit, like Agnus', is made to impress. Actually, everyone's clothes are. Even my daft brother took the time to wear his best when he'd usually throw on a Metallica T-shirt like it's the only thing available.

Elsa is wearing a soft blue dress that compliments her eye colour. Dad and Agnus are in dark suits they usually reserve for business—because that's what this is about: business.

I've chosen a black tulle skirt that stops at my knees, fish-net stocking, and boots. I also have a white T-shirt—with no sayings on the front—and a black denim jacket. My hair is straight, hitting just under my chin as usual. The only thing I gave up is the black makeup.

I think you missed the memo about makeup. It's supposed to make you prettier, not uglier.

No, it's not because of his words. Ronan Astor doesn't affect my decisions and never will. Not even if I wear his engagement ring.

The reason I went with normal eyeliner, a touch of mascara, and baby pink lipstick is simple: to impress.

Because once today ends, my plan will come to fruition.

I smile at Dad, and it's a real one, a thankful one. When Knox and I faced death, he saved us, had us call him Dad, and insisted we continue to even after his nine-year coma.

He's the only dad I've ever had, and I've never shown him my thanks. This is my chance to do it properly.

"I want to do this, Dad. I don't mind."

"Teal…" Elsa pleads.

"Shall we?" I motion at the door.

Before any of us can do anything, the double doors swing open like in some fairy tale, and there stands a tall man wearing a butler's suit complete with white gloves and a dispassionate smile. "Welcome to the Astor Estate."

Only this isn't a fairy tale—or perhaps it is, with a twist.

In the end, the hero won't win. The villain will topple everyone's lives over.

What everyone doesn't know is, the villain wasn't always a villain. Once upon a time, they were a victim.

"We always come here for Ronan's parties," Knox whispers to Elsa and me. "What's with the formality?"

"I thought you don't go to parties?" Dad gives him side-eye.

Knox grins. "I'm still your favourite son, Dad. Admit it."

My father shakes his head with slight exasperation as the butler leads us through a large hallway filled with medieval portraits. Usually, for the parties held here, there would be guards near all these so none of RES's students ruin them.

We're led to a large dining table. This one is always closed and off limits for partygoers. That's done for a reason.

The room is like a scene from a period film. Golden chandeliers hang from above, and the chairs surrounding the huge table fit for an army are high and meant to swallow tiny people like me.

At the head of table stands the lord of the estate. Earl Edric Astor, member of the House of Lords, a ruthless investor, a faithful husband.

And a fucked-up human being.

He smiles at us, reaching out his hand so his wife can rise from her chair and stand on his right.

She's elegant and pale, almost like one of those Victorian era maids who were forced to marry an influential lord.

Something in my chest stings upon seeing her, her radiant smile and wasted beauty. What has she done to have to be married to a monster?

Ronan stands at his father's left, grinning like an idiot. I don't meet his or his father's gazes. If I do, I might start having those signs that could trigger my episodes.

"Welcome, Ethan." Edric motions at the seat. "Please. I'm honoured to have you amongst us."

Dad, Agnus, and Edric exchange pleasantries. His wife,

Charlotte, hugs Knox then Elsa. When it's my turn, I force myself to remain still in preparation for the physical attack— and I kind of fail. Instead of hugging me, she eyes me up and down, but with no maliciousness. It's more like…pure interest.

I fidget then stop myself when I realise I'm doing it. *Damn.* Did I just feel nervous or something? I don't do nervous—not usually, at least.

Her lips pull up in the warmest smile I've ever seen on a human being. It rearranges her features, making her appear younger and softer. When she speaks, there's a distinguishable French accent. "I love your sense of fashion."

Usually, when people say that, it's with a venomous undertone. Not Charlotte.

She pulls me close and wraps her arms around me. "I'm so happy to meet you."

I pat her back awkwardly, almost mechanically, and just then, my eyes meet Ronan's dark ones. His grin wavers for a second as he watches me and my hand on his mother's back.

Then his attention slides to my face. If eyes had a language, his would be saying he wants to trap me and smear my lipstick in a dark library corner about now.

I shake my head internally, forcing that image to go up in smoke. It's all I've been thinking about since yesterday. There's a slight chance Ronan will ruin my plan. Contrary to my original assessment, he's not a gigolo. He's only using the gigolo image for other purposes, and since I don't know what those are, I can't form a counterstrike this soon.

The way he touched me and how his usual shallowness slipped means he might have more depth.

But that doesn't mean I'll give up on the plan. I've finally gotten here, and no rich spoilt boy will take away my justice.

The more he watches me, the harder I glare back.

If he thinks I'll be the one to break eye contact first, he must not know who he's dealing with.

His girls and shags don't even compare to me. He's lived in one world, and I'm an entirely different one altogether.

Charlotte breaks away, shutting down the glaring competition. We all take our seats, and as I settle beside Dad, my gaze strays to the head of the table.

Edric motions at one of the staff, and like magic, dishes appear in front of us. They contain many colours with different compelling smells. Knox dives into the food and loses the connection with his immediate surroundings.

Dad and Agnus are chatting about business and stocks. Ronan whispers something to Knox—probably about the 'usual' parties—and they both laugh under their breaths.

Elsa keeps sending me pleading signals over the table even as she speaks to Charlotte.

Me? There's this black smoke that keeps swirling around my head and a shadow perching on my shoulder.

I can't fight it off as I watch him, hear him, his voice with that distinguishable tenor. It's changed a little, but it has been more than a decade, after all.

He's still the same: confident, arrogant, and a wolf in a sheep's clothing.

Back then, I could do nothing about it.

Now, I'll slaughter his legacy, crush his name, and make him bleed.

My phone vibrates in my jacket and I pull it out under the table, thinking it's a notification from one of the newsletters I'm signed up for, or perhaps the club. My heart flutters at the thought. It's a long shot, but what if they accept me? What if they —

My shoulders drop when I see the screen.

It's a text from Ronan.

My attention slides to him. He's still joking and playing with Knox across the table; when the hell did he have time to text?

Also, I have no clue how he got my number, though this isn't the first time he's texted me. He sent me one last night, too.

Today's text says:

Ronan: Do as agreed.

I scroll up to last night's texts.

Ronan: My father will ask if you agree to this engagement, and you'll apologise and say you don't. If you feel like it, some tears are encouraged, but it's not mandatory.

Teal: Why would I do that?

Ronan: Because if you don't, I'll figure out your secret and crush you with it until you wish you'd never gotten in my way. Mmmkay?

Teal: What makes you think I have a secret?

Ronan: We all do, *ma belle*. Some are just more destructive than others.

I didn't reply to his last message, and I don't plan to reply to this one.

Sure, secrets are scary, but there's no way in hell he'll be able to figure out mine. Even Knox doesn't know all about it, and that says something since we've shared everything since our mother's womb.

As soon as I tuck my phone in my jacket, Edric's cool, posh voice fills the dining room. "As you're all aware, we're here to start a relationship between our families. I'm honoured to have ties to you, Ethan."

Dad tips his head. "So am I, Edric."

The latter smiles, and I tighten my hold on the napkin in front of me. "Before that, we have to get the youngsters' approval—modern times and everything. Ronan, do you agree to be engaged to Teal?"

His son's lips curve in an almost manic smile. "Of course. It'd be my honour."

His honour?

The fucking liar.

Why does he get to fake his feelings so perfectly like that? Why can't I do that?

"Teal?" Edric asks and it takes everything in me not to rise out of my seat and lunge at him with a fork—or better yet, a knife.

My gaze focuses back on Ronan, who's watching me with that same smile.

"Absolutely." I mimic his smile. "It's an honour."

Congratulations scatter all around us, but the one I focus on isn't Agnus as I initially thought I would. No—it's the boy with a previously disgusting symmetrical face.

Previously because I can't conjure the disgust anymore, no matter how much I try to.

His smile is still in place, but his entire demeanour sharpens. His eyes darken, his shoulders strain, and his hold on the spoon tightens.

Those are all small, almost imperceptible changes, but the signs are there, and they point to one thing.

The start of a war.

Wars are Death's playground. It's where he harvests souls and leaves the remaining ones desolate.

You're always a victim of war, whether by losing a loved one or your property or both.

And right now, Ronan appears ready to make me lose everything.

Not that I'm scared of him. I'm not. Because what he doesn't know is that I'm also ready to make him lose everything.

His hand disappears under the table, and soon after, my phone vibrates in my pocket.

I hold it in my lap and read the text.

Ronan: You made your hell, and now I'll ruin you.

Not as much as I'll ruin you.

I meet his glare with one of my own as I type.

Teal: Bring it.

FIVE

Ronan

The team comes to a halt after the assistant manager calls for a time out.

The air is grim like the grey clouds, and the school's pitch appears like a scene from an apocalypse—minus the bodies.

Our football team attracts all the ladies' attention. They always appear at our practice, calling our names and cheering us on. I grin at them as they stand by the sidelines, and they wave and scream my number, thirteen.

That's right—my number. Needless to say, I'm the most popular. My fucker friends can claim otherwise, but they're wrong, so they don't count.

I head to the bench with Aiden and Cole and snatch a bottle of water before Cole can get it. I'm in the middle of downing it when I meet those black eyes that should belong in some gothic tale about black magic and sucking people's souls into nothingness.

Teal stands behind the school stadium's barrier with Elsa and a miserable-looking Kim—because Xander isn't here and she's kind of too soft for that fucker.

She waves at me anyway—Kim, I mean—and I wink, grinning even though I'm close to crushing the bottle of water between my fingers.

Teal isn't even watching us. She's focused on Coach, who's yelling at a freshman, asking him if he wants to be on this team or not.

Her phone is snuggled between her fingers, almost forgotten, but not really. Soon enough, her concentration goes back to whatever voodoo spell is in there.

After her display at dinner last week, she's been acting as if nothing happened, as if she didn't fuck up my fifteen-year plan that includes not getting married.

Nothing is over, though.

That tiny girl with black hair and eyes, and possibly a black heart, has riled up a part of me I've been keeping hidden for so long I actually thought maybe it'd start disappearing, but nope, it came back reeling from the dead.

And now she'll fucking pay for it.

"What has that bottle done to you?" Aiden asks from his position on the bench. He's also sipping from a sports drink, but his entire attention is on Elsa. There's even a slight smirk on his lips; his male ego is happy she's made it a habit to show up to watch him practice after being against it for months.

Cole sits beside him, wiping the side of his face with a towel. We're all wearing blue Elites jerseys and shorts since we're starters and are playing against the second string, which will take over next year once we've all graduated.

Knox is jesting with the goalkeeper, and I seize the opportunity his absence provides. I barge between Cole and Aiden and wrap an arm around each of their shoulders, grinning at them suggestively.

"Withdrawals, Astor?" Aiden raises an eyebrow.

"Nope, been smoking my usual stash just fine. Thanks for asking, though."

"He meant sex withdrawals," Cole elaborates. "You haven't thrown a party in a week since your parents are back."

"Nah, I'm doing fine." Lie—about the partying, not the sex part.

"If you were, you wouldn't be clingy like a stripper." Aiden glares at me. "Not interested."

"Fuck you, King," I say, but I don't remove my arm.

"I might be interested." Cole raises an eyebrow. "Depending on the circumstances."

"You keep your kinky shit away from me, Captain," I warn.

"Are you sure?" Cole drawls. "You never know when it'll be useful."

His gaze strays to the spectators and he smiles at Teal. She tips her head in acknowledgment before focusing on her phone.

The fuck?

I stare between him and her then back again. Now that I think about it, Cole and Teal have been getting disgustingly close for some time now. It's almost unnoticeable, but he's possibly the only one amongst the horsemen—or the entire male population—that she exchanges words with.

In the beginning, I thought it was because they're both nerds, but even if I don't know her—yet—I know Cole. He doesn't take a step without calculating a thousand years ahead—no kidding, he's probably writing a financial plan for his fourth generation by now.

Cole is kind on the outside, but he doesn't actually let people get close. The fact that he did with her is…interesting. Interesting for me because that means he'll give me indispensable information.

"What do you know about Teal?" I ask them both, because Aiden practically lives at Elsa's house now and might know more about her than he lets on.

"If Marquis de Sade and Snow White had an offspring, it'd be her," Aiden says.

"What else?" I probe.

"Why are you asking us about your fiancée?" Cole nudges my side.

I grin. "I'm trying to get to know her and figure out what type of flowers she likes."

"She prefers dark chocolate." Aiden appears serious. "Elsa buys her packs all the time."

"Give me more. I want to woo her." I wiggle my brows.

"Could've fooled me." Cole smirks.

"You know something, don't you?" I narrow my eyes at him.

"I might."

"Tell me."

"Why would I?"

"Because we're friends."

"I might be friends with Teal, too."

"I came first."

"Now you're starting to sound like a clingy ex." Aiden points his bottle at me.

I flip him off and face Cole, speaking in a dramatic tone. "Remember all the shit I did for you?"

"Like what?"

"Like throwing parties so you could shag and no one would hear the screams."

He raises an eyebrow.

"What? You thought I didn't hear them?" I grin.

"Told you, Captain." Aiden smirks.

"You too, King." I squeeze his shoulder. "I might have some footage."

"No, you don't." Aiden scoffs. "If you did, you would've used it for your cause about now."

Fuck. I really should've kept some footage. Surely Lars and his conniving mind would've made it happen. He might even have an entry about it in his little black book.

"Besides…" Cole tilts his head. "Why should we do the work for you? Where's the fun in that?"

It's times like these I wish Xander was here. His playfulness balances their arsehole behaviour, but he had to fuck it up with alcohol and disappear for a while.

Wait, is it because I'm surrounded by these two fuckers that I'm starting to have these buried, unusual thoughts?

Those are only excuses and you know it.

"Who told you I haven't done my homework?" I smile. "I'm a lot more than noble. I'm the nobility itself, and there's a manual that says we always get what we want."

"And yet you still can't find an answer." Aiden cocks his head too, so now I have two pairs of eyes judging me.

"Of course I can." *Lie.*

I've watched Teal for a week. She's either in a 'fuck off' mode or an 'I don't care' mode. She doesn't smile, doesn't do any club activities. Her only friends are Elsa and Kim, and she rarely speaks. Her head is usually buried in her phone, reading articles about medieval torture devices.

I charmed Mrs Abbot, the librarian, and found out which books Teal borrowed from the school's library. They're all about wars. Every last fucking one of them.

Why would the nerd only read about wars? Who fucking knows. Cole does read about war, but that's not all. He has philosophy and psychology books. It speaks to his personality a little.

What does it mean if you only read about wars? That you're fucked up, that's what, but that conclusion still doesn't give me any way in with her.

Me being with other girls didn't bother her. I've hugged a few, slapped a few on the arse when she was in view, and she just walked past me as if I and the girls didn't exist.

Being a dick didn't work either. I made sure to slam into her and made her fall to her arse. She merely pulled herself up, gathered her books, and continued on her way as if nothing happened.

Her lack of reaction is beginning to grate on my

fucking nerves. Her disinterest and mighty attitude has started to scrape against my walls, and even I don't know how I'll act if those walls somehow end up falling and letting everything break loose.

"You're used to girls falling at your feet." Cole's voice pulls me out of my head. "It's time someone tells you no."

"She didn't say no—she said yes." The fact that I don't know why she's so insistent about this bloody marriage is probably why I'm on edge.

Sure, she wants to help Ethan, but with her psycho personality, I'm almost certain that's not all.

I focus on her again as she stares at her phone.

What the fuck are you hiding, ma belle?

"Yes can mean no." Aiden takes a sip of his drink. "Ever thought about that?"

"What do you mean?" I ask.

"You've known me for years, haven't you, Astor?"

"I have."

"You know when to stay away and when to get close, and you just act like you don't know sometimes to be a dick."

"Who? *Moi?*" I feign innocence.

"Like that." Aiden points at me. "Your game is strong."

"What he's trying to say is"—Cole twirls his finger—"think with the other side of your brain. Let it loose."

I grin, and my cheeks hurt with the motion. "No idea what you're talking about."

"You'll have to figure it out. Otherwise, you'll just continue to lose." Cole speaks in a calm tone. "Either you make the first move or you have to follow someone else's first move."

In other words, either I go all the way or I lose.

"And think about the kinky stuff, and the…screams." Cole's lips curve in a suggestive smirk. "It might come in handy."

"Real talk, Captain." I dig my fingers into his shoulder. "What will it take for you to tell me what you know?"

"Information," Aiden says matter-of-factly. "Give him something he doesn't know about the subject of his obsession, though I doubt you have any valuables."

I grin, and this time, it's genuine. Since I found out about Cole's hidden tendencies and figured another thing out, I planned to hold on to this piece of information until I needed a serious favour from him, but I'm at the end of a road here, and I need to carve a way out. "I might have."

Cole's head tilts. "What?"

"*Une seconde, mon ami.* If I give you what you want, will you give me what I need?"

"I might."

"Not good enough for the shit I have. It's all documented and with evidence."

He narrows his eyes before quickly going back to normal. "Fine."

Of course Cole would choose his battle instead of anyone else's. He's Cole, after all.

Friends? Fuck that. Those don't exist when it comes to himself.

"You go first, Captain."

Teal insisted she doesn't have a secret, but as I said, everyone does.

And when I have hers, nothing will save her from me.

She'll wish she'd never said yes.

SIX

Teal

Since I turned eighteen a month ago, I've been waiting for this moment—or rather waiting for the response.

The letter with the black envelope and red writing.

The acceptance.

The possible solution to all the fuckery that's been happening in my life.

I adjust my mask as I walk through the hall of the club.

It's more exclusive than the palace and needs more intervention than MI6's agents. I first got my ticket here a month ago after I convinced one of the random men I met at a pub that we could meet here.

It was, of course, a lie. Spending one night with him had already been too unremarkable.

He was the last one. I've been dissatisfied for a long time now, and I realised after that night that I should stop. It was all a waste of my time.

I cut out all my random escapades a few days before the official engagement with Ronan. I wouldn't call it that official, though. People know about it, but it's not announced vastly, and I refused the ring until we're at least out of school.

Not that this game will go on until then.

The reason I stopped the encounters has nothing to do with the engagement and everything to do with me.

It's been more than a week since that dinner at the Astor mansion. Ronan still lives his life as if nothing happened, and I get to live mine the same.

After all, it's just a contract, a convenience, a link between our families and a thread to my plan. Nothing more or less.

I meant it—he can bring it. Nothing will sway me, and there's no way in hell he'll have me abandoning what I started.

Holding the acceptance letter between my fingers, my insides hum with excitement as I follow the girl down the hall with red carpets and walls covered in black flowery wallpaper.

It's the theme of the club, *La Débauche*. As its name suggests, it's for debauchery, depravity and…fantasy.

I first discovered it in my trips through the dark web. Then I found one of its members on *Tinder* and hooked up with him that night. That meeting got me my entrance recommendation.

Since then, I've been coming here to be part of the *Audience Society*, the voyeurs who watched the titillation of the human mind through their bodies.

It was fascinating. It was the first time I thought of something as that in…forever.

Watching those girls fall to their knees in front of stronger, bigger, and older men always had me rubbing my thighs.

I've had sex before, but I've never once had an orgasm or gotten wet enough to make the experience pleasurable. I've always chosen older men, at least fifteen years older than me and experienced, and still…nothing.

I was starting to think I was broken beyond repair and that I'd never feel the ecstasy Elsa and Kim keep talking about. I thought the feeling was foreign, just like me.

La Débauche's scenes brought back some of that faith and the possibility of more.

That's why I applied to be 'Debauched'. One night, one

stranger, and that's it. I was rejected two times, but today, I received my acceptance letter.

The greatest policy here is anonymity. The reason I found Richard on the dark web is because he posted a shot of the invitation card in his public profile.

Here, no one knows who you are or where you came from. There are no names, just numbers. No faces, just black masks like the ones from costume parties. All women wear black satin gowns, and all men wear black trousers.

That's it.

That's all that's needed.

As soon as they confirm you're over eighteen, the sky's the limit.

I have no idea how they accept people here, but it seems to be a tight process. I don't even know how I got in. Even with Richard's referral, it seemed so farfetched at the time, but I still threw in my letter anyway, hoping for something different.

That's all I've been doing my entire life, wishing the shadow weren't a normal state of mind and that different didn't actually mean crazy.

Different just means…special.

That's what Knox and Dad tell me, but the problem lies in believing them.

This club is different. It's more than different; it's an open door to many things I never thought were possible.

And now, I won't only be watching—I'll participate.

Not exhibition-style, though. I applied for a private session because, well, I might like to watch, but being watched is a different thing altogether. It means being bare, and I don't like that.

The attendant, wearing a maid's outfit and a mask, motions at a room. "Through here, Ms 115."

I walk past her. The room has the same black wallpaper and red carpets. There's no window like the other rooms I participated in, no bed or sofa, not even a chair.

The attendant reaches her hand out. "Have you filled out the form, Ms 115?"

"Uh…yeah." I finally release the acceptance letter that has the form attached to it from between my sweaty fingers.

The form is a checklist about what I won't allow and what I'm good with. I'm not good with anal, flogs, crops, any extreme pain, or being tied down, and that's it.

I wanted to ask for a thirty or forty-something man, but they didn't have an age option. However, all I've seen so far is older men who know how to handle a woman. *La Débauche* attracts a specific type of dominant males who have been in this depravity game for far too long.

"Do you want to review it one last time?" she asks.

"I-I'm okay." *Shit.* Why the hell am I stammering? I wanted this. It's my last chance at normal before I pass the point of no return.

She hands me a black blindfold. "As you requested."

I take it from her with trembling fingers. "Thank you."

"Please wait for Mr 120 on your knees." I nod, and she smiles. "I wish you a lovely night."

And with that, the door clicks closed behind her.

With one last breath, I sink to my knees on the thick red carpet, gripping the blindfold like it's a lifeline.

Considering what happened in the past, this is the last thing I should do, but oddly enough, the moment I wrap the blindfold around my eyes, turning my world black, a sense of clarity falls over me.

I don't think of Dad, Knox, or even Agnus, and what they would feel if they saw me in this position. I only think about those scenes I watched, the anonymity of it, the throbbing tension and that need for more.

Therapy didn't work, so maybe this will. It's a different type of therapy—the titillating kind.

The door opens, its click loud and deafening in the silence

of the room. My breathing quickens as the air fills with another presence.

I don't see him, but that doesn't mean I don't feel him.

Just like in the past.

I inhale through my nose and exhale through clenched teeth. This is different. This time, I consent to it.

This time, I want it.

Is it sick to want something that used to terrify the fuck out of me?

Or maybe it's sick that I've run after it ever since I realised what sex is all about.

The presence stops in front of me. I don't move even as I feel his shadow falling over me.

It's strange how the other senses kick into gear when sight is gone. I think people don't understand just how important your eyes are.

Now that my world is black, I hear every pulse in my ear and feel each breath going into and coming out of my lungs, and I sink into the scraping of the gown against my bare skin. As per the club's policies, I'm wearing nothing underneath, and because of that, the buds of my nipples strain against the cloth. I have no doubt they're visible for him.

Does he like it? Appreciate it?

For some reason, I can't smell him. I do smell myself though— the lime scent. No idea why it feels like it's coming from him, too.

Does he also smell of lime and citrus?

A hand falls on my shoulder, and I stiffen, my old signs trying to push against the intrusion. I breathe deeply, camouflaging that need.

It's big, his hand, but it's not calloused, just slightly so. It feels like the type of hand that will soon flip me over and fuck me against the ground.

Shit.

Why do I want that?

It's too fast even for me, and yet there's this unusual longing for Mr 120's touch. Could be because of the blindfold or how good his skin feels on mine.

He slips the gown's strap down my shoulder, the touch slow and sensual. For a second, I hold my breath, unable to stifle the pleasurable sensation crawling up my throat.

As he does the same with my other strap, my breasts slip out with a gentle bounce. They're heavy and aching, and… strange. I've never had my breasts hurt this much, and he hasn't even touched them yet.

It's the anticipation.

The sick, thrilling anticipation.

Those same fingers clutch my jaw and lift it so I'm staring up—or my blindfolded eyes are anyway. The easy way he handles me is a sign of experience. He must've done this a thousand times before. I instantly feel safe at that thought.

His fingers trail down my neck, pausing at my collarbone to squeeze slightly. I stop breathing for a second, my thighs pressing together.

God. He's only touching my collarbone and I'm ready to spread my legs wide for him.

He cups my breasts with both hands, and I purse my lips, trying to keep in the foreign sound that's trying to escape.

The pads of his thumbs run over the tips and I jolt in place as a zap of pleasure shoots straight between my legs.

Holy. Shit.

Is that supposed to feel that good? He's merely touching my nipples—that's all. Just touching them. He's not twirling or squeezing or anything.

I've always had sensitive nipples, but this is a new level.

He twists the tight buds. This time, I can't hold in the sound, and I let the moan fall free in the silence of the room.

I don't even know what's happening to me, but my back arches, pushing my breasts into his expert hands.

Pinching one nipple, he teases the other with a feathery touch. It's so soft and yet so damn painful. I never thought nipple play could get this unbearable or out of control.

It's like I'm losing all common sense and my body only listens to this stranger's ministrations.

My belly dips and an odd type of stickiness coats my thighs.

Am I...wet?

How on earth did that happen? And what the hell is this sweeping sensation forming at the bottom of my stomach?

He twists both nipples again, making me whimper and squirm. He goes back to the gentle caress just to pinch again. My pussy stings and I'm tempted to reach out and touch that ache.

The moment I do, he stops his ministrations.

No, no.

Why did he...oh, is it because I'm touching myself?

"I-I'll be good," I murmur, my voice so sexual it almost doesn't sound like mine.

I let my hands drop to my sides again. He makes no sound or move, and I start to think I ruined the whole thing.

But then he returns to torturing my nipples. With each brush of his skin against mine and every cruel pinch, I moan aloud.

It's too raw, too real.

Just too much.

He squeezes my nipples one more time, and my moan breaks into something so utterly foreign I stop making sounds altogether for a second.

It's like being attacked from the inside out and I need to push it outside. The wave is so sudden and violent it steals my voice.

I grip the stranger's arms, his fingers still pulling on my nipples as my pussy contracts and more juices coat my thighs.

Holy. Hell.

I think I just…came.

For the first time in my life, I had an orgasm, and he didn't even have to touch my most intimate part.

What would he do if he got to that? Break me?

And why the hell am I getting so hot and bothered at that idea?

Even as the wave slowly subsides, I don't release my hold on him. My nails dig into his forearms—they're strong, feeling veiny to the touch, as expected from an older man.

I sigh, my heart rate slowly leaving the dangerous range and going back to normal.

My nipples still ache and throb, probably because he still hasn't released them yet. He runs his thumbs over the tips again as if testing that they're still hard and hungry for more.

This is one of those moments I wish I could have with a real person, not a stranger or in a fantasy or in a club.

But people like me aren't supposed to have these things.

They were stolen a long time ago, and like any missing object, it's impossible to get them back.

Something similar to shame sinks in my chest at the thought. How come I've become the girl who searches for normal in places that are nowhere near normal?

I shake my head internally. I'll have all the time to think about that later. Now, I just need to focus on my night, make my teenage mistakes, and then move along.

"Huh." His voice echoes around me like doom. "I didn't know nipple orgasm was actually possible."

I swallow so hard the sound is audible in the quiet of the room.

No.

I heard it wrong.

I must've. It can't be him.

It just can't.

I reach for the blindfold with trembling fingers, my pulse roaring in my ears like a disaster looming in the distance.

The moment I pull the black cloth over my head, a gasp leaves my lips.

He stands right in front me, wearing nothing but black trousers from which a V line is peeking. He's lean, but his chest muscles are developed to perfection, adding a lethal edge to his previously approachable appearance. His hands are still playing with my breasts even as a wicked grin curves his lips.

I feel something break inside me as he speaks.

"Bonsoir, ma belle."

SEVEN

Ronan

I never thought there would be a day when I'd consider Teal beautiful.

She did have some sort of external beauty. Elsa calls her snow white with her tiny features, porcelain skin, and naturally red lips, but it was never quite *it*, you know. It's not the type that grabs you by the gut—or rather by the dick—and refuses to let go.

As she kneels in front of me, half-naked, her gown bunching around her waist and her huge black eyes staring up at me, I see it.

Her beauty.

It's a special type, the kind you not only want to stare at but also want to trap somewhere so you're the only one who sees it. It's kind of sick, but it fits her.

Everything about her is beautiful, from the flushing of her cheeks, the parting of her lips, and the slight perspiration covering her pale skin to the erratic rise and fall of her chest that causes her generous tits to push further into my hands.

Her pale pink nipples are red from my ministrations, and I still can't let them go. My dick strains against the sorry excuse for trousers, and I inhale a deep breath while taking in her confusion mixed with the scent of her arousal.

Well, fuck.

I've fucked more girls than I could count, and none of them—absolutely none—had this effect on my dick.

Ron Astor the Second is ready to rip someone in half, and not just anyone.

Her.

The girl who orgasmed by just nipple play. The girl who appears like a robot but is actually turned on by a simple blindfold and the teasing of her nipples.

When Cole mentioned this place, I almost didn't believe him. Teal might appear like a goth with a tendency of calling out Satan in night-time rituals, but she's Ethan's good girl. After all, she wanted the engagement for his sake.

Surely she wouldn't be in a place that's fit for Cole's defective brain. But then, sure enough, I saw her.

Here. Wearing a black gown and waiting to be devoured.

Since Cole's family owns this business of debauchery, and he's the one who accepted her application so soon, it didn't take me long to not only become a member but to also have her as my first meal.

Teal Van Doren is more than what meets the eye, indeed. I didn't know I needed to read her fantasies until I had them on paper in front of me.

All laid out for my pleasure reading.

I begrudgingly release one of her swollen nipples and continue tracing the other as I reach into my pocket and retrieve my phone.

"Say cheese." I snap a picture of her dazed, flushed state.

That manages to snap her out of her stupor. Teal pushes back so abruptly she nearly falls over.

To my dismay, I lose all feel of her nipple as she rises to her shaking feet. Her tits bounce with the motion, giving me one last view before she pulls up the straps of her gown, covering them and herself.

Hiding those beauties is a tragedy that needs to be mourned.

She runs a hand through her straight hair. To her credit, she does regain her composure and adopts her haughty default state, but it's not soon enough to hide the slight tremble in her fingers or the goosebumps covering her arms.

No one can hide involuntary bodily reactions—not even with her level of emotional blankness.

I rattled her. One point for me.

"What the hell are you doing here?"

"Being debauched like you." I grin. "Actually, I'm the one doing the debauchery, but details."

"Phones aren't allowed h-here." She bites her lower lip, trapping it against her teeth as if reprimanding herself for stuttering.

And suddenly, a thought I never had becomes my sole purpose in life. I want my teeth on that lip. I want to lick it, bite it, then devour it.

But that's kind of a wrong thought, isn't it?

It's probably this place and her earlier state; they're playing with my fucking head.

As if you never knew you had this in you?

Shush, thoughts.

"I guess I kind of snuck it in." I lift a shoulder as if saying 'Oops'. "You're really special, though, aren't you, *ma belle?* Nipple orgasm is so hot."

"Fuck you." Her cheeks flush, but it's not entirely embarrassment; there's also a hint of rage.

I grin.

It's the first show of emotions she's ever given up. Anger is good; anger makes people commit mistakes. That's why I make sure I'm rarely angry, if ever. I might feign it, but I always stay the fuck away from it.

Anger is the source of all evil.

Teal here is ashamed of her orgasm—or rather the one who caused her pleasure. Since she can't say that out loud because it'd mean admitting it, the pent-up frustration is turning into what resembles rage.

"I'm happy to oblige, *ma belle*. I can come up with other types of orgasms we can try out." Lie—I don't need to come up with them. My perverted head has been filled with them since the moment I walked in here and saw her kneeling on the floor.

"But first," I continue, "I need you to tell your daddy and my daddy that you're calling off the engagement."

"That won't happen."

I scroll through my phone, feigning a sigh. "Then I guess Ethan can see what places his daughter frequents. Are you sure you want to scar him with the image of your tits? Don't get me wrong, they're wonderful tits, but they're not fit for your dad. Unless…you have a daddy kink?"

She gulps audibly, her delicate throat moving with the motion. One day, I don't know when, but I'm going to grab her by that throat and fuck the living shit out of her until she can't move.

Okay. That was too explicit even for my perverted brain.

"Besides," I continue. "I assure you, Earl Edric Astor wouldn't approve of a daughter-in-law who likes to be treated like a slut. Since I'm a gentleman, I'm giving you the chance to walk out of this unscathed. We both get what we want. Win-win."

We stare at each other for a second. I watch her body language for a sign. Her chest that used to rise and fall heavily is now serene, calm almost.

Good. She learnt her place.

Just then, she pounces on me. No kidding—she jumps at me like a flying animal, her legs wrapping around my waist as she lunges straight at the phone in my hand.

Well, fuck me.

Out of all the reactions I expected from her, this was the last. Fuck, it wasn't even on the list. She didn't let her height keep her down when she made the decision to come at me.

A fighter.

Why the hell do I want to break that or somehow engross myself in it?

Her face reddens as her gown bunches up her thighs in her struggle to reach my hand. Even by using my body as some sort of a ladder, she can't reach the phone.

I keep it up. When she thinks she's got it, I throw it to the other hand, making her cheeks redden more, her chest rising more. Her breathing turns harsh, causing her tits to strain against my bare chest.

When she realises she can't reach it, she scratches my arm with her black-painted nails. The sting burns my skin and I react immediately, slamming her back against the wall.

A yelp escapes her throat, but before she can react, I grab both her wrists in one hand and pin them above her head, securing them with a hand.

Now, I have a tiny frame wrapping her legs around my waist, her chest against mine, and her arms are confined.

At my mercy.

Or the lack thereof.

"Let me go," she hisses, but her gaze follows my hand that's clutching the phone as I let it fall to my side.

I motion at the angry red scratch marks on my forearm. It's like I've been attacked by a kitten—a small, furious kitten.

"You hurt me," I say with a dispassionate tone.

"You want a prize for that?" She strains, trying to get free, but I'm pinning her so thoroughly she's barely able to move.

"No. I'm more interested in justice. You hurt me, so I should hurt you back, don't you think?"

To her credit, she tries to hide it, but her eyes widen the slightest bit, and to my fucking surprise, it's not out of fear.

A spark just passed through the dim colour of her eyes, almost like a shooting star in a moonless night. It disappears as soon as it appears.

Well, well, well.

Looks like Teal Van Doren has perfect control over her expression. But there's something she's not quite successful at controlling—something that permeates the air with a musky, distinctive smell.

"Are you turned on by the prospect of being hurt, *ma belle?*" I smirk, drawing out the words slowly.

"You wish."

"You did come by nipple pain just now. Does the thought of pain make you soaked?"

She purses her lips but says nothing to deny or to confirm.

"You know." I slide my phone into the pocket of my trousers and reach my fingers to lift her chin.

Her lips are pink, full, and have this heart shape that could use some devouring or could be wrapped around Ron Astor the Second—I'm not picky.

She glares at me as if she wishes she could bite my eye out with her teeth. I wouldn't put it past her. She's a bit crazy, and fuck me, it's starting to grow on me.

"You don't have to hide it. I can feel your arousal on my stomach and smell it in the fucking air."

She clenches her thighs then loosens them with the intent to come down. I slam her against the wall again.

The moment she gasps, I crush my lips to hers. She tastes like…madness, the type you can never get away from or with. It's the type that gets under your skin, and soon enough, you don't know whether you're losing your sanity or your life.

Her lips tremble as if she doesn't know what to do or how to do it. Her tongue moves tentatively against mine before it stops. She doesn't kiss me back, but I don't allow her the chance to.

For the first time in my life, I fucking feast on someone. Using my grip on her jaw, I squeeze it open so I can claim her tongue, bite it with my teeth, suck it with my lips. I steal her breath and her damn sanity just like she's been doing with me.

She stirred up my ugly side, and now she has to become its target.

I, Ronan Astor, the most attentive lover you could ever find, want to break someone—but not just anyone.

Her.

I want to smash her tiny body against mine until she can never find an escape. And I want her to enjoy every second of it.

Tiny teeth latch onto my lower lip then bite—hard. Both of us taste the strong metal as she shoves away from me.

In her attempts to pull away, she stumbles to her unsteady feet. I expect her to fight me, to curse me, but she simply stares at my lips, at the blood she left there, as if she can't look away. Then she wipes the blood off hers, still not breaking eye contact with my lips.

It's like she's in a trance and can't break free.

Seeming to realise that, she turns around, and as I warned her she would, she runs.

It's useless, though. She can't run away anymore.

Different times. Different circumstances.

They say you should find what you love and keep it close.

The same can be said about what you hate.

EIGHT

Teal

I don't know how I get home.

One moment I'm running out of the club, and the next I'm hiding under my covers.

My breathing is choppy and harsh even though it's been an hour since I arrived at my room. Even longer since his hands were on me, and yet that's the only thing my body thinks of.

The way he took control of me, how he brought me to orgasm.

God, I can't believe I came by just the teasing of my nipples. Shouldn't there be a natural law against that or something?

I wish all my arousal had disappeared when I saw his face—his stupid symmetrical face—but it didn't.

Not even close.

Those aristocratic features were nowhere near boring at that moment, or ordinary. All I saw was the one person, the first person who made me feel.

Really feel.

I felt so much it was unbearable. That's why I still can't come down from that high even now.

Then he grabbed me, trapping me, and although the signs of an attack nearly swept me over the edge, they didn't.

They freaking *didn't*.

Usually, I'd have an episode if someone as much as tried to cage me. It brings back dark memories, thoughts, and smells, but at that moment? When he took all my will against the wall, I felt a strange sense of awareness. My nipples hurt even more than when he touched them.

They still do. They're sensitive, throbbing, and sending tingles down to my core.

A shiver snaps through my spine and I curse myself, throwing the covers off and breathing heavily. So what if he touched me and it somehow didn't suck? So what if he's more than his gigolo image and has more depth? And he does have depth. The moment his smile disappeared—which is rare as hell—it was almost as if a different person altogether emerged.

A person who finds sick pleasure in trapping me, subjugating me to his will and mercy.

Still, that doesn't change anything.

Ronan Astor is only a pawn in my game, a domino. That's it.

That's *all*.

He took that picture of me, and he'll use it to threaten me to end the engagement and my damn plan. If anything, he's my worst enemy now, and I'll deal with him as such.

I retrieve my phone, determined to read an article or two then go to sleep. Tomorrow, I'll deal with the mess that is Ronan Astor.

I won't allow him to step on me even if it's the last thing I do.

Of their own accord, my fingers hover over the Instagram app. I don't even use Instagram—or any social media, for that matter—but the other day, I made an account. It has zero followers, is following one, and lacks any profile picture.

The only reason I started it was to see what he posts in my quest to read him.

Ronan's Instagram is a translation of his bubbly, energetic

personality. It's filled with pictures of him and his friends half-naked. Most of the shots are in pools with bikini-clad girls, and he always showcases that signature sickening smile.

A smile that hides more than it shows.

I hover over a picture of him from the side taken without his notice. It's after one of the games and he's wearing the team's blue uniform. The stadium's lights shine on him as he throws his head back in deep, radiant laughter that glows on his entire face.

How can he fake that? Even I fell for it, and I don't understand human emotions all that much.

How could someone be so carefree and yet bottling up so much inside?

It doesn't make sense.

Either you're on this side or that—it can't be both.

I scroll down below and find a picture of him leaning down to hug his mother's shoulder. She's smiling at the camera, and his grin in this one is almost too boyish, softer than the others.

The caption says: *Her ladyship. A woman after my own heart.*

Interesting. I keep that information for later use.

I'm about to exit when he posts a picture. I click on the notification so fast I'm scared I actually alert him to my presence.

It's a selfie of him lying on a bed, half-naked as usual, as he places a hand on his stomach—the same stomach I wrapped my legs around not long ago. The same stomach I rubbed myself on so he'd release me while having a crazy thought of *What if he doesn't?*

The caption says: *In the mood for some debauchery.*

Swallowing, I click on the picture to study his messed-up hair and the slight smile on his face.

It's like we're still in that room. He's pinning my wrists against the wall as my nipples brush against his naked chest and my core is sticky with arousal on his stomach.

My hand snakes under my pyjama shorts and cotton underwear to find my folds—my wet folds.

It's still such a weird sensation to be wet. I have a toy and I touch myself, but it's felt so bland, so uninteresting, even, that I started to wonder if I'm somehow asexual.

Right now, though? As I stare at his face, at his hand on his stomach where I was not long ago, there's no asexuality whatsoever.

I rub my fingers over my clit and my lids flutter closed. Rich brown eyes invade my thoughts, and I moan then hide my face in my pillow to muffle the sound.

He's gripping me by the wrists, pinning me, making me helpless as he dry-humps me over and over again.

He's kissing me hard and fast and he's touching me, flicking my clit, twisting my nipple —

I come.

I don't even know how it happens, but my body shakes and I free-fall into a feeling so addictive I want to restart all over again.

My eyes snap open, and I find his face in that picture.

What the hell is he doing to me? Why am I letting him?

I pull my hand from between my sticky legs, feeling disgusted that I let him, a pawn, get to me this way.

He won't.

Absolutely won't.

I start to tuck the phone away then notice I clicked like.

Oh no.

No, no, no.

I remove it immediately. He probably receives a thousand notifications, so surely he didn't notice it.

Just when I'm about to throw my phone to the ground, it vibrates with a text. I startle, my heart nearly jumping into my throat when I make out his name.

Ronan: Hey, stalker *winking emoji*

He noticed. Oh, god, he noticed.

What is wrong with me today?

But fuck him, really. I won't reply.

When I ignore his text, he sends another.

Ronan: How-about-no98 is an interesting username, by the way.

I glare at the phone as if I can wrench him out of it and punch him in the face.

Ronan: Also, your scratch still hurts. Want to come kiss it better?

Teal: I should've scratched you harder.

I curse myself as I hit Send. Why the hell am I even indulging him? I broke so many of my patterns today, and it's all because of him. I should stay the hell away from him to avoid any other disaster.

Ronan: Pain. Yum.

My legs clench, and the orgasm from earlier feels like it's rising to the surface all over again. Just how can he elicit this reaction from me?

But if he thinks he can get me out of my element and receive no retaliation, he has another thing coming.

Teal: You're not my type. Get over yourself.

Ronan: And what's your type, *ma belle?*

Teal: My type is at least fifteen years older, experienced, and doesn't smile the entire time like a gigolo on crack. In short, not you.

I feel a weight slide off my chest as I send that text. I needed to remind myself of that fact as much as letting him know, because that's what's bothering me about the whole thing—the fact that he, someone not even close to being my type, is invading my thoughts this much.

There's a long pause before he sends his next text.

Ronan: And yet you came when I only touched your tits.

Teal: That's because I didn't know it was you.

Ronan: Is that why your arousal still coats my stomach?

My cheeks heat and I curse him all the ways to Sunday.

Ronan: It's all dried up, but it's there. You saw it on that IG pic. I'm not washing it off.

Teal: You're sick.

Ronan: I like to think I'm not sicker than you, *ma belle*, but I love the competition.

Ronan: Cancel the engagement and I might fuck you.

I might fuck you? *Might?* As in his gracing me with his damn cock? The arrogance of this bastard.

Teal: As if I would ever want to fuck you.

Ronan: I think we should both agree that you did tonight.

Teal: I did not.

Ronan: Sure. Whatever helps you sleep better at night.

I can almost imagine his smirk, and I want to smash his face and this stupid feeling of embarrassment with it.

Ronan: Night, *ma belle*. I'll dream of your orgasm face.

I throw my phone to the side, seething, my heart beating so hard it's nearly dangerous.

He thinks it's fine to play with me? He'll see what playing means.

NINE

Ronan

There's this thing about breaking habits that messes with the human brain.

Or that's what Cole says. I believe him, anyway, because he reads more than the pope reads the bible.

My point is, breaking my habits is what's making me weird. I can see it loud and clear now.

I went from throwing a party every other night, smoking my stash of weed, and fucking exotic girls to living like a priest.

The partying part can be overcome. Not only does Lars no longer bitch at me to stop, the absence of night fun also means Mum is home. I get to have breakfasts and dinners with her every day. Needless to say, her presence matters more than all those other strangers who only exist in my life because I have money and status.

Mum being here also means Dad is around, too, and that kind of sucks, especially since he's been watching me more closely lately.

Lars and I have put on an Oscar-level performance each time he's asked about a missing item.

Or rather, I put on the performance and Lars follows along. It's become our thing since that night.

The excuses usually follow the same pattern of *What? We had that? We must've given it to friends.*

Dad reminds me that we don't have that many friends, and I tell him of course we do. They just visit when he's not around because they seem to love me. It's like he's baiting me to admit something, and for some reason, it doesn't feel like he's interested in the partying part.

The only untouched things are Mom's paintings, which she's spent years collecting. She studied art before she had tremors and had to stop drawing altogether.

Or maybe that's the version of things my father came up with to convince her to remain a housewife—or rather his bloody secretary, whom he paraded around the globe.

Anyway, back to the point, the lack of sex is the reason behind the shitshow a few days ago at *La Débauche*. If I'd been fucking like a normal human being, I would've never had those thoughts about Teal or sent her those texts.

Or dreamt about an affair between her mouth and Ron Astor the Second.

Now is the time to fix it.

Then, I'll corner her and have her visit my father and tell him all too politely that she's breaking off the engagement.

I drag Claire behind me to a storage room at the back of the library. She giggles as we sneak through the rows of books.

Claire is one of the few I've fucked more than once. As long as I bring her to orgasm, she lets me do whatever I want.

Except what you really want to do, you mean?

Shush, thoughts.

As soon as we're away from prying eyes, I flip Claire's dark brown hair over her shoulder. "Strip for me."

She licks her lower lip and I wait for her to refuse, but she throws her uniform's jacket away then unbuttons her shirt. I reach into her lacy bra and twist her nipples, and she sighs.

Sighs? Really?

I ignore that and tease her nipples some more. She leans into me, breathing with delight. Fuck, it's like I'm caressing her.

Not like a certain someone who detonated all over the floor after I only touched her nipples.

But this isn't about her.

I lift my hand and grab Claire's jaw then open her mouth using my fingers.

"Do you want me to blow you?" Claire asks in a sultry voice that's…wrong.

So damn wrong.

I can't even get Ron Astor the Second to wake up for her.

I-I'll be good.

Her voice barges into my mind like a fucking train wreck.

"Say I'll be good," I tell Claire.

"I'll be good." She runs her tongue over her upper lip and fingers my tie. "Aren't you like *sooo* overdressed, though?"

"That's not the tone." I smile. "Say it right."

Her brows furrow. "What do you mean?"

It hits me then like doom with all the damning sounds. It's not her voice that I want to hear or her face that I want to see.

In all the years I've been fucking my way through the female population, I always had that sense of dissatisfaction. I brought them to orgasm and had mine in return, but there was always something missing.

I ignored it for years, pretending it was wrong.

But that night, when Teal rubbed all over my stomach, I realised what I've been missing.

It's the depravity of the act.

I have never in my life been as hard as I was while her body was wrapped all over me.

And I mean fucking *never*.

Since he witnessed that scene, Ron Astor the Second has become picky and refuses to get hard for anyone.

It's not Claire's fault; it's his.

I'm about to push her away when the door opens. Light

comes through the slight crack before those slender fish-net-stocking-covered legs come into view.

Teal is breathing heavily as she glues her back to the door, closing it behind her, and clutches her chest, seeming oblivious to her surroundings.

She bends over, her harsh breathing filling the dim space, but I can make out her dishevelled state, the parting of her lips even as her hair falls on either side of her face.

Is she having some sort of an attack?

Now that I think about it, she's always had these moments where she disappears to the middle of nowhere and no one can find her.

"Um, excuse us?" Claire places a hand on her hips, turning slightly to face her. "This spot is occupied."

Teal's body jerks, her head snapping up. The blackness of her eyes appears even more desolate with the lack of light.

The moment she sees me, her expression softens, but it only lasts for a second. The rest of the scene in front of her becomes clear—Claire half-naked, my hands on her chest—and just like that, Teal's features turn into a blank façade.

Unfeeling.

Empty.

She wants me to think none of this affects her? Fuck that.

"I didn't know anyone was in here." She starts to turn around.

"You can stay and watch." I smile. "Right, Claire?"

The latter nods, too eager to end this and go tell her friends she fucked Ronan Astor. Girls here use me and I use them back—win-win.

Teal doesn't make a move to stay.

Someone is running away.

My lips rise in a smirk. "Unless something about it bothers you?"

"You flatter yourself." She faces me fully, her hands hanging limp by her sides.

"How about we give my fiancée a show, Claire?" I grin at her. "She's a bit of a voyeur."

I think Teal's jaw clenches, but it disappears all too soon.

"Absolutely, Ron," Claire says breathlessly.

"On your knees, love." I'm speaking to Claire, but my attention is on the girl by the door. "Suck me off and make it good so my fiancée can get some pointers."

Claire sinks to her knees without any protest, her fingers playing with my belt.

Come on, ma belle. *You know you want to stop this.*

Teal's gaze remains uninterested, detached even as the situation progresses before her eyes. Her hands tremble a little; it wouldn't even be noticeable if I wasn't watching her like a hawk.

Claire is now unbuttoning my trousers, and I groan. "How do you feel watching your future husband being blown by someone else, *ma belle*? Does it turn you on?"

Teal's gaze strays to Claire's fingers before it slides back to my face. "There's one type that turns me on, and I'll see it tonight in that place we both know so well. This time, I'll make sure you don't ruin it. Maybe I'll make you watch, too, for pointers and all that."

I grin even though my jaw clenches.

Well played, fiancée.

But does she think I would mind having some older man touch her, bringing her to orgasm by just teasing her nipples and watching her face flushing as she trembles all over?

I don't care.

Fuck—I *do* care.

Why the fuck do I care?

I'm about to stop Claire when Teal barges towards us. It's like that night when she jumped me in a second. A knee-jerk reaction.

She grabs Claire by the hair and pulls her back. The girl shrieks as she falls on her arse. "What the —"

"Leave." Teal glares down at her.

"No, you leave, you freak." Claire rises to her feet, about to attack her.

Teal stops her with a hand to her face. I don't know how she does it, but she appears normal even though her body is shaking with rage or agitation—or both. It's like her face can't catch up with her emotions.

She pushes her out of the closet, throws her jacket after her, and slams the door shut in her face, cutting off all Claire's shrieks and protests.

When she faces me again, the blankness is still there, but her hands are balled into fists by her sides.

"There goes my BJ for the day." I keep my voice light-hearted. "Did you kick Claire out to finish the job?"

"Dream. On."

"Aw, you've never given head before? I can help with that." I point in front of me. "The first step is to get on your knees."

She crosses her arms over her chest.

"Oh, wait." My lips curve in a smirk. "You like pain with that, too?"

She says nothing.

I button my trousers back, and she watches the movement as if my dick will jump on her or something.

Truth be told, he does want to do that.

"If you didn't plan to take Claire's place, why did you kick her out?"

Her eyes harden, but she huffs and looks the other way.

"Huh. Is it because—"

"I don't know."

"You don't know?" I approach her until once again she's against a surface and I'm towering over her.

I'm starting to like this position, maybe even love it.

She seems to realise this fact as well since her nails dig into her arms.

Teal doesn't back away though. She has this adorable habit of glaring even when she's cornered.

There's so much fight in her, and I want to explore it inch by agonising inch then maybe break it.

Definitely break it, so I can see what's behind it.

"All I know is," she says in a neutral voice, "if you do that again, I'll also be having people go down on me in front of you. I'm your fiancée, and that makes me your equal, not your toy. If you disrespect me in front of other people, I'll do the same."

I smile, but there's no humour behind it. "What makes you think I care?"

"Then continue. By all means, let's see who's the biggest exhibitionist between the two of us. For the record, I never lose."

Fuck. This girl.

"You're not going to *La Débauche* tonight." Or ever, for that matter, but that's for another day.

"Why not?" she taunts. "I can have someone strip me as I get on my knees for him. I feel like recreating the scene from just now."

I grab her by her nape and she stills, her breath hitching. Fuck me, just one touch and she's already this responsive.

What would it be like if I pinned her down and ate her out like she's my last meal? Or better yet, if I fucked her without holding back, like I've always wanted?

"L-Let me go."

"You might want to make that a bit more convincing," I whisper.

"Ronan…"

"*Oui, ma belle?*"

"If you don't let me go—"

"What? You'll leave another love bite like the one on my lip?" I tap the slight cut that's slowly healing.

Her gaze follows my finger and she swallows, her breaths crackling in the silence of the closet.

"Does it turn you on to know you hurt me?"

"What? No." Her voice is the lowest I've ever heard.

My little crazy beauty.

"Then is it the prospect of being hurt in return?" My finger traces up and down the skin of her nape, and that's when I feel the shiver that overtakes her.

When she says nothing, I lean in to whisper, "You don't have to hide your crazy from me, *ma belle*. Show it, and I promise to feast on it."

She shoves me away, her cheeks turning red. I chuckle as she opens the door and bolts outside.

"You have a week to break off the engagement," I call after her in my charming tone.

She doesn't turn back and runs to the nearest exit.

This is the second time she's run away from me, but there won't be a third.

TEN

Teal

"**H**ey, Agnus." I smile for the first time today. Knox likes to tease me by saying I smile only once a day, and I'm hoping he doesn't catch on like Elsa has and realise who I smile at.

I snap the seatbelt in place as the car swerves in the streets.

Agnus has raised Knox and me as if we were his children. When we were eight, Knox and I were kidnapped by his brother, Reginald, though I wouldn't actually call it kidnapping. Knox and I were running away from the brothel in which Mum worked. We were starved and cold, *so* cold; I can still feel the chill on winter nights even when I'm under covers.

Reginald was this posh driver who offered us food if we met his mistress. Knox didn't like it and said we shouldn't go, but I took Reginald's hand and we went into his car.

We had our food. We ate so much until I thought we were going to burst, but being hungry dirty kids, we continued to eat because we never knew when we'd eat next.

Then, Reginald's mistress showed up—Dad's dead wife, Abigail—and she was a spitting image of how Elsa looks now.

She was kind and showered us then gave us new clothes. I didn't speak, not even once, but Knox kept thanking her and being his charming self.

What we didn't know was that she was mentally ill and only fed children who looked like her dead son. The moment she found out I was a girl who had my hair cut short, she kind of flipped.

Knox and I were trapped in an underground basement for days or weeks, I still don't remember. We barely ate, and she once cut our knees so we'd have the same injury as her son.

Back then, Knox cried, even as he hugged me and told me everything would be okay.

I didn't.

I was too numb, and it wasn't because of that incident. I didn't speak either. All I kept doing was licking my lips to taste the last of the chocolate we'd had.

Then Dad showed up.

People think knights are your love interests, but mine is Dad, Ethan.

He saved us from his wife and was about to take us back to Mum, but Knox begged him not too.

I just shrunk back, my whole body shaking at the thought of having to return to that life in the brothel and go through everything that came with it.

Even though it's been more than ten years, I still remember the first time Agnus spoke to me. Dad was busy talking to Knox, and then this man crouched in front of me and asked in a soothing tone, "You don't want to go back?"

I shook my head so hard he smiled and made me stop.

"Can you say that?"

"Don't take us back, please." It was the first time I'd spoken in weeks, and it was because of Agnus.

He didn't hug me, though. Dad did, and maybe that's why I see him as my knight.

Agnus is different. I watch his side profile with a small sigh. I never considered him a father. Weird, I know. After all, he's the one who took care of Knox and me during the years Dad spent in a coma.

He never acted as a father, either. He's always been efficient at getting things done and that's all.

Over the years, the initial admiration has been developing. I don't know at which point I am exactly, but all I know is that I enjoy his silent company, and the fact that he never smiles or shows emotions is a plus.

What? Everyone has different tastes.

"Thanks for picking me up, Agnus."

He merely nods.

Little to no words—another one of his qualities. Oh, did I mention he's Dad's trustee and right-hand man? He's the one who managed Dad's steel empire when he couldn't. He's the one who's helping Dad snatch his place back in the business world now that he's returned.

There are practically endless positive qualities in Agnus.

"Will Knox and Elsa be there at dinner?" he asks without taking his eyes off the road.

"Knox is out with friends and Elsa is with Aiden, so I assume no."

"Perfect."

Of course he'd find it so. They make too much noise at the table, and while Dad is amused by it, Agnus never is.

Tonight, it'll just be the three of us, peaceful and perfect.

I also dislike a lot of energy. It messes with my senses and exhausts me.

Like a certain arsehole from earlier. I can't believe I acted that way with the girl who was kneeling at his feet.

So what if she sucked him off? It's none of my business.

He's a pawn, just a damn pawn.

But sometimes, pawns can flip the entire game. Dad has won several times by just using his pawns.

I shoo the thought away.

Why am I allowing that bastard to ruin my alone time with Agnus? I study him again, his strong hands and face.

Memories of other hands touching me, feeling me up, and trapping me barge into my mind.

Get out of my head, damn you.

"Are you going to tell me what's going on?"

I startle at Agnus' question. I was too caught up in my fantasies about Ronan, and I nearly forgot about him.

Way to go, Teal.

I tuck a strand of hair behind my ear, knowing full well it'll be untucked in seconds. "About what?"

"The whole engagement idea."

"I told you—I'm just trying to help Dad."

"I see."

He knows I'm lying, damn it. I don't want Agnus to have that idea about me, but at the same time, I refuse to come clean. This secret will follow me to the grave. Neither he, Dad, nor Knox will be hurt by this.

It's only me and the shadow on my shoulder.

"I really want to help Dad, and I might have something else going on. I just want you to trust me."

"I'll consider that if you tell me what's going on." He doesn't miss a beat.

"Agnus, come on, everyone needs to have their secrets."

"Not when it can harm Ethan."

"I'd never do that."

He gives a curt nod, and just like that, the subject is gone. I have no doubt he'll dig after me, which means I need to be extra careful about my moves.

Agnus has zero tolerance for anything that could harm my father. He nearly turned against Elsa when she was proving to be a problem in Dad's path to success.

That's probably why the two of them don't really get along.

My phone vibrates with a text—Ronan.

He sent the picture he snapped of me in the club. My cheeks heat at the position I'm in—a position I've never been in my entire life. Submissive, confused…aroused. His finger is pinching my nipple, and I nearly feel the touch in my throbbing breasts.

Ronan: Since you ruined my getting-off session, I'll jerk off to that picture.

The image of him wrapping his hands around his dick and wanking off to my picture causes my stomach to dip. Why the hell would that have this effect on me?

I loathe male masturbation, so why do I not hate it when he does it?

My phone vibrates with another text.

Ronan: Then maybe I'll send it off to Ethan and my dear father. Come on, end this, *ma belle*, and I promise you the world.

Ronan: Just kidding. I promise you pain.

Teal: What type of logic is that? You're okay with touching me when I'm not your fiancée but not the other way around?

Ronan: Ding dong, you finally figured it out.

Teal: Why?

I allow myself a curiosity I would've never followed if it were any other person.

I'm a strategist; my eyes are always on the end goal. I don't allow myself to swerve in the middle of the operation.

But Ronan is the exception to all rules.

He's a damn anomaly with his stupid grin and his punishing hands and the contradictions in his personality.

Ronan: Because the title comes with burdens. I don't want to fuck with burdens. Sort of like how you don't want to fuck normal.

I mark the text as read but don't reply.

Ronan: This is your final warning. End the engagement before I do it. Mmmkay?

My shoulders stiffen as I exit the chat. He's been

threatening me for so long now; it's time he knows I am *not* to be threatened.

"Agnus?"

"Yes."

"Can you drop me somewhere?"

I hit the number on my contacts list and smile for the second time today.

Ronan should not have messed with me. If he bites, I'll always bite back.

ELEVEN

Ronan

"**W**hat does it mean when a girl cockblocks you?"
Cole doesn't lift his head from the book; it's one he's been reading a lot lately, titled *The Anatomy of Evil*. He has phases where he spends a long time reading a certain book until he memorises the whole thing.

"You mean something similar to how you're now blocking me from reading?"

"It's not the same, you can't fuck books." He raises an eyebrow, and I hold out a hand. "Don't even voice that thought, Captain. Now, back to my question: why?"

"Why are you asking me? Why not ask the others?"

"Because Aiden is shagging Elsa—not that he shares wisdom—and Xander is at rehab, so you're all I've got." I pause, grinning. "Besides, you're the smartest."

"Nice save."

"What am I if not a good sport? Isn't that right, Captain?"

He flips a page, momentarily ignoring me. I tagged along with him and we're now at his house, or rather his stepfather's house, Sebastian Queens. The future prime minister of the United Kingdom and one of Dad's allies. He likes to keep everyone who matters near—like Teal's foster father, Ethan Steel.

Cole's room is impersonal with a bed and a desk and nearly

nothing memorable. He does an impressive job of keeping it boring and filled with books.

Unlike me, Xander, or even Aiden, Cole doesn't like having people over.

Told you, he's kind on the outside, but a dick on the inside.

"If I answer your question," he says, "are you going to leave?"

"Depends on whether or not you'll bluff me." I need to get that out there because the fucker has a tendency of telling you what you want to hear just so you'll disappear, kind of like how I throw out smiles to maintain peace.

Still sitting on his bed, he leans on a fist but doesn't release the book. "Give me details."

Fuck yes.

I drag his desk chair over, flip it around, and sit down so my arms are on the top. "So here's the thing: my friend was about to get a blowjob, and this girl interrupts me—I mean *him*, not me. As you know, I have no problem getting sex. He's a loser."

"What other friends do you have aside from us?"

"Just someone. Also, I have Lars."

"Lars is thirty years older than you. Are you sure you want to consider him a friend?"

"I do, and you're so fucked, Captain. I'm telling Lars, and he's a snob who holds grudges and writes about them in his little black book, so no tea for you, *and* he won't lend you novels from Father's library."

"Then maybe I shouldn't be helping with your…I mean, your *friend's* problem."

"I'm kidding, Captain. Just kidding." I give him my best smile. "So where were we? Right, my friend and the girl who cockblocked him."

His expression doesn't change. "Did your loser friend let her cockblock him?"

"Why are we calling him a loser?"

"You did—I'm just playing along." His lips twitch in a smirk. "He's your friend, after all, right?"

Dick.

"Yeah, he let her."

"Did he at least use her mouth instead?"

"No." And not because I didn't want to; it was because she ran. Why the fuck did I let her run?

"We should call your friend a pussy instead of a loser."

I feign a grin. "Is that all the advice you have?"

"She was probably jealous."

"Right? I knew it."

"Or she's playing a game."

Damn. "How do you know which is which?"

"That's the question all philosophers ask."

"And the answer?"

"There's no answer, Ronan. You have to live with the fact that you won't understand how women's brains work."

"So how should he react?"

He raises an eyebrow. "By not being a pussy. If you get a chance, seize it. I mean, *your loser friend* should seize it."

I grab a pen from the table behind me and throw it at him to wash away his smirk, but he catches it above his head. His smirk turns into a full-blown grin.

"My information helped after all." He twirls the pen between his index and middle finger. "Don't you think you owe me?"

It's my turn to smirk. "Don't you think you owe me more? Imagine if I didn't tell you about how *she* acted in front of your secret admirer."

"Next time, when you tell me something, don't do it when Aiden is around."

"Why? You think he'll change his mind?"

"Like fuck he would."

There's a knock on the door before it opens and Silver peeks inside. She's different out of our school uniform. At home, she's in a pink mini-dress that moulds to her curves and puts emphasis on her tits that Xan and I have been tricking her into showing us since we pre-pubescent.

Girls like Silver used to be my type: blonde, put together, hot as sin, and from my social standing.

Now, it seems no one is my type.

Correction—Ron Astor the Second thinks only one is his type, and there's nothing I can do to change his mind.

"Dinner is ready." She barely makes eye contact with Cole before focusing back on me. "Hey, Ronan. Join us."

Cole's face remains the usual—bored, like he'll commit suicide because of how dull the world is—but he stops twirling the pen.

"Ronan was just leaving," he says.

"Blasphemy. I wouldn't miss your mum's cooking for the world." She's a bestselling author and yet still finds time to cook the best meals. Silver's mum is hotter, but Cole's mum is homier, softer and Mum's friend. If I were Silver's father, I would've had both. Just saying.

I jump up and wrap an arm around Silver's shoulder. "Is it only me, or do you look so hot even in house clothes?"

She grins and flips her golden hair. "What can I say? It's my default."

I steal a glance at Cole and he mouths, "Leave."

I pretend I didn't see him as I walk with his stepsister down the hall.

He catches up to us and whispers so only I can hear. "Leave before I break that arm."

"Silver, did you hear someone talking?"

"I don't think so." She smirks, and I smirk back.

I'm starting to feel how Aiden did all those years. This sense of power over Cole is euphoric.

My phone vibrates. It's a text from home.

Lars: We have a situation.

After kissing Cole's mother on the cheek and pissing her son off one last time, I leave their mansion.

I arrive at home in record time. I called Lars on the way here, but he didn't pick up, which means he's busy doing what-the-fuck-ever and doesn't have time for a phone conversation.

This better not be what I think it is.

The moment I step into the house, I feel it—the change in the air, the shift in the atmosphere. Even the usual jasmine scent Mum loves so much seems to dim, swallowed by a different type of smell.

Something potent and yet unnoticeable.

Lars appears at the entrance and nods in the direction of Dad's office. I don't have to be told twice, and I take two steps at a time, only stopping myself from running because staff members shouldn't see an earl's son running.

Pretty sure they also shouldn't help him throw parties or hide his weed stash, but semantics.

I'm near the office when it opens, and two men emerge. One is my father, and the other is his younger brother, Uncle Eduard.

Unlike my father, Eduard is an energetic man in his late thirties. He works in the imports and exports branch of my father's business. He's basically Father's right-hand man, aside from being his most beloved brother.

He dresses in eccentric colourful suits—his way to attract attention. Today, it's dark purple with some mosaic-coloured cloth at the breast. While Father is tall and broad, Eduard is lean and has scrawny shoulders. His looks are average at best: round nose and slightly bulging green eyes, as if they're not able to fit in their sockets. The genetic difference between him and my father is noticeable. One looks every bit the aristocrat he is, while the other appears like a charity case—which he was at some point, being a stepson of the Astor family.

The moment he sees me, Eduard abandons Father's side and clasps me in a hug. I freeze for a moment, meeting Dad's eyes, and then I wrap my arms around my uncle, patting him in that 'people with titles don't hug' awkward way. Even my father shakes his head at that.

He never managed to get Eduard to quit this habit. He never will.

"Look at you, nephew." Eduard pulls back to look me up and down. "You've grown."

I grin. "You're still the same."

He laughs, the sound like a song gone wrong before ending on a smashing note. "That I am, nephew."

"It's a surprise to see you here." I stare between him and Dad, hoping one of them will explain his sudden return from the other side of the world. I thought he was responsible for the Australian branch and wouldn't return anymore.

"Edric called me back." Eduard squeezes my shoulder. "Isn't it wonderful?"

"Indeed." I keep my attention on my father.

"I'm busy, so your uncle will take care of the London branch from now on."

"Busy with what?" I ask before I can stop myself. "Your touristic trips or dragging Mother all around the globe?"

"I will not be questioned by you." He levels me with a glare.

When I was younger, Earl Astor's glare meant I needed to shut the fuck up and do as he'd told me.

I always did.

Until one of his glares changed my life for fucking good.

"Eduard, let's have some tea." Father smiles at his brother, motioning downstairs. "Lars has your favourite ready."

"Lars. How lovely. I forgot you always have him around." Eduard squeezes my shoulder one last time. "We have so much catching up to do, nephew. I'm looking forward to it."

"Not sure you'll have any time for me, Uncle. My father doesn't mess around with business." I stare at said parent. "I'm going to Mother since you're *busy* as usual."

He opens his mouth to say something, but I'm already striding down the hall to my parents' bedroom.

Eduard's voice echoes behind me as he soothes my father, telling him I'm at that age and he should be patient with me.

Fuck them both.

Fuck their names and titles and business.

I stop in front of my parents' bedroom and take a deep breath. Mum can't see me at my worst, or she'll sense it.

She always does. Since I was a boy, she'll stop and stare at me and say, "*Dit moi tous, mon chou.*"

I don't know when I stopped doing that, telling her everything that's on my mind, I mean, or being *son chou*. No, that's a lie—I know the exact moment; I just never wanted to associate it with my mum.

She's light. That moment is darkness.

I suck in a deep breath and knock on the door. There's no response. I knock again, and when there's nothing, my heart races.

She can't possibly have fainted like the other time…right?

"Mother?"

No response.

"I'm coming in."

I push on the door and go inside, but there's no sign of her in her room. I check the bathroom, but she's not there either.

Fuck. Where did she go?

Mum rarely leaves her room, if ever, and whenever she does, it's for the adjoining office she uses to answer emails and such.

She doesn't have friends to speak of either. Dad and I are her entire world, as she once said.

I'm about to check the office when I pass by the closed door of the balcony. Sure enough, Mum is standing in the sun, her blonde curls falling to her shoulders as she laughs. I haven't seen her laugh like that in...years.

And the reason behind the laugh is none other than the tiny girl who's crazier and prettier than I ever thought.

Teal fixes a ribbon on Mum's dress and says something that makes her laugh again. The rare English sun shines down on both of them, making Mum's hair and eyes shine and giving a glint to Teal's black gaze.

She's smiling. It's demure and discreet, but it's there. A smile—a fucking genuine one at that.

Could be because of the meeting with Dad and Eduard, or it could be everything that happened over the days since that tiny thing barged into my life.

I know one thing for certain: she won't be able to leave this time.

Cole was right—it's time to seize the chance.

TWELVE

Teal

I was never one for small talk. It causes my skin to itch. Besides, I'm too awkward for that.

Human interaction has always been my weakness; that's why I keep it to an absolute minimum.

However, as I sit with Charlotte, I don't think of the situation as small talk, but more like afternoon tea. Or rather something more pulling and extraordinary.

It takes me a long time to connect to people—if I ever do—and it takes them ages to warm up to me. That's what happened with Elsa and her friend Kim.

Charlotte is different.

She has an elegant finesse about her that makes me feel more welcome than my skin allows.

Despite our recent acquaintance, she talks as if we've known each other for ages, as if Lars making us tea is a daily occurrence. She didn't even protest when I offered to do her makeup and pick her dress.

People with titles like Charlotte dress up in the house, sort of like in the Victorian era.

I didn't feel the hours passing by. The reason I'd come started to fade away too. Soon enough, I found myself talking to her, and not due to what's expected in these situations.

Me, talking. Me, striking up a conversation.

At first, I think it's because I feel sorry for her. After all, Charlotte is a victim in all this, and she doesn't deserve what will happen at the end of the tale.

But eventually, I realise I do enjoy her company, right around the time I start telling her about Knox's pranks and Elsa's new love.

"How about you?" she asks in her feather-light, soothing-to-the-ears voice.

"Me?" I pause in tying the ribbon on her waist. I've always had a thing for clothes and appearances, even if mine lean towards the eccentric type.

"Yes. Do you have a new love like your sister?"

"No…I don't." What the hell is up with that hesitation at the end?

Charlotte's beautiful face falls a little, but she pats my hand. "Don't refuse the idea too soon. You never know."

"How…" I peek up at her. "What does it mean to love? I mean, I know I love my dad and Knox, but I've read there's a different type?"

I purse my lips as soon as I say the words. Why am I pouring out my issues with understanding emotions on a woman I just met and barely know?

Charlotte smiles; it's bright and a little weak, but it reminds me so much of her son. There's no question about from whom he got that radiance.

"I wish there was a textbook explanation for that, but I can promise you this: the moment you encounter love, you'll recognise it right here, *chérie*." She places a soft hand above my left breast.

I stop myself from telling her I feel things but mostly fail to recognise them. There's no fixing that; even the therapy didn't work. It only gave me a few pointers, and sometimes, those don't give the right answers.

Human emotions are weird.

Charlotte drops her hand and sighs. "I also felt as confused as you when I first met Edric."

My nails dig into the ribbon, but I soon unclench them. "Really?"

"You know, our marriage was also arranged."

"It was?" How come none of the articles mentioned that?

That's the second miss on your part, Teal.

"Yes. His father and mine were business partners, but here's the plot twist." She leans in to whisper. "Edric was supposed to marry my eldest sister, Céline."

"Oh."

"I know. I kind of stole my sister's fate." She laughs, the sound gentle and non-intrusive. "But there's another plot twist—my sister eloped with Papa's guard, like in a soap opera, and I had to save the family's honour by marrying this arrogant Englishman Papa brought to our house. I hated Edric so much back then. He was too proud and controlling, wouldn't take no for an answer while I was a free spirit."

I'm caught off guard by her words. "You hated him?"

She rolls her eyes. "To death."

"Then how did you end up marrying him?"

A sly smile lifts her lips. "I destroyed his walls and found the man under the surface, not the one he shows to the public, and that man inside is the one I never knew I needed. We've been married for twenty-three years, and they've been the happiest years of my life."

If they've been married for twenty-three years and Ronan is eighteen, then they stayed childless for several years. I wonder why. Edric is the type of man who would make sure his rotten legacy lives on, so I'd have imagined they got married less than a year before Ronan's birth.

I keep the question to myself because I'd sound awkward as fuck if I voiced it.

"That's why I want you to keep an open mind, *chérie*. You never know what you'll find unless you destroy some walls."

What is she suggesting, exactly? That I knock down her son's walls? If that's the case then it's already happening—only it's not in the romantic way she's hoping for.

And he doesn't know it yet.

"*Bonsoir.*"

My shoulders stiffen at the sound of the voice that's starting to appear in my dreams—not my nightmares, my fucking dreams.

Ronan strides in through the balcony's doorway, still wearing his uniform, minus the tie and jacket. The top buttons of his shirt are open, hinting at the bare skin I once rubbed all over while —

I internally shake my head to rid it of that image.

He leans in and presses a kiss to his mother's temple. It's soft, tender, and Charlotte sighs in delight.

"You look beautiful, Mother." He takes her small hands in his and kisses the knuckles.

"It's all thanks to Teal." Charlotte motions at me then at her dress and makeup with pride.

My cheeks heat.

Damn it. Am I blushing? I don't even do blushing.

"Is that so?" Ronan fixes me with a glare. "Don't ruin my mother's face with your black kink."

"That's rude," Charlotte scolds.

I pretend his words don't jab as I run my finger over the containers of the makeup. If his mother weren't here, I would stab him in the eye with a brush handle.

"I'm just kidding." He grins at his mum.

"That's not something to joke about, *mon chou*." She rises up on her tiptoes to stroke his hair back.

I stand there in the midst of the mother-son bonding, and it's like I'm shoved out of my skin.

For my whole life, a mother was the only thing I never had. The woman who gave birth to me and Knox doesn't count; she's the devil.

She's the reason I can't recognise half my feelings and run away from the other half as if they're on fire.

Seeing Charlotte treat Ronan with so much care and affection in her blue eyes makes me hate him even more.

He doesn't deserve a mother like her just like Edric doesn't deserve her as a wife.

"Mother, do you mind if I steal my lovely fiancée?" He's asking her, but his lunatic grin falls on me.

Before I can protest, Charlotte speaks first. "Why, of course I don't mind."

She takes her son's hand and puts it on top of mine. The shock of his skin heightens when he threads his fingers in mine, smiling at his mother. He tightens his hold around me, and I suppress a wince at the force of it.

Charlotte strides away with a smile and a suggestive "Have fun, kids."

As soon as Ronan closes her bedroom door behind us, I yank my hand free of his as if it were burning me—and in a way, it was.

He grabs me by the arm so abruptly I swallow a shriek. "D-don't do that."

"Do what?"

Startle me. It brings back memories.

Instead of voicing that, I bite my lower lip and adopt my no-nonsense tone. "Touch me. I don't like it when you touch me."

"Let me count all the fucks I give." He pauses, pretending to count with his free hand. "None."

"Where are you taking me?" I try to wriggle out of his grasp as he drags me down the hall. His strides are so long and quick, and I'm panting to keep up with his pace.

Damn tall people and their legs that go on for freaking miles.

"You fucked up, *ma belle*, and it's payback time."

My breath hitches and his grip on my arm is tingling. Problem is, I can't figure out why the hell it's tingling. Is it fear? Anticipation? Or maybe something worse?

Ronan pushes a door open and shoves me inside. I stumble and nearly fall, but I catch myself against the wall for balance as the sound of a lock echoes in the distance like doom.

I swallow, lifting my head to take a quick inventory of the place. Considering the bed with dark sheets, the framed pictures, and the football, this is his room.

Ronan stands with his back against the door and his hand reaching behind him—for the lock he just turned, no doubt.

I force my hands to fall on either side of me so I don't reveal the tremors plaguing my body.

This is not a real trapping. I can get out at any time.

Any time.

I chant those words in my head over and over again.

"I assume there has been a miscalculation?" He smiles, but now I'm certain he's hiding a lot of fuckery behind it. "As per our agreement, you were supposed to pay a visit to my father and end the engagement, not play dress-up with my mother."

"Our agreement?" I scoff. "I don't remember agreeing to anything."

"Really?"

"You assumed everything yourself."

"Does that mean you won't end it?"

"Absolutely not. And if you threaten me with that picture again, I now have an ally in Charlotte." I pretend to sniffle. "How do you think she'll feel if I tell her you took me there by force? I don't look compliant in that picture."

His jaw ticks, but his grin widens. I'm starting to think Ronan smiles more when he's trying to camouflage something. "You think my mother will believe you over her only son?"

"We won't know until we put her in that position." I feign care. "She seems like a soft woman—I'd hate to scar her with the fuckery going on in your head."

He pushes off the door, and something inside me screams at me to run, to bolt, even jump from the window, anything but stand here like prey for the taking.

I'm not prey.

I'll never be prey again.

Jutting my chin up, I meet his gaze with my tenacious one.

Men don't intimidate me because I lack that normal streak of shame and embarrassment. However, as Ronan strides towards me, I can't help the locking at the bottom of my spine or the dancing emotions crawling up my arms.

"And what do you know about the fuckery in my head, *ma belle?*" He's still smirking, stalking, making me all too aware of him and his presence.

His overpowering presence. Just like that night at the club.

The only difference is that I see him right now, and that's probably why I can't get out of his orbit.

"You still haven't taken a tour in there, but I'm willing to change that." He stops in front of me and grabs my chin.

The gesture is soft, almost like a feather's kiss. His thumb and forefinger take control of my jaw, and just like that, it's almost like he's clutching a marionette's strings.

"Remember what I told you about how you'll pay?"

"I won't pay for anything." I'm surprised by my calm tone.

"Do you honestly think you have a choice?"

"Of course I do. I have a choice in everything."

His grin disappears, and any attempt he was making to stay normal evaporates in the air surrounding us.

Everything turns heightened—the rise and fall of my chest, the heat radiating off him, his smell like spice and fucking damnation. He's all I breathe, all I see, and all I can focus on.

I don't attempt to free myself from his clutch. I'm that

marionette ready to be moved, to be controlled, to be completely at his mercy.

Snap out of it, Teal. This is Ronan—a pawn, not a fantasy.

"I thought you didn't like touching your fiancée, the title bothering you and all that," I try in my most neutral tone. This is the last chance I have to get rid of whatever influence he has on me.

"I lied."

"What?"

"Or rather, I changed my mind."

"You can't change your mind."

"Of course I can." He glides his index finger over the curve of my jaw as his thumb rubs my lower lip. "Now, I'm curious about something."

I clamp my mouth shut, but he shoves his thumb between them and presses on my lower lip then smears my lipstick like he did that first time he touched me at the library.

Just like then, a tremor shoots through my body—only this time, there's something more potent, something dangerous.

He's not smiling.

He's not even attempting to smile.

"I'm curious to see how far I can take your fantasy list."

"W-What?"

His gaze remains on my lip as if he's entranced by the back and forth of his thumb over the tender skin. "You know, the checklist you left for me at *La Débauche*. Your little depraved fantasies."

I never understood what the expression *Dig myself a grave* meant until this moment. I wish I could summon a hole and disappear into it.

Yes, I figured he saw that list, but I thought he'd forgotten about it, or better yet hadn't paid it much attention.

My darkest secrets are on that list, secrets no one should see, least of all Ronan.

"And yes, I do remember them." He smirks. "I learnt them by heart."

Oh, God.

Oh. My. God.

"Now, let's see, it starts with something like…" His eyes glint with pure sadism, the type I've never seen on his face, not even when he taunts.

His hand trails down my chest, slow, sensual even. I stop breathing altogether when he rips my shirt in the middle.

"Stripping you bare."

THIRTEEN

Teal

The sound of tearing cloth fills the air as buttons fly everywhere, scattering around us.

For a second, just a moment in time, I'm too stunned to react.

For a second, I stare at him with wild eyes, as if that will make this situation a bit more understandable.

It doesn't.

A second is all it takes for him to yank my jacket and shirt away, leaving me in my bra and uniform's skirt.

A gust of air envelops my skin, and my heart resurrects back to life as if it had an attack—or rather an arrest.

The clothes fall to the ground with a soft whoosh, thrusting me back to reality.

I cross both arms over my chest—trembling arms, tingling fucking arms all covered in goosebumps and the promise of the unknown.

"What the fuck are you doing?" My voice is merely a whisper, not attempting to sound angry.

I should be; deep in my heart, I know I should be, but I can't even muster up the courage to do it. There's something about the way he ripped my clothes that's making me weak in the legs; I'm surprised I'm able to remain standing.

"Making the fantasy come true." He grabs my arms and shoves them both to either side of me.

His force is havoc-wreaking—it's the type you can't escape even if you try. It's the type that shakes my thighs and turns me into that marionette I can't push out of my head. Only this time, it's the good type. The pleasurable type.

Ronan wraps a hand around my wrists and imprisons them behind my back. My breasts are thrust in his face, praying for attention.

"You have beautiful tits—did you know that?" He licks his lips like he's about to dive into a meal as he unclasps the strap of my bra. My breasts spill free with a gentle bounce, and the look in his eyes darkens as if he's about to devour me.

Own me.

No, no.

This is Ronan—he can't do that.

"Stop it." I choke on the words, my voice so weak it's pathetic.

"Another one of your fantasies." He wraps a finger around a nipple and twists so hard I gasp and moan at the same time. "Stop means more, doesn't it, *ma belle?*"

Oh, God. Why the fuck did I write that? Why the hell does he remember it?

If I'm sick and he's attuned to my sickness, what does that make us?

I don't want to think about the answer. Something tells me it'd be a lot worse than the situation I've gotten myself into.

"You know…" He trails off, twisting my nipple again and making me fidget with the need to keep in the sounds clawing to escape. "This is the first time I've wanted to break someone." He pauses, pinching again, until the searing pain takes over my entire body and my nerve endings tremble with the need for more. "No, that's a lie. This is the second time. The first was when you knelt in front of me and moaned like a good girl.

You're not a good girl, but you turn into one when I corner you."

"Ronan…" My voice is choppy, fragmented, and I have no idea what I want to say. His name feels foreign on my lips, newer, *maddening*.

"Do you want to come, *belle?*"

I swallow past the thickness in my throat, unable to stop feeling the sensations he's eliciting in my nipple, the ones going straight to my aching core.

I don't stop to think about the fact that he's trapping me and blocking any exit I might have.

Perhaps that's what I want, isn't it? The lack of damn escape.

This is so fucked up, especially with everything that's happened in the past, but I nod slightly.

A week or so ago, I didn't know what it meant to come, but now, I can't stop thinking about it, about *him*—his hands, his skin…the whole damn thing.

"I'm going to need words," he muses.

I stare up at him with a pleading look, or that's what I hope for anyway; I'm pretty sure I'm glaring at him. "Don't make me say it."

"But I want to hear it. You have your fantasies, and I have mine." He pinches again and I collapse against his chest, biting my lip. "The words, Teal, or I can continue doing this all day. I'll edge you close but never give you release."

He can do that?

I peek at him, testing to see if he's for real or playing with me. Judging by the dip in his brows, he seems dead serious.

"Just do it."

He crushes my nipple between his thumb and forefinger. I cry out as the pain takes over me.

I wish it was only the pain, but no, the pain brings something else—something that ends with arousal between my shaking thighs.

"That's not the tone. Say it right."

"M-Make me…"

"What?"

"Come," I breathe the word. "Make me come."

The word is barely out of my mouth when he pushes me back. I yelp as I fall against the bed. The shock of it leaves me speechless, unable to utter a word.

"Manhandled." He raises an eyebrow. "Remember that in your pretty little list?"

"Screw you." I stare at the wall, at his stupid football uniform peeking out of the closet—basically anywhere but at him.

I try to remind myself that those fantasies weren't supposed to happen with him. They were meant for my very older and experienced men.

Besides, they were just that—fantasies. Aside from the club, I never thought I would experience them, especially not with someone who doesn't fit any of my criteria.

How come he was completely off my radar and now he's the only one on it? How come I see his face when I close my eyes at night and even dream about him?

I never dream about men. I only have nightmares about monsters—or rather one monster in particular.

"Do you realise how beautiful you look right now, *belle*? You're all splayed out and ready for the taking."

My cheeks heat, but it's not out of embarrassment about my position.

He called me beautiful.

He thinks I'm beautiful.

Why the hell is my heart skipping a beat for that? I don't want Ronan to think I'm beautiful. I couldn't care less about it.

…right?

He kneels in front of the bed and parts my legs. I gasp as my skirt rides up to my waist, exposing my cotton underwear.

"Oh, look at that." He runs his middle finger through my

folds over the cloth. I try to clench my thighs, but he slaps them apart, making me yelp.

"You're wet and soaked and ready for some fucking."

"Stop saying things like that," I murmur.

"Like what?" He teases my entrance through the cloth and I arch my back. "Like how hard I'm going to fuck you until everyone hears you beg for more? How loud I'm going to make you scream as you come?"

If my cheeks were red before, they must've turned to crimson by now. Never in my life did I think I would be brought to the edge this brutally or that I would be so turned on by dirty talk.

Ronan hooks his fingers in either side of my underwear and slips them down in one go.

"Keep your hands on the sheet." He speaks so commandingly it causes a tremor to shoot down my spine. "If you don't, I'll stop."

Before I can ask what he'll stop, his face disappears between my legs and he swipes his tongue from my clit down. My back arches off the bed at the mere contact.

"Jesus fucking Christ," I pant.

"Not him." He emerges, licking his lips like a lion about to start his meal. "*Me.*"

And then he's back to lapping against my folds fast and hard. As if that isn't enough to drive me insane, his tongue thrusts in and out of my opening suggestively, fucking me, devouring me.

"You're so delicious, *belle*. I could eat you all day long."

A thousand shivers explode on my spine. I reach for his hair, needing the contact, needing to torment him as much as he's owning me. I'm close, so close to that wave I felt when he was torturing my nipples at the club.

The wave only he can bring.

No orgasm I've brought to myself has been as satisfying as that time—not even when I picture him doing it.

The moment I grab a handful of his hair, his tongue leaves my folds.

I whimper at the loss of contact. "W-What? Why…?"

I can't even speak like a normal human being.

"Told you I'll stop if you don't keep your hands on the sheets."

I let go of his mane of hair and slam my hands back on either side of me, panting as if I've been running up a hill. "I'll be good."

His eyes darken with indecipherable emotions. It's like the rich brown wants to become black, potent, and wild with fury.

I might not understand the emotion behind the change, but I know something tickled him in some way.

"Repeat that." He speaks low against my core, and I feel the vibrations on my sensitive skin.

"I-I'll be good," I whisper.

That's all it takes.

He curls his tongue against my hypersensitive clit, and it's like he never stopped.

It's like he's able to throw me over the edge without even trying. It's my fantasy, and yet he's smashing it, ruining it, moulding it so it's almost his, not mine.

And in some way, it's even better than my original one.

My back snaps upright as he wrenches a strong orgasm from me. Tiny shivers crawl up my spine then explode all over my skin. It's not my first orgasm, but it feels like it is; it's stronger and owns me whole.

Just like the one who brought it out of me.

I hide my face in the pillow to erase the sound. It comes out like a muffled shriek, something you'd hear in dark alleys late at night.

I'm still riding my orgasm when a sharp slap hits my pussy. I shriek, my eyes fluttering open. I stare, incredulous, as Ronan's face emerges from between my legs.

"Why…why did you do that?" I pant through my pain mixed with agonising pleasure.

"Don't hide your screams again or it won't just be my palm against your cunt. Let's try again, and this time, scream."

He yanks my legs apart, stretching me wide before his lips go back to my swollen clit. He doesn't even bother with taking it slow. It could be because I've never been so turned on in my life, or it could be because of his maddeningly fast pace.

It could be both.

This time, the wave hits me harder and much quicker.

I scream, my head rolling back and my eyes fluttering closed. "Ronan…oh, Ronan…"

"That's right. Me." He nips on my tortured clit. "Just me."

I writhe on the bed, my nails digging into the sheet, unable to keep quiet or still. He's turning me into someone even I don't recognise.

"Ronan…"

"What do you want, *belle?*" He speaks against me, the vibration of his voice turning me delirious. "Maybe you'll get inspiration after another orgasm." He licks me from the top to the bottom of my slit, and I shiver. "I still can't get my fill of you."

"I-I'm…I'm…"

"What?"

"S-sore."

"So?" He emerges from between my legs and suggestively licks his lips.

The fact that he's licking me off him should be repulsive, but it isn't.

Shit, why isn't it?

"You know, it should stop me. It did in the past. I don't make girls sore—I make fucking love to them, but not with you, *belle.* I want to fuck you like a dirty little whore."

The words should offend me, but they're making me wet. Why do I love the sound of that on his lips.

"You like being mine to use." He grips my thigh tighter. "Don't you?"

He climbs on top of me, flicking my tormented nipple on the way before he grabs me, pulls me up so I'm sitting up half-way, and slams his lips to mine.

Unlike the other time, he doesn't stop to take it slow. He invades me, conquers me, and most of all, he tastes of me: slightly sweet, a lot dirty.

I never kissed before. I liked to get it over with, and kissing got in the way of that. Any form of intimacy did.

The fact that I can't get enough of Ronan's kiss should be alarming—and it is. I just can't seem to get enough.

There's not enough kissing, not enough touching.

There's simply not enough.

I'm starved for more.

So much more.

"You taste like fucking sin." He breathes against me. "But do you know what will taste better?"

I shake my head, barely able to focus.

"My cum down your throat."

FOURTEEN

Teal

"**M**y cum down your throat."

I must be out of my mind, because the moment he says those words, I nearly moan.

It could be because I hardly cared about right or wrong before. It could be because I hoped for this somehow.

Either way, his words ignite a fierce tendril of desire within me.

Ronan grabs me by the arm and swings me over so I fall in front of the bed. Just like he kneeled to eat me out, I'm now on my knees, my nipples throbbing, my pussy aching, and my flimsy skirt is still around my waist, ruined by his fingers and my own arousal.

He slides to the edge of the bed and swings up to a standing position, towering over me like a god.

A death god.

I see it now, his name—the reason he's nicknamed Death. It's not because of his playing or any of that. It's the way he finishes lives without making a sound.

He's discreet but ruthless.

Appears loveable but is actually domineering.

Death.

And he's now after me. I'm his next target, and for some reason, I think he'll never let me go or be finished with me.

"Remember the blowjob you ruined today?" He raises an eyebrow.

I scowl up at him, not wanting to recall how that girl was in the same position I'm in now, on her knees, with no purpose but to please him.

No. I'm not her.

I'm no one's replacement. I'm me, and Ronan is lucky. He's damn lucky he gets me on my knees for him.

I'm only doing this because he already dropped to his knees for me not two minutes ago.

If you offer a god a sacrifice, he'll let you go.

I don't know why those words pop into my mind, but now that they're there, I can't get rid of them.

Besides, it's not a sacrifice. If it's that then I need to give up something valuable, but I'm not.

If anything…something is pushing me to do this.

"Did you get turned on while she was undressing me, ready to take my cum?" He grabs my chin, lifting my head up. "Or were you angry because it wasn't you?"

I leave my lips in a line, refusing to answer him. He won't get to me, and he sure as hell won't get me to admit what I felt then, not when I don't even like admitting it to myself.

"Unbutton me, *belle*. Make it good."

"And if I don't want to?" I whisper the question.

"Then I might tie you down."

My eyes widen. "No. You read my file—it's my hard no."

"Then start unbuttoning."

I stare at him for one second.

Two.

Three.

He reaches for me. "We'll go with my plan."

"I'll do it." My voice quivers as my shaking fingers undo his belt then the button of his trousers.

The fact that he plans and will go through with his threats pushes me into a different state of mind.

It's like going through a dark forest, but instead of being afraid of its ghosts, I'm slightly eager to meet them, see them.

Touch them.

He releases my chin and strokes my hair out of my face—to get a better view of me, I suppose.

I pause once his trousers slide down his muscular thighs and pool around his legs. He remains in dark blue boxers that mould around his tight skin. I've seen his thighs before at games and in his extravagant selfies, but it's the first time I want them on me. I don't care how, but I want those thighs to crush me between them, want to find out if they're as strong as they look.

"Pull my dick out." His voice wrenches me out of my fucked-up thoughts.

I will my fingers to stop trembling as I do just that.

Oh, God.

Ronan always—always—brags about how big he is, and I kind of hoped it was because he had some sort of a complex issue and was trying to hide his dick's true size.

Well, the evidence is right in front of me.

He's big, so big a shiver of fear goes through me. I'm no virgin, but this thing will hurt.

It'll hurt so much.

Why the hell are my thighs clenching at the thought?

"I-I've never given a blowjob." I don't know why I say it, but I want it out there.

Yet I don't meet his gaze as I say that.

Something is definitely wrong with me.

"Who said anything about a blowjob?" He grips my chin, once again forcing me to be trapped by his glimmering gaze. "I'm going to fuck your mouth, *belle.*"

My core becomes slick with arousal and my pulse roars in my ears.

Holy shit.

I might need my therapist after this.

No sane person would feel this turned on by those words, right?

Before I can react, he grabs his cock with one hand and gathers my hair in a short ponytail with the other then pushes the tip against my lips.

The first thing I taste is the distinctive salty pre-cum, then him, then I'm gone. I don't even wait for his order before I open my mouth.

In return, he doesn't pretend to take it slow.

The first thrust hits the back of my throat—all the way in. I choke on my own spit and my air supply vanishes.

I place both hands on his thighs, nails scratching his skin in an instinctive attempt to push him away.

He forces my head down with my hair, suffocating me. Tears fall on my cheeks as I beg for air. I don't cry; these are different tears. Lust tears.

"Drop your hands," he orders.

I do. I just do. I don't stop to think about it anymore. The moment my limp hands hit the floor, he pulls out, allowing me a large gulp of air before he pounds in again and again, stealing my breath and my sanity, too.

My chest tightens, my core tingles, and the need to come hits me again.

He's turned me into a nymphomaniac. I can't stop thinking about coming, and about the fact that I'm about to make him come, too.

I'm bringing him pleasure, as he brought it to me.

"That's it," he grunts, trapping his bottom lip under his teeth. "Make my dick nice and wet so I can slide it inside that tight cunt of yours. That cunt wants my dick, doesn't it, *belle?*"

A sob tears the air, and I realise it's mine as I nod. I don't mean to, but I'm nodding. I can't stop nodding.

He's ruining me, corrupting me, and I'm enjoying every second of it.

This is different from any of my fantasies.

This is the best fantasy I could've had.

"Today, when you walked in on me and that girl, I wasn't hard for her. I was hard for you." *Thrust.* "I wanted to fuck you." *Thrust.* "Ruin you." *Thrust.* "Own you."

I'm so glad his cock is blocking my mouth or I would be screaming right now.

When I'm with him, I let go of all of my inhibitions as if they were never there, as if all those chains and walls are of my own making.

He's setting me free in ways I never thought possible.

And I hate him for it.

I hate that it's him, of all people, who's making me feel this type of strange belonging and absolute abandon.

He's my enemy.

He should be my enemy.

But as he fucks my mouth, uses it, brutalises it, I can't help asking for more, wanting more.

I would never get on my knees for anyone. It's a humiliating position and a symbol of weakness, but with him, it doesn't feel like one.

With him, it feels like a position of power where I'm giving him as much pleasure as he's giving me.

He says he owns me, but I'm owning him as much as he owns me.

With every thrust into my mouth, he steals a part of me, and I steal a part of him too.

The part he never shows to anyone else.

It's a shift in dynamics, a play of power. Just because I'm on my knees doesn't mean I lack power; it only means I'm earning it in a completely different way.

A knock sounds on the door. "*Mon chou?* I brought Lars' scones."

Both of us freeze at Charlotte's voice—and by freezing, I

mean Ronan stops at the back of my throat, keeping me there by my hair.

Black dots form at my peripheral vision due to the lack of oxygen. I struggle for breath, and maybe that's why the haze doesn't wither away even with someone else's presence. I'm still drifting, riding the wave, needing more of it.

"I'll be right out, Mother." He sounds normal, or at least a bit normal considering the circumstances. He focuses back on me and whispers in a lust-filled voice. "How do you feel about someone walking in and seeing you this way, all choked with my dick?" I shake my head frantically, but he just smirks. "You want to be my fiancée, but you're my whore now." His hold on my hair turns stronger, more controlled. "Made only for me."

Those words make me lightheaded, and it's not only because of the lack of air.

The more he speaks to me like that, the wetter I get. The more depraved he becomes, the deeper I fall into his web.

He goes back to thrusting in and out of my mouth, faster and harder this time. He uses my hair to guide me, not allowing me any movement outside of his approval.

I'm a marionette in his hands, a wanton, willing marionette who can't get enough.

His shoulders become rigid and his head tilts slightly back. I can't help staring up at his masculine beauty and complete control as he stops powering into my mouth. Something salty hits the back of my throat then drips on my chin, mixing with the drool and tears covering my face.

Ronan grunts, watching me intently, almost as if in a haze himself as he pulls out of my sore mouth. He gathers his cum with his thumb and coats my lips with it, smearing it all over, as if he doesn't want to miss an inch, doesn't want to waste a drop.

When he nudges my mouth open, I don't hesitate to take his thumb inside and suck it clean. He laps his single digit against my tongue, groaning deep in his throat.

The sound does something to me. I feel pride, because I'm the reason behind that. I'm the reason his godlike features crease with satisfaction.

I feel lust, because even after two orgasms, I'm greedy for more. I want his hands all over me again. His strong, lean hands that know how to wrench me out of my self-imposed fortress.

There's another emotion I can't quite pinpoint, one that snaps my shoulders together and makes me want to run and never return.

"Ronan?" Charlotte's voice comes again.

The spell breaks as he pulls up his boxers and trousers, and just like that, he appears normal, not like someone who just fucked up my entire universe.

He throws me one last quizzical glance and motions for me to stay quiet before he heads to the door.

I remain slouched by the bed, my heart almost beating out of my chest as I watch his back disappearing around the corner.

For the first time in my life, I feel used, and yet so utterly pleased.

That's when I take the time to finally admit I'm in so much trouble.

FIFTEEN

Ronan

The upside of pretending since the day I was born is that most people can't see the real me.

Hell, even I can't see that bastard sometimes. It worked just fine for years, and we're talking about a lifetime subscription.

The difference between me and, say, someone like Teal—who's currently glaring at me from the top of the stairs at her house—is that she can't hide.

She's too real, too raw, even if she has this 'fuck off' aura. She can't fake or say things she doesn't mean, and it's why she's never fit in the hypocritical game of RES's halls.

When girls did everything to fit in, she just followed what she liked. She never once laughed or smiled because it was expected. She's a socially awkward bean with a twist. Most socially awkward people don't want to be in that category, whereas Teal likes it—if anything, she might even take pride in it.

Her glares are real, too. They're probably the most real thing about her, the way her thick brows scrunch and her skin reddens with pent-up anger. Without words, she communicates that she hates having me here. She hates my guts and my existence, basically.

Get in line, belle.

For the past week, I've been picking her up for school, despite her protests and jabs and attempts to throw me under the bus like a mechanic every time an adult is around.

She tries to brush past me, ignore me, pretend I don't exist. When that doesn't work, she attempts to make me look bad.

Teal still doesn't understand that she can't win against me in the peopling game. I'm way too loved, too approachable, and I don't give off the deceptive calm façade like Cole. For that reason, people like me and naturally gravitate towards me.

It's not a gift. It's a commitment I made to myself when I decided I'd never be alone.

Not for one second.

Not even for a blink.

To accomplish that, people needed to take a liking to me. Before I knew it, I was becoming the epitome fantasy of any person looking to socialise.

Teal and I are opposite that way. She's a loner by choice, never by force. She wasn't bullied into it, because even when people called her a social outcast and Satan's worshipper, she didn't give them the time of day. She just rolled with it and gave them the middle finger.

So how come someone like her, someone who doesn't fit in my image of peopling, can consume my thoughts?

I haven't stopped thinking about her. After the day she left my house with her clothes and hair dishevelled and her lips swollen from me fucking her mouth, she became Ron Astor the Second's fantasy come true.

Every night, I dream of her black eyes as she stared up at me, and I can almost still taste her on my tongue.

I can still hear her tiny voice saying *I'll be good.* Fuck. I've never loved words as much as those, never thought of a girl as much as I do of her.

Thankfully, I have the best solution to get rid of this unwanted attention. If I get close enough, I'll eventually tire of her. The reason she's occupying my thoughts is that I still know little to nothing about her aside from her being manhandled kink and her bad taste in men.

I should be her type.

Anyway, that's why I've been showing up every day since. She's starting to slip away by avoiding any alone time with me, probably scared about what I'll do with her.

My head has been going into overdrive since that day, obsessing about the best way to fuck her so thoroughly she'll forget everyone before me—and after me.

Wait. She gets people after me? I don't like that thought.

Knox clasps my shoulder as she huffs and goes back to where she came from. She'll buy more time before she has to go to school—it's her pattern. Doesn't matter. Sooner or later, she'll come for me.

Pun intended.

"Never mind her. She's always like that." Knox grabs an apple from the bowl on the table and crunches loudly.

"Has she always been like that?" I grab an apple myself and toss it in the air, pretending to be nonchalant.

Knox and I have been getting close over the weeks, but he's been distant lately, even during football practice. He also doesn't like talking about his sister, which I understand considering the sibling relationship.

But something tells me he's trying to hide something else.

Holding a secret for so long gives me certain perks; the most important of all is that I get to sense when someone is hiding something.

Knox, for instance.

"Why are you asking?" He takes another huge bite. "You want me to tell you her deepest, darkest secret so you can use it against her?"

I lift a hand in the air, pretending to wave a white flag. "I just want to end an engagement neither of us wants."

Or at least, I *didn't* want it. I'm not so sure anymore. The thought that she could be with someone else as soon as we're over makes me want to grab her by the throat and fuck her until she no longer thinks about anyone else.

I've never had those thoughts about a girl before or even viewed sex that way.

For me, shagging was another way to keep people close, to never spend nights alone. Even when some fucked-up ideas barged in, I usually shooed them away without a problem.

Not with Teal.

It's almost as if she brings them to the forefront of my messed-up brain.

Knox chews slowly. "She does want to be engaged."

"Why would she?"

He lifts a shoulder. "I wish I knew. You think I want my sister with a womaniser like you, mate?"

"Then we can help each other."

He raises a brow. "Or you can do right by my sister."

Fuck that.

"We're not in the middle ages anymore, Van Doren."

"Apparently, your father thinks otherwise."

I sigh, pausing before I throw the apple. "At least give me something about her so I can treat her right."

Or rather, learn her better. Even after seeing her in her most intimate moments, she's still a puzzle. It's the way she shuts down, immediately building up fortresses and walls.

Knox chews, looking me up and down. "Don't startle her."

"What?"

"Don't come out of nowhere and surprise her. Don't touch her when she's not aware of your presence. She has a bad reaction to that."

A few things click into place—the way she jumps slightly then instantly hides it, the way she was breathing heavily as she sought refuge in that closet.

She has some sort of attacks.

But she didn't have them when I pinned her to the wall. Was it because she was already aware of me?

I fully face Knox. "What's the reason?"

"Childhood trauma."

"The stuff with Elsa's mother?" When Knox and I were getting close and smoking weed in dark corners at parties, he told me about how he and Teal became a part of Ethan Steel's family and what his wife did to them.

I suspect something similar happened to Aiden, but the fucker never talks about it.

"Nope. Something deeper." He tosses the finished apple in the bin. "That's all for your psychological class of the day."

Something deeper?

What's deeper than being kidnapped by a mentally deranged woman, being made to pretend to be her dead son, and being cut by her? Teal and Knox have faded scars on their knees—evidence of those times.

He places a hand in his pocket and his eyes droop a little as he shoots me a glare. "I know you don't want this engagement, but hurt my sister in any way and you'll see evidence of my origins. *Our* origins."

Street kids. A prostitute's offspring who don't even know their father because even their mother doesn't.

That is the reality of the Van Doren twins. Everyone knows it, Edric included. Just because Ethan Steel became their father doesn't mean it changed their origins. And yet, Edric agreed to the engagement for a partnership with Ethan.

He didn't care who he had to throw me to.

Earldom 101: selling out your children for arranged marriages like whores.

"Just a piece of advice," Knox says.

"Yeah?"

"Don't fall in love with her."

I laugh, tossing him the apple. "That will never happen."

He catches the fruit above his head. "Good, because it'll never be reciprocated. T doesn't know how to feel."

He says it with an edge of sadness, like it's bothered him for a long time and he doesn't want others to be caught in the same position.

Just then, she descends the stairs. This time, she's accompanied by Agnus, Ethan's partner or adviser or what-the-fuckever. She's asking him about some of her stuff and he replies with curt, detailed descriptions of everything.

Then something happens, something that makes me grip the table so tightly I'm surprised my tendons don't snap.

When they're at the base of the stairs, she stares up at him, and her lips curve into a sensual smile—soft, warm, fucking angelic.

I know it's honest because she can't fake a smile to save her life. I know she means it because her entire body is angled in Agnus' direction.

My type is at least fifteen years older, experienced, and doesn't smile the entire time like a gigolo on crack. In short, not you.

Her words play at the back of my head in a loop.

My gaze snaps to the man she's spent the last ten years with, the man she's smiling up at.

Her fucking type.

It takes everything in me to plaster a smile on my face. I push off the table and stride towards them. Her smile falls and she shoots me a 'stay away' look.

Stay away? Stay fucking away?

I place a hand on the small of her back, and a slight shiver goes through her body as she remains completely still.

There. Much better.

"Agnus, right?" I grin at him, showing my teeth.

He gives a curt nod, pretending, like I am, that it's the first time we've met.

"If you'll excuse us, I'm going to drive my fiancée to school now."

"Agnus can do it." She tries to wriggle away, but I dig my fingers into the tender skin of her waist, making her wince under her breath.

"I'm sure he's a busy man." I smile. "Right?"

"Yes, indeed." He ruffles her hair, and she blushes so furiously her pale skin turns rosy. "Call me if you need a ride home."

I grind my molars, but I speak through my usual smile. "No need. I'll do it."

And with that, I drag her with me outside. In just a few seconds, my mood has gone from grey to black. No, not black—red, and fucking murderous.

"I told you not to pick me up," she protests.

"And I told you that's not how it works."

"Let me go, Ronan. I can't keep up."

I stare back at her as we reach the entrance. I'm clutching her by the wrist, and she stumbles on her own feet in her attempt to catch up to me.

Instead of letting her go, I slam her against the wall. She gasps as her back is flattened against the blunt surface. "You don't need me to pick you up because you have Agnus?"

"Well, yes." She stares up at me despite the tremor in her voice.

"*Well, yes?*" I laugh, but there's no humour behind it. I know she sees it too, because she swallows, her black eyes filling with what resembles fear.

Fear is good. Fear means she knows her fucking place.

"So does that mean I'm ruining your daddy kink, Teal?"

"Screw you, okay? I won't allow you to talk about Agnus that way."

"And in what way should I talk about him? Is he the reason behind your fantasies, *ma belle?* Is that it?"

"I don't have to tell you anything."

I grip her by the chin and force her neck into a bent angle so I'm glaring down at her. "Forget about him, starting right fucking now."

"Or what?"

"Or I'll make you regret it."

Something sparks in her features, a challenge, a 'game on' of sorts before she puffs out her chest. "No."

"Oh, Teal." I caress her skin, my voice calm and touch gentle though my insides are on fire. "You're fucked."

SIXTEEN

Teal

In the past, when I used to walk through RES's halls and see couples whispering to each other or kissing in corners, I'd breeze straight past them.

I made a decision to be around Elsa as little as possible when she's with Aiden. He cares about no one when he starts tonguing her as if they're in private. I even avoided Kim when she started going out with Xander because they gave off this soulmates vibe that I've read about in books and makes me roll my eyes so hard.

There's no such thing as soulmates. It's all a chemical reaction, a rush of dopamine, a high, and like any high, it'll eventually wither away.

When I told Elsa and Kim those exact words, they laughed at me. They thought I didn't understand. Well, they're the ones who don't understand, and with time, I'll be able to say 'I told you so.'

The downfall of that plan, and of my thoughts in general, is a moment like this one.

Ronan has his arm around my waist as we walk down the hall, and no matter how much I elbow him, he won't budge.

If anything, he glues himself more tightly to my side, as if we were born attached at the hip. Even Knox and I weren't.

His closeness is a dent in my plan. The way I keep inhaling his spicy scent and basking in his warmth is dangerously close to that addiction state. You know, the one that comes after the high I already established is beneath me.

Not only that, but since he cornered me at my house, he's been acting as if nothing happened.

He's still smiling at girls—and boys—and everyone who crosses our path, teachers and school staff included.

Despite his Death nickname, he's loved here. Scratch that—he's not only loved, he's also worshipped, and like any god, he has a religion and an altar for sacrifices. He has followers—other than the ones on Instagram and Snapchat—and fanatics.

Said fanatics, mainly the female population, keep shooting me glares the more Ronan pulls me to his side, parading me around for the world, or rather the school, to see.

I don't like attention, and it's not because I prefer staying under the radar like Elsa, but because attention is kind of stupid. What do you do with attention? You can't even eat it.

Also, people who thrive on attention like the arsehole who's digging his fingers into the flesh of my hipbone are shady as fuck. You never know what they're actually hiding.

I thought he was a gigolo, fake, shallow, but I learnt the hard way that Ronan Astor is more than what meets the eye. He's the disaster you never see coming. He's a monster hidden under the popularity and the picturesque smile and family.

His *damn* family.

The fact that he's unpredictable has put me on edge since that encounter in his room with his mum on the other side of the door.

I don't like admitting this, but he rattles me. He's putting dents upon dents in my plan, and I need to stay the fuck away from him to keep my sanity and protect my clear course of action.

But at the same time, when he slammed me against the wall earlier, warning me to stay away from Agnus, I couldn't help provoking him.

I'm not the type who provokes people—if anything, I walk straight past any provocation—but with him, all my domino pieces are shuffled and knocked down.

There's no order or strategy, there's only…the unknown. It's like being thrown into a dark maze covered in black smoke.

Truth is, I want to dip my fingers into the other Ronan, the one only I can see, the one who's not running for a popularity vote.

Why would I want that? I don't know.

He's not helping either. He hasn't uttered a word, not during the ride here and not now.

You're fucked.

He said it. I heard him. Why isn't he acting on it?

Do I have to wait long for his retaliation?

Do I have to see a doctor for being excited about his retaliation and how far he'll take it this time?

"Wannabe bitch," whispers Claire, the girl from the other day, as she passes me by.

While I usually don't give them the time of day, I'm on the edge of myself, and I don't allow bitches to walk all over me.

So what if I started this for a plan? Everyone needs to know their damn place.

"Hey you." I stop, forcing Ronan to halt too.

The girl and her friend glare back at me then bat their lashes at Ronan.

"If you have something to say, why don't you speak out loud for everyone to hear?" My voice is calm, neutral even.

I realise a small crowd has started to gather, but I couldn't care less. This isn't about them; it's about me.

My self-worth. My dignity.

"I don't know what you're talking about." Claire feigns innocence, still giving Ronan that 'fuck me' look.

"Aside from the fact that you stole Ronan from her." The friend, a tall blonde girl, places a hand on her hip.

"Ladies." Ronan grins, his tone is that loathsome happy-go-lucky one. "Don't fight. Everyone gets a share."

Everyone gets a share?

Everyone gets a fucking share?

I'm surprised my face doesn't combust from the amount of blood rushing to it.

But then again, why should I care? He can give all the shares he wants as long as I get to my end goal.

He doesn't matter.

"She doesn't seem to think that way, Ron." Claire pouts like a fucking kid with issues.

Ron.

Of course they call the man-whore that.

Before he gets a chance to speak, I slide myself out of his hold and stride towards Claire until I'm nose to nose with her. "Do you know why?"

To her credit, she keeps her posture straight, pretending I don't scare her. After all, the female population in this school agree with her, not me.

"I happen to be his fiancée. Ever heard that term?" I stare down my nose at her. "Google it, and then we can maybe talk about it."

Claire's face creases with a scowl, but her friend points a finger at me. "You're only his fiancée because he's forced to. Arranged marriage. Google it."

"I did, and that's how I managed to officially own him while all of you beg for scraps." I stare at her then at every girl watching me with either mouths agape or malice in their eyes—or both. "If any of you threaten me, you won't like how I'll react. This is my first and final warning."

And then, I grab Ronan and drag him away from the scene. I expect to find him grinning at the others, offering them his apologetic smiles or whatever he does to seem like an innocent gigolo, but his gaze is entirely on me.

Just me.

Those rich brown eyes with a slightly colourful hue, those brows arching a little. For the first time ever, he's not smiling or smirking or grinning on the school grounds. If anything, he appears...a bit pissed off?

I have no time to focus on that as I push him down the hall. Once we're near class, I let him go.

The other girls are watching from afar. Half must be spooked since they think I offer sacrifices to Satan—good. At least that will keep them off my case. The other half seem to hate me even more and are plotting my demise.

Screw them all.

I didn't come this far for those little bitches to ruin what I've worked for.

Do you honestly think that's the only reason behind your public display of ownership?

I ignore the voice in my head, not wanting to dig into these emotions going through me all at once. It's hard to comprehend one emotion at a time, let alone all of them.

"What was that all about?" Ronan grabs me by the arm, forbidding my entrance into the class.

"Nothing." I try to step inside again.

This time, he pulls me behind him and slams my back against the wall of a dark corner near the teacher's room.

Damn it. What's with him and pinning me to walls?

And why is my spine tingling with anticipation?

When I meet his gaze, it's a bit blank, a bit unreadable, a bit shadowed. "I said. What the fuck was that all about?"

Is it so wrong that my entire body comes to life whenever he looks at me that way? Whenever he sheds his mask and shows me his true, raw self?

Only to me. Not anyone else but me.

Still, I use my stern tone. "Don't you dare disrespect me in front of others, Ronan. I don't react well to it."

"Obviously." His fingers dig into my arm, and although his skin is separated from mine by my jacket and shirt, it's almost as if he's gripping my bare flesh and engraving himself into it.

"Let me go," I hiss, watching our surroundings. Teachers wouldn't react well to this scene.

"Not before we clear things up."

"What things?"

"Like your stupid belief that you own me." His voice is cold, cruel even. "You don't own me, *belle*. It's the other way around."

I lift my chin. "Is that what you think?"

"That's what it is, and if you challenge me again, I'll prove it."

"Prove it how?"

"Considering your show just now…" He trails off. "You don't want to know that."

"Ronan," I warn.

"Teal." He grins.

"Fuck you."

"I'll be doing more than fucking you if you don't heed my warning."

"What are you talking about?"

He places his arm against the wall by my head and leans down so his face is a mere breath away from mine. My breasts heave an inch away from his jacket.

"Stay away from Agnus, and this is, as you said earlier, your first and final warning."

The sense of provocation hits me again. I want him to kiss me, to bite my lip and draw blood. I want him to devour me like this is the last day on earth and I'm the only one he wants to spend it with.

But most of all, I want him to breathe life into me.

"And if I don't?" I murmur.

"I'll be doing a lot of fucking, and not with you." His face and voice are neutral. "You're welcome to the front-row seat since you're into voyeurism. I'll put on a show for you as I fuck Claire and her friend while you watch and know it won't be you."

Something red and hot bursts inside me. It could be my own blood or my veins or rage; I don't know. All I know is that I can't shut up. I have to give back what he served.

"After that, you can watch my show." I run my fingers over his tie. "I have a dial list, you know. All the men who fucked me will be open for a redo, and guess what, Ronan? They're my type—older, experienced, and aware of how to make a woman feel good."

Thick silence lingers between us for a second too long.

I expected Ronan to act on that since he did before. I expected him to tell me fuck no, or kiss me, or anything.

Instead…he's smiling.

Why the hell is he smiling?

"You do that, *belle*."

What?

"Now if you'll excuse me, I'll go schedule my threesome." He pushes off me.

The emptiness of the air on my skin is like being abandoned, being thrown away.

It's one of my most hated feelings in the world.

"I'm not kidding." I speak to his back. "I will do it."

He glances at me over his shoulder. "I'll do it too."

And then he's walking again. Damn it. Damn it.

It wasn't supposed to go this way. Why the hell isn't he stopping me? He should, and I would stop him in return.

Unless the arsehole actually wants to do this?

He can't…be serious.

"Ronan." I grind out his name, expecting him to ignore me, but he turns around and faces me.

There's still that loathsome smile on his face, the one I want to burn to ashes. "What is it, *belle*?"

"Is this another game?"

"I don't know. You tell me, because I don't play fair."

"Just because you have a dick doesn't mean you're the only one who gets to do things."

"Just because you have a pussy doesn't mean you're the only one who gets to do things," he shoots back without missing a beat.

It's a challenge. He's challenging me.

"What do you want?" I snap. "Tell me."

"I want *you* to tell me."

"How the hell would I know what you want?"

"Figure it out. You started this."

"I started this?" I repeat, incredulous.

"You did. Now, as you fix it, I'll go get my dose."

This time, I don't stop him as he disappears into the class, even though something in my chest shrivels and dies.

Fuck him.

He's not the only one who doesn't play fair.

SEVENTEEN

Ronan

The best-laid plans start with a scheme. It can be something as simple as planting a seed for trouble.

Like I did yesterday.

Teal has been ignoring me since I announced my threesome plans with Claire and her friend. When she thinks I'm not watching, she glares at my back.

She can't resist glaring. It's in her personality and the only way she can purge away her emotions.

Sometimes, her brows will furrow when I'm in her peripheral vision, as if she can't comprehend what's going on. She realises something is wrong, but she can't figure out how to fix it.

What she doesn't know is that she'll fall in line sooner or later.

My fucking line.

I spent the entire evening with Knox at their house last night, making sure she didn't go out for whoever the fuck is on her contacts. I'll do something about those suckers later. It'll start with erasing them from her life and end with no future contact with them.

For now, she needs to admit her fault, realise what she's done, and promise she won't do it again.

There's something about Teal aside from how real she is.

She also goes bonkers when she doesn't understand shit. This situation isn't something Google can answer for her, just like it can't answer my questions about her. There's nothing about her and Knox on the internet except the fact that they're Ethan's foster children. The whole thing is suspicious as fuck, and while Knox isn't any help, there's another family member who is.

I find Elsa right before her track practice, the only time the fucker Aiden leaves her alone.

She's on her way to the pitch when I wrap an arm around her shoulder and fall in step beside her. "How is my favourite Ellie?"

"You have many Ellies?"

"Just three." I grin. "And you're the best out of them all."

"You're incorrigible, Ronan."

"Your compliments warm my heart."

She looks me up and down. "Shouldn't you be at practice?"

"It got cancelled. Don't tell King."

"Why not?" she whispers, as if this is an elaborate plot.

"He's a dick all the time, while I only get to be a dick now and again."

She laughs, poking my side. "Don't let him hear you say that."

"Our secret. My life depends on it—seriously."

"If you know that, why do you keep provoking him?"

I lift a shoulder. "Because it's fun."

"Fun, huh?"

"Speaking of fun or the lack thereof, I still cry into my pillow every night because you refused to marry me and threw me to your foster sister." I feign sadness. "I thought I meant more to you than shallow fun, Ellie."

"Hey, Teal is great."

"Is she, though?"

"She is. She's just misunderstood."

"Misunderstood, really? Surely you heard about the horror story she started at school yesterday?"

She smiles awkwardly. I hit the nail on the head with that one. "She's just protective and doesn't like being provoked."

"Do you think she wants this whole engagement thing?"

"She said she does."

I don't miss the way Elsa's face scrunches as she says those words. She doesn't believe her.

That's…interesting.

"Do you think she's lying?" I feign nonchalance.

"No, but…" She stares up at me, biting her lip. "You're my friend, too, and I think you need to know this."

"Know what?"

"I think Teal has always had a crush on Agnus."

Fucking Agnus again. The next time I see that man, something childish and out of character will happen—or criminal, depending on my mood.

"For the record, I like you best, Ro." Elsa pats my hand that's dangling on her shoulder. "Agnus is manipulative as hell, and I don't like that he's important to Dad's business. If I have to pick a side, it'll undoubtedly be yours."

I place a hand on my heart. "I knew you loved me. Now, about that threesome Aiden shouldn't know about…"

"Stop it." She chuckles.

"I swear my dick is bigger than his."

"How would you know that?"

"Shower, Ellie. Ever heard of it? Aiden and I have taken them together more times than I could count."

Her cheeks redden. "I didn't need that image."

I waggle an eyebrow. "Yes, you did. Now, let's plot the fun we'll have without him."

"Without who?" Aiden's voice cuts into my plan like a devil's sword. He yanks my arm off Elsa's shoulder and plants himself between us as he holds her to him by the waist. "From today onwards, you're not allowed near Elsa when I'm not here."

"Question is, how would you know if you're not here?" I taunt. "Nice jersey."

He cuts me a glare and I grin. He changed into the team jersey and shorts before he found out practice was cancelled. Since I'm still in my uniform, it means I knew all along and didn't tell him.

Pushing Aiden's buttons. Good times.

"Elsa was just agreeing to the threesome," I continue. "You're welcome to watch."

Elsa motions at me to shut up, seeming worried about my safety. I expected Aiden to threaten my life and remind me of the grave he's been digging for me since the beginning of the year, but he smirks instead.

The fuck? Is he immune to it now?

No, come on. Provoking Aiden so he shows his non-poker face is one of my recent favourite hobbies.

So, I go with it and snap my fingers. "This means you're cool with it, right? Ellie, I meant it about the size, and —"

He cuts me off. "How is your fiancée, Astor?"

I smile. "Probably performing some satanic rituals."

"Hey!" Elsa scolds me.

I pretend to grin back. What Elsa doesn't know is that I need to keep up the façade, need to make everyone believe I don't give two fucks about Teal—even she needs to know that. She needs to realise there's no way in fuck she'll become my weakness like Aiden is parading his around in the form of Elsa.

I don't have weaknesses. I have people.

Lots of fucking people who fill every corner of my life.

So what if Teal stands out from that crowd? So what if I've been looking for her during lunch break and haven't found her? I won't show it or ask about her.

She'll be the one who'll admit her fault and come back to me, not the other way around.

I'm an earl's heir. We never show our true emotions.

"I see," Aiden muses. "That must be why she's with Cole then. You know, for pointers."

What the fuck is she doing with Cole?

As if reading my mind, Aiden's smirk widens. "You know his rituals. They can get…interesting."

"Uh-huh." I don't know how I manage to get that out with how firmly I'm gritting my teeth.

"They're in the garden, near the back."

Cole is with Teal in the garden, where he usually reads alone like a creep. What is he doing there with her?

And what is she doing with Cole instead of coming to me?

"I didn't ask." I smile at Aiden.

"I'm just saying. They were cosy." He's talking to me, but his lips are whispering the words against Elsa's forehead. "Send me updates."

And then he disappears with his girlfriend down the hall, and not in the direction of the pitch.

For a second, I stand there, processing Aiden's words. He could be lying to get a rise out of me, but that's the problem: he doesn't—lie, I mean. He likes chaos, but not to the point of making things up.

Cole and Teal are cosy.

I run a hand through my hair. *Fuck!*

"Hey, Ron." Claire's soft voice barges through my head before she grabs me by the arm. "You look tense. Do you want me to loosen you up? Reese would help, too."

I stare at her face, but I'm not seeing her. My dick is so flaccid, Ron Astor the Second is about to start weeping—and not in a good way.

Claire and her friend do shit for me now. I never even planned to fuck them, and my challenge to Teal yesterday was only that—a challenge. I never planned to act on it. I'm almost sure she never meant to act on her threat either.

So what the fuck is she doing with Cole?

"Later, Claire." I push her and her disappointed expression out of view as I hurry to the other entrance of the school and towards the garden.

I try telling myself Cole isn't her type. She prefers older and fucked up.

Still, cosy. Aiden said *cosy*. What does cosy mean? They're sitting together under the tree and reading poetry? They're talking—which is as cosy as Teal would get? Maybe they're writing their own book titled *How to be Fucked Up, and Other Questions*.

Even as I tell myself that, my blood boils with every step I take. They're not even in view and I'm about ready to cut a bitch and murder a fucker.

I try not to think of small things, like the fact that Cole was the first one she openly greeted when she first transferred to RES.

Or how when we watch games at Aiden's house, he's the only one she'll willingly sit beside, and how she even listens to him when he speaks.

He's not her type.

Then I recall the fucking fact that he's the one who accepted her into his club and that he knew she'd be there that night. *A coincidence*, the bastard said.

There's no coincidence with Cole. He plots everything to a T then pretends it's been a coincidence all along.

The fucker.

My feet come to a stop of their own volition. Sure enough, Cole and Teal are sitting on the same bench, reading from a book.

They're reading from the same fucking book like in some period drama.

Teal tucks her hair behind her ear. It's useless. Her strands are too silky and will fall over her face in no time. She smiles up at Cole, and the fucker smiles back as if this is some sort of cheesy teen film.

My vision turns red.

I don't care if this is planned by Cole and Aiden; they'll all learn their places—starting with Teal.

A hand grips my arm, stopping me in my tracks. I stare down at Silver's calculative features, her bitch mask in place and ready for trouble.

"What are you doing here?" I ask.

"Aiden sent me a text to meet him here."

Of course he did. That arsehole is out for blood while he's shagging his girlfriend somewhere.

"He's not here," I mutter while gritting my teeth.

"I can see that." Her gaze doesn't leave Cole and Teal as she releases me and folds her arms.

"What are you going to do about it, queen bee?"

"What makes you think I'll do anything?"

"Come on, Silver, it's me. We both know you're plotting trouble in that pretty little head of yours." I grin. "How about a collaboration?"

She raises a brow. "A collaboration?"

"Cole and Teal think they can play everyone, but they didn't consider us, did they?"

Her lips curve in a smirk, and I smirk back.

I warned Teal. I told her she's fucked, but she didn't listen.

If words didn't put her in her place, action will.

EIGHTEEN

Teal

Researching on Google is tricky. You have to know which resources to believe and which to chalk up to rumours.

Like the latest gossip about the Astor family. I wonder if Ronan knows about his uncle's return and where the mighty earl is rumoured to have taken Charlotte the past months.

Not that I should care if Ronan knows or not. He's an Astor, after all. If some forums on the internet know, he probably does, too.

Dad and Agnus always tell us to stay away from the internet's rabbit hole since it says more lies than truths, but there's no smoke without fire.

I can already see the Astor family's demise, because I'll make sure of it.

The only person who makes my chest do some strange stuff is Charlotte. I wish I could do this without implicating or hurting her, but as they say, there are no victories without sacrifices.

I'm so sorry, Charlotte.

Maybe I should stop the hypocritical stuff and not visit or text her anymore.

I switch to the article about the correlation between death

and fear. It's about how humans are instinctively afraid of dying, even those who are suicidal.

Fear of death is a foreign concept to me. Why would you be scared of something that will eventually happen? It's coming anyway, so might as well make the trip towards it worthwhile.

"Death and war. Interesting."

My head rises at Cole's serene voice. He slides beside me, clutching a book called *Calila e Dimna* that has animal illustrations on it.

"Interesting book," I say.

"I know. I finally got my copy." He motions at my phone. "But it's not as interesting as your article."

I stare back at my phone. *Death and Fear in Times of War.*

I make the screen go black, not because I'm ashamed to read about it, but because Cole's book seems more fascinating.

Cole is in his uniform, minus the jacket, and the sleeves of his shirt are rolled to beneath his elbows. With the calm expression on his face, he seems like one of those handsome book nerds whom the girls admire from afar. It's for different reasons than Aiden. My sister's boyfriend doesn't care—at all. Cole does, but in a dispassionate kind of way.

When I came to RES, he approached me first and talked to me as if we'd known each other our entire lives. We also share certain…tendencies.

While our interactions are easy and raise no alarm, I know Cole always has a purpose up his proper sleeve.

He sold me out once, and if he thinks I didn't figure it out then he doesn't know who he's dealing with.

I might not be that good at deception, but I know how to lure someone to the battlefield.

"Tell me about your book," I say.

"It's old tales, or rather fables, translated to Arabic then Spanish in the twelve hundreds." He opens the first page, running his fingers over the words.

"What does it talk about?" I motion at it.

"Philosophy told in the form of animals. For instance, the lion is the king, and there are others who represent different roles."

"Such as?"

"The ox and the bull. What do you think they represent?"

"Cunning? Force?"

His lips quirk in a small smile. "Probably. Each fable has a purpose."

"Just like every piece in chess and dominos?"

"Exactly."

I raise an eyebrow. "Hey, it's sort of like this entire school."

He mirrors my gesture. "Possibly. We all fulfil a role."

"What role do I fulfil in your game, Cole?"

"Woah." He pretends to be taken aback. "You do me injustice, Teal."

"How about *your* injustice? You think I don't know you told Ronan about the club?"

"Why would you assume it's me?"

"You're the only one from school I saw there. It doesn't take a genius to figure it out."

"Not the only one. There's someone else you're forgetting about."

"That someone else wouldn't tell Ronan."

His lips curve again. "How can you be so sure?"

"I had a deal with her. Besides, you're the only one who plays games."

"Noted." He flips the page as if he's been reading the entire time. "However, in my defence, Ronan would've figured it out anyway, so I thought I might as well tell him and gain favour."

"He wouldn't have figured it out if you hadn't told him."

"Oh, he would've. Ronan is like a dog—a trained one. He smells things from afar and doesn't stop until he finds his prey. If I hadn't told him, he would've followed you, stalked you, broke in, hacked your phone and emails, and eventually gotten what he wanted. I simply made it easier for everyone."

I huff. He makes it sound as if he's the angel in this tale and we should all bow down in thanks and possibly offer some sacrifices at his altar.

"Because of you, he now has me by the arm, and do you know what I'm tempted to do, Cole?"

"Tell me. I'm all ears."

I allow myself a cunning smile. "If you ruined my fun, what stops me from ruining yours?"

"I didn't ruin your fun—I made it happen. Can't you see that?"

I stare incredulously. "You made it happen? How the hell is being involved with Ronan making my fun happen?"

"Teal, even you can admit that Ronan has added an interesting flavour to your life. I'm just being a good Cupid here."

I scoff even as I boil on the inside.

Cole doesn't understand that he ruined much more than he knows. My plan, for instance—it used to be so clear, but now it's all murky water and feelings I can't even begin to comb through.

"Tell me about Ronan," I say.

"Tell you about Ronan?"

"After what you did, the least you can do is give me information. Why does he act different sometimes?"

He chuckles. "Oh, you saw that part."

"So you know about it."

"The three of us do, but he doesn't like to show it. We barely get it once a year during Halloween. May I ask how you managed to poke it out?"

"I'm trying to figure out how to tuck it back in, not poke it out."

"Are you sure, though?"

Yes. No. I don't know.

That arsehole is turning me into a version of myself I don't like or understand. There's this foreigner who's taking over my body and leaving me without any thoughts.

The worst part is that I want to understand. Deep down, I want to sit with him, talk to him, touch him.

Just be with him.

"Do you want to know what I think, Teal?" Cole flips another page.

"No."

"I think you do like it," he continues, ignoring my reply. "Maybe you don't like that you like it. Maybe you don't like the effects it'll have on your plan—and, by the way, I'm all ears if you care to share."

"Hard pass." He'll just use it in his own game.

I haven't even told Knox about it, and it'll remain tucked between me and the shadow over my shoulder.

"He's here," Cole whispers, and I know who he's talking about without having to lift my head.

The hairs on the back of my nape stand on end and I tuck a strand behind my ear then quickly drop my hand down. Why am I acting like the girls who are always praying for his attention?

"Read with me." Cole points at a highlighted line.

I am the slave of what I have spoken, but the master of what I conceal.

"Why are we doing this?" I murmur.

"Because we can?"

Because we can? That's so intriguing about Cole's character. Does he always do things just because he can?

Is he one of the people who like watching the world burn?

"*Salut.*" Ronan's voice cuts into my bubble. I take a breath before I look up.

Nothing would've prepared me for the scene in front of me.

Ronan has Silver glued to him by the shoulder as she stares up at him with dreamy bloody eyes.

Silver with her blonde hair and provocative beauty—the type Ronan has gravitated towards in the past.

What the...

"So, Captain, Teal." Ronan grins at us. "Silver and I were going to drink and smoke and fuck. Who wants to join?"

"Yes, join us. Teal?" She stares at me, her eyes screaming, *You broke a code.*

Silver and I aren't friends or even close, but we have an arrangement. Why is she doing this now?

I didn't break the code. *She* did.

Cole remains still, flicking his gaze at them then back at his book. "Teal and I have a book to read."

Sure, I can go on with Cole. If I really want to spite Ronan, I can grab Cole and kiss him and then see all hell break loose, but I can't fake things like that.

I can't stare at him in the eyes and pretend he's someone else.

Or wait...maybe I can.

It's pretence, after all. An eye for an eye.

I'm a firm believer in justice. He started this whole mess, and he keeps making it worse.

I throw one last glance at Silver's French-manicured nails toying with Ronan's tie and then place my palm on Cole's cheek, making him face me. "We can do something more fun than reading."

Something flashes in his eyes, something like sadism. It vanishes as soon as it appears. Before I can take the next step, a strong hand wraps around my arm, and I gasp as he hauls me to my feet.

Ronan stares down at me with raging eyes on the verge of breaking hell and all of its friends loose. "What the fuck—and I mean, what in the actual *fuck*—do you think you're doing?"

"I told you." My voice is calm. Too calm. "I might let you do things to me, but disrespect me not. I am not your damn toy."

I push at his chest and storm out of the garden, my chest heaving and my heart nearly bursting out.

As I arrive at the car park, I place a hand on my chest, willing it to stop beating this hard, this fast.

What the hell is wrong with you, heart? Why are you coming back to life?

And for who? A fucking gigolo? Couldn't it be someone, I don't know, more available?

Someone trips into me from behind and I yelp, my lungs constricting. The person apologises and moves along.

I slump against one of the cars, holding a hand to my heart, and I realise I just wished it was Ronan who bumped into me. When it wasn't, my heart might have died a little.

"What do you think you're doing, Teal? If you want the bitch façade, that's what you'll get." Silver's voice cuts into my thoughts.

She walks like a model to face me, her arms folded and her face full of malice. I wonder if that's what I would look like if I had the ability to show emotions.

I mirror her stance, widening my legs and crossing my arms. "Funny, because I thought the show back there was you being a bitch."

"You've seen nothing, Teal. Don't make me show you."

"Do you honestly think I'm scared of you? If you stab, I'll stab right back."

She attacks then. Her hand shoots up and she pulls me by the hair, nearly ripping it from its root.

I do the same.

We're clutching each other by the hair, but instead of feeling the pain, all we offer each other are glares.

"We had an arrangement," she manages to mutter.

"And you ruined it."

"Oh, I did? Are you hearing yourself?"

"I told you at the club I'd stay out of your way as long as you stayed out of mine, and what did you do? You were running your claws all over *my* fiancé. My —"

I cut myself off before I say more, before I admit that seeing her with him has put me entirely off balance, that I might've even felt small in comparison, that maybe she fits him more than I'll ever do. Silver is the daughter of Sebastian Queens, the most probable future prime minister. Her mother is a member of parliament who's a smart, beautiful and eloquent. Even her stepmother, Cole's mother, is a bestselling, genius author who's known for her intelligent storytelling. Silver is the epitome of everything an earl's son should be with. Her outfits are always pristine, she smells of Chanel and is a social media goddess with picturesque family and life. She even plays the fucking piano.

I never feel small. I don't allow myself to.

What on earth is Ronan Astor doing to me?

"You were there first." She grunts. "I'm not a nice person, Teal. Don't test me."

"I'm not a nice person either."

We glare at each other for long seconds, and then we release each other at the same time.

"Stay away, and I will," she warns, putting her hair back in place with utter elegance that resembles Charlotte's. While Ronan's mother is soft, Silver is all rugged edges and plays the bitch role all too well.

Elsa and Kim already categorise her as such. In fact, the entire school considers her queen bee. After seeing her at the club, it's hard for me to look at her from that perspective.

"I thought you didn't like him." I study my black nails. "It seemed that way at the club."

Her cheeks redden. "Shut up."

"I'm only saying it as I see it, Silver."

"Oh, you want me to say it as I see it, too?" She straightens, and since she's taller, she uses every inch to look down at me. "You're afraid of Ronan, Teal."

"Me, afraid?" I scoff.

"Yes. You know he can barge through the whole goth and satanic exterior and see the real girl inside, and you don't want that, so you picked up the defence and decided to protect your walls. But you know what? You can't protect your walls and claim him at the same time. One of these days, you'll have to choose." She flips her hair. "But what do I know, right?"

I continue staring at Silver's back as she heads to her car.

Her words swirl in my mind, but their impact is a lot worse than she aimed for. She wanted to make me feel guilty so I'd go to Ronan and leave her plan alone, but a different realisation hits me.

I realise I am feeling after my vow not to ever feel again.

And I realise I need to get rid of these feelings.

Only one way to go about this.

NINETEEN

Ronan

T hat night, I mope around at the Meet Up.

Okay, maybe mope around is the wrong word. I'm sulking like a whore without clients.

And who gets to witness my misery? The three other fuckers I don't want near me right now.

Xander just returned from rehab and is grinning like a fucking idiot with those dimples someone should get rid of to give the world some peace. What's so special about them anyway? They're like holes in his cheeks. I've always thought they're overrated with the ladies.

Even Kimmy loves them, secretly or openly or whatever you want to call it, but we all agree that Kimmy and Elsa have terrible taste in men. And by we all, I mean Lars and me when I slur stories to him whenever I'm stoned.

Like now.

This shit is good.

I take a drag of the joint and close my eyes, letting it submerge me into its hold. I'm not a junkie. Unlike common belief, I don't smoke weed every day. I only do it when I don't want to be in my head or when I want to throttle someone and I know I can't.

Lars PMSes and writes about me in his little black book

when I smoke in my room, especially now that his favourite earl is in the house. Lars is a fucking traitor. I'm removing him from my list of people. I'm also removing Cole and Aiden.

These two fuckers are lucky I'm in no fighting mood or I would've jammed both their faces against each other.

Or not.

Violence might cross my mind once and again, but I don't act on it—or rather I have enough self-control to never act on it. That whole package comes together: an earl's heir, a noble title, expectations, and a good boy tag.

Maybe if I hadn't been fucked up at a young age, I would've grown into that image. Maybe I wouldn't be smoking my joint and imagining her disappointed, angry obsidian eyes staring up at me, as if I let her down and scared her at the same fucking time.

I glare at Cole, who's sitting beside Aiden, leaning his head against his fist and reading from that same book he had when they were together earlier.

That book is going down.

"We should all agree that my pussy suggestion is the best," Aiden tells Xander, who's sitting on the armrest of my chair and twirling a ball.

"Your suggestions are never the best." Xan rolls his eyes. "If anything, they're the worst."

"They are the best." Aiden's lips tilt in a smirk. "Ask Nash."

Cole flips him off without looking up from his book.

"Nash is a petty little bitch, so his opinion doesn't matter anyway." Aiden points at me. "Ask Astor. I gave him the best tip today."

I nod without saying a word.

"And you sent that text to Silver," Cole says. It's not a question; he's dead sure about it, and I'm a hundred percent certain he's planning Aiden's demise as we speak.

Usually, I'd watch their clashing with a grin. I even instigate it at times, but now, I want Cole down, not Aiden, in a grudge-like, I'll-haunt-you-for-eternity kind of way.

"Wait." Xander pauses twirling his ball. "Drama went down today, didn't it? Damn. I can't believe I missed it. Updates, anyone? Ron?"

"You tell me nothing." I continue glaring at Cole. "Why should I tell you?"

"Come on." Xan jokingly hits my shoulder with his. "You're still salty about that? You have a big mouth, Ron. If I told you anything, it would've been in the *Daily Mail*."

He and everyone on the team like to think I don't keep secrets, and I perfected that image because I don't want them to throw their darkest secrets on me. I don't want to be the vessel of those because they only bring me down.

That's why whenever any of them tells me something, I make sure the entire team knows, so they'll stop dumping their shit on me.

I'm already bubbling with one secret. It keeps expanding and becoming larger than life with time, and if I add others, I'll just snap. I'll just let it all go.

And I can't do that to my mother. I just…*can't.*

"Here's the condensed version of what went down," Aiden starts in a semi-bored tone. "Nash here was trying to start a battle by spending time with Teal, and Astor brought Silver and started his own war after making us believe wars are beneath him. Astor has been trying to make us think he doesn't care about his new fiancée who has a tendency towards satanic rituals and sarcasm, but he is actually contemplating the best way to kill Nash and bury him without anyone finding out. Oh, by the way, Nash is contemplating the same while pretending to read that book, because, as I always say though no one believes me, Nash is a petty little bitch."

"Damn." Xan throws his ball in the air then catches it. "I can't believe I missed all of that."

Cole doesn't even lift his head from his book, because if he did, he'd show his real emotions, and he's not the type to do that.

Lucky for me, I have my beloved joint. It erases all emotions whether I like it to or not. My expression must look serene, happy almost.

"So…" Xan pokes me. "New fiancée and stuff, huh? Since when do you take your father's orders?"

"I don't." I drag a long inhalation and check my phone.

Nothing.

Absolute desert. She hasn't replied to any of my texts.

Yes, she ignores me sometimes, but not to this extent.

On a scale from one to ten, how dangerous is climbing someone's balcony?

I'd take pointers from Aiden and Xan, but fuck them basically.

"But you're engaged to her, right?" Xander insists.

"I am, and if some fucker gets in the way of that, I won't stay still."

"Do I hear a threat?" Aiden smirks.

Cole lifts his head slowly even though he's still leaning on his fist. "Is it? A threat, I mean."

"You tell me, Captain. Play in my half of the field and I'll crush you."

"Woah." Xander chuckles, pointing at me. "Death is coming out. He's coming out. Hold on to your tits, bitches."

"Show him, Astor." Aiden grabs Cole's shoulder. "He deserves that side of you."

I glare at Cole, and he glares back before saying, "I thought you didn't want Teal?"

"I thought it's none of your business."

"Of course he wants her," Aiden scoffs.

My glare snaps to him.

"What?" He feigns innocence. "I'm just saying if you want

pointers about chasing and conquering, I can give you pointers from the King household manual of cease and desist."

"That sounded so fucking wrong," Xander says. "You know that, right?"

"How do you think my dear cousin Lev got Astrid? We both take those genes from Jonathan. I'm not an alien. My father is only more interested in business. Imagine if he wanted a human being."

We all pause then shake our heads with distaste.

Jonathan King is better off without any human presence near him.

"See?" Aiden raises a brow as if proving a point. "Now, back to Astor—you want help with your fiancée?"

"I don't need help. I just need you all to fuck off."

And for her to answer my texts.

There's still no reply. She didn't even see the fucking messages.

Cole stares at me funny for a second before he stands up and heads in the bathroom's direction.

"Hey, Knight," Aiden starts. "Give him pointers. I still vote for chase and conquer, but maybe Knight's pussy ways work."

"Fuck you, King." Xander grins. "You're just jealous because you can never have my connection with Kim."

"I can live with that."

"Do any of you have a lighter?" I ask.

"I have Nash's." Aiden dangles it in front of me. "Why?"

I stagger to my feet, snatch the lighter, and set the book Nash just left on his chair on fire. A smirk tugs at my lips as the flames eat it up. I heard he had so much trouble getting this book here with all the translation issues and limited editions and blah fucking blah.

He shouldn't have read it with Teal. He shouldn't have sat with her and allowed her to palm his cheeks.

I'm the only one whose fucking cheeks she's allowed to palm.

"He'll kill you." Xander chuckles under his breath.

"Way to go, Astor." Aiden squeezes my shoulder. "You're fit to be my friend."

Neither of them tries to stop me.

I throw the burning book and the lighter in the fireplace on my way out. "Give Captain my fucking regards."

I don't wait for their replies as I step outside. The cold air seeps under my uniform's jacket and the shirt.

An arm wraps around my shoulder as soon as I'm in front of the Meet Up.

"Yo." Xan grins at me. "You okay?"

While Aiden and Cole share sadism and sociopathic tendencies—among other things—Xander and I have always been the closest.

He's the only one who knows about my secret. I told him a few years ago when he found me hiding at a party—when I never do that. It was so suffocating, and I felt like crashing my car to feel something other than numbness. I blurted it out, not everything, but the part that weighed on me.

Xander has kept my secret since then. We might tease each other, but he always has my back, and I have his. I lied earlier—I'm not mad he didn't tell me his secret. Besides, I played Cupid in his tale with Kimmy. That's how much his support means to me.

That's why I felt kind of empty when he went to rehab. Of course, I'll never admit that to the fucker or he'll record it and show it to my great-grandchildren.

"I'm fine," I say.

"No, you're not. You barely talked in there, Ron. It's so unlike you."

"It's the weed."

"Not a certain Teal?" He waggles his brows suggestively.

"Fuck off."

"Nah, I'm really interested to know about the girl who's stealing your heart."

"She's not stealing my heart."

"Your sanity, then?"

Probably. "She just hides so much."

"Hides?"

"Yeah, I feel like I can't reach her."

"You know, Kim tried to hide from me before, and do you know how I was able to see her when no one else could?"

"How?"

His face softens. "I took that moment and really saw her. Not my prejudice of her, not my misconceptions. Just her."

"How the fuck am I supposed to do that if she's hiding?" Teal is so different from Kim. The latter has her heart on her sleeve in a way. Teal is a closed off gate.

"Then you're not doing it right."

"That's not an answer. You're a terrible councillor, Xan."

"Screw you, mate." He squeezes my shoulder. "I'm here if you need me."

"Save the pussy moments for Kimmy."

He flips me off with a grin, and I return the gesture as I head to my car then stop in front of the door.

I bring my phone up and stare at it. My subconscious is having this crazy thought that if I stare at it long enough or hard enough, it'll magically light up with a reply.

The screen lights up, and I pause.

That tactic actually works?

My hope is crushed when I make out Knox's name on the screen. I was going to pay a visit to their household anyway, maybe murder Agnus if she's spending time with him. I'm sure Lars will be up to covering up murder if I give him his favourite tea for Christmas.

"Yo, Van Doren," I answer.

"Have you seen Teal?"

"Funny, I was going to ask you that same question."

"Ah, fuck, okay."

"*Ah, fuck, okay?*" I repeat, bemused. "What is that supposed to mean? Where is she?"

"Probably purging somewhere."

"Purging."

"She does this sometimes. She disappears to purge by swimming or running and then she returns better. It's just how she rolls."

How she rolls? Why the fuck does he make it sound as if it's normal?

And why do I feel like swimming and running aren't the ways someone like Teal purges?

"Where does she usually go?" I ask.

"We don't know. We never do."

Well, fuck.

TWENTY

Teal

There's nothing I hate more than running.

And it's not only because of the physical activity of it, the shortness of breath, or the screaming of the muscles demanding I end the torture.

It's the memories that come with running.

Knox and I ran as hard as our small feet could carry us when we decided Mum's roof wasn't the one we'd stay under.

We ran and ran in the dirty streets. We ran after we stole food from the market. We ran after we heard a policeman's whistle, even if we hadn't done anything. In our small minds, we believed the police would find us for the stolen food and take us back to Mum.

It would've happened. We could've been forced to go back.

We didn't because we ran.

Naturally, all my memories of running are rubbish. Whenever I think about running, my brain fills up with fucked-up shit like maybe now we'll get caught, maybe now they'll take us back to Mum and she'll make me do—

I shake my head as I forge on in the park. I stopped counting how many hours I've been running. I pause for water and to catch my breath, but the moment I can run again, I do that. I run.

I let my legs lead me somewhere out of this place. It's transported me back to Birmingham, provoking loathsome memories and shit I don't want to think about, but it also eradicates the present.

It erases the predicament I'm in—or rather, that's what I like to think.

I stop, throwing my body on a bench, and a cat hisses then jumps away, glaring at me for disrupting his peace.

My breathing is jagged and choppy and out of control. I retrieve a towel from my bag and wipe my forehead.

The night has turned into morning and it's now the afternoon. It's been an entire day since I last had human interaction.

At least with humans I know.

I spent the night running, then I went to the forest and ran some more, and now I'm back to the park.

Dad and Agnus already know, but they probably didn't expect me to be gone for an entire day. That's why I chose a night they were spending working in the office.

Even if they do figure it out, they'll understand. They know I need this.

My therapist used to call it a coping mechanism. I call it purging.

You know, human beings are like sponges. They soak up so much, and there comes a time when they have to expel those feelings so they don't suffocate—or worse, snap.

I need to purge more than the average person because when that darkness creeps in, I can't shut it out. I can't look the other way and pretend it's not happening and the world can go on.

That type of darkness not only glides under my skin, it also possesses my head and puts crazy ideas in there, like maybe, just maybe waiting isn't the greatest tactic. Maybe I should make them feel how I felt before I stopped feeling altogether.

Maybe the shadow on my shoulder will finally stop crying.

But no. I can wait. If I suffered, he can suffer.

If I bled, he'll bleed.

My heart rate escalates at those thoughts, and I've never hated my heart the way I do now.

Despite all the purging, I can't get those stupid brown eyes out of my head. I can't chase him away from my thoughts.

The harder I run, the faster he barges in. The longer I torture myself physically, the more I yearn for his hands on me, feeling me, touching me, owning —

I shake my head and take out my phone. Ronan Astor is an arsehole, and that's all there's to it.

I power on my phone to send a text to Knox and let him know I'll come back later.

When my screen lights up with a few texts, I'm not surprised. Elsa and Knox tend to worry even when I make sure to tell them where I'm going beforehand.

Elsa: Kim and I are having a girls night if you want to join.

Knox: Why didn't you tell me you disappeared? I had to hear about it from Dad. You're losing twin privileges, sis.

Knox: Text me back that you're okay.

I reply to both of them, thinking I'm done with texts, but then a dozen other messages appear at the top.

My heart does that stupid thing whenever his name comes into view. God, what's wrong with me?

The first text was an hour after I left school.

Ronan: When I told you to figure out your mistake, I meant to figure out your fucking mistake, not get together with Cole. Spoiler alert: that made your situation way fucking worse.

He sent another text soon after.

Ronan: Where are you? Why is your phone turned off?

He laid off for an hour before sending another one.

Ronan: Teal, don't fuck with me or I'm tying you the fuck down when I find you. Answer your damn phone.

Ronan: If this is your version of playing hard to get, it's working. Reply to my texts or answer my calls. We need to talk. Stat.

His next text was a few hours later, at eight.

Ronan: Do you know where I am? At the Meet Up. You've been here before, but do you know the story behind it? It's the place Aiden inherited from his dead mother. It's the only place where we get to be ourselves and just talk. Usually, I'd do most of the storytelling. I'm not talking right now, though. I'm thinking about you while smoking weed and contemplating the perfect way to get away with murder and if I can melt Cole's corpse with acid. No idea what that makes you, but it's something close to being the cause of murder. If you don't want to become one, how about you answer me?

My lips curve in a smile before I can stop it. He has a way of making you feel like you're there with him. I can absolutely imagine him being a bastard about what happened with Cole, but it's not like he's innocent in the whole thing.

The following text came soon after.

Ronan: What's with all the purging Knox mentioned? What are you doing? I just confirmed that the fucker Agnus is with Ethan at the company or I would've cut a bitch. You're not at the club either. That's a good save, for your sake, not mine. Why do you need to purge? And I can't stress this enough, but fucking answer me.

I bite my lower lip, my heart beating fast and loud. I can't believe Knox told him that. It's supposed to be our secret. Why does everyone think Ronan is good to be privy to my life?

Myself included, because even now, I'm tempted to reply to that text and come clean about all the shit I think about when I'm in this mental state.

He has that effect on me, Ronan, the type where I want to bare myself and just be out there with him.

Which is the worst thing that could happen to someone like me with someone like him.

I might have snagged this arranged marriage, might have fought tooth and nail for it, but the truth remains: he's an earl's son.

I'm a prostitute's offspring.

A few hours later, at night, another text comes from him.

Ronan: You're infuriating—has anyone ever told you that? You're so infuriating it's on another level. You're so infuriating I'm tempted to do shit to you. But I don't have you here with me, so I'm rubbing one out in your honour, *ma belle*. I'm jerking off to the memory of your lips wrapped around my dick as I fucked your face like the other time. When I see you again, I'm fucking you whole.

My mouth hangs open and the cold air forms goosebumps on my skin. I can't fight away the image of Ronan masturbating, and not only masturbating, but masturbating for me.

When did I become such a fan of male masturbation? And not any male—him.

Another text came this morning.

Ronan: I didn't sleep because of you. Happy now? I'm not. Happy, I mean. Lars isn't happy either because I made him stay up all night listening to me spouting rubbish. He's writing about me in his little black book and hid my stash of weed. No more weed for me at home. It's all because of you, *belle*. I'm going to take it out on your pussy the next time I see you, which better be in the first class of the day at school.

An hour later.

Ronan: You're not here. Why aren't you here? And why do Elsa and Knox think it's fine that you're purging or what-the-fuck-ever? You better answer me or I swear to fucking God…

Ronan: Okay, that sounded threatening. I don't want to threaten you, but I fucking will if I have to.

Ronan: That text didn't help my case, but fuck it. If no one told you, I don't stop, so I'll search and find you, and yes, that sounds stalkerish, but fuck it again. I'm finding you and punishing you.

I scroll to the next text as if my hands are on fire. Reading the progress from angry to pleading and back to angry touches something inside me. It's a feather-light touch, but it's deep and raw and all I want is more.

The next text is a few hours later.

Ronan: Okay, fine. I shouldn't have threatened that stunt with Claire and her friend. I don't even know her name. I think I fucked her once, but if I don't remember her name, she's clearly forgettable. Anyway, that's not the point. I never planned to go through with it. The sex part, I mean. I wanted you to come clean, so how about you do that, and then I'll fuck this whole messed-up day out of our memories?

I narrow my eyes. If he doesn't remember Claire's friend's name but remembers Claire's, does that mean she's a memorable fuck?

Damn. I can't believe that's the only thing that remained in my mind after that entire text.

Ronan: I visited your house again. Agnus was there. I threw his phone in the rubbish bin. Knox told me I'm being childish, and I told him to fuck off. (Btw, I burned Cole's newest book toy yesterday too. I had two accomplishments in less than twenty-four hours.) If you didn't look at Agnus with those damn smiley eyes, I could've spared his phone, but oh well, RIP phone. What do you see in that creep anyway? Elsa says he's a psychopath, like a real one who manipulates people and has no emotions.

Ronan: Wait…is that your type? Is that why you were with Cole? Come on, pick a type—daddy kink or psycho kink.

Ronan: I'm better than both. Just saying.

I laugh out loud then hide the sound with the back of my hand. He's an anomaly. A serious one.

And he's the only one who makes me laugh even when he doesn't intend to.

The next text came two hours ago.

Ronan: It's been exactly twenty-four hours since you disappeared on me. Congrats on the ghosting effort, but it'll come to an end. I'm going to hire a PI and even the MI6 to find you. Brace yourself.

His last two texts came an hour ago.

Ronan: I'm at the Meet Up and I kicked everyone out to smoke weed and think about you in peace. I miss you and I'm going to fuck you when I find you, my crazy *belle*. Oh, and my calls have started with the PI. I'm going to convince Ethan to file a missing person report. You're going down.

Ronan: I fucking miss you, though.

My chest squeezes so hard after reading the last words, so hard I'm surprised my heart doesn't tear out of my ribcage and jump out of its confinement. How can he say words like that so easily, as if he was always meant to say them to me?

How can he get to me so effortlessly when no one else could?

I stand up before I even realise it. This time, I don't pretend it's normal or that it's a phase.

It's not, and I'm completely fine with it.

I'm completely fine with Ronan finding me and punishing me and everything in between.

Because the truth is, he's not normal, and neither am I.

And maybe, just maybe, that's completely fine.

TWENTY-ONE

Teal

By the time I arrive at the Meet Up, it's night-time. It's only when I push the door open that I actually take a second to think about what I'm doing.

I came here for Ronan.

He's also the only one here. I confirmed it when I spotted his car parked outside without a trace of the other guys' vehicles.

I can do it. I can absolutely do this.

I draw deep breaths in and forge ahead. One foot in front of the other.

One step.

Two steps.

Three steps…

It's not that hard, and it's probably the first time I've thought about steps while I'm taking them.

It's like the club all over again—me on my knees waiting for someone to set me free, even if just for the night.

The person I got was the last one on my mind, but maybe, just maybe, like Cole and Knox say, I needed that without even realising it.

Or maybe I'm making a huge mistake.

My thoughts come to a screeching halt and so do my feet

when I stand at the entrance of the Meet Up's small lounge area. There's a soft yellow light bathing the place, casting a cosy glow on the furniture, yet it feels lonely too.

Ronan sits on the sofa, still in his uniform, minus the jacket that's thrown over the armrest. The sleeves of his shirt are rolled up, exposing his veiny, strong forearms as he inhales from a joint.

His other hand is holding his phone up, and he glares at it as if contemplating cracking it to pieces.

All the doubts I had—and still do—evaporate at that sight. He's waiting for a reply while staying alone.

Ronan isn't the type of person who likes loneliness. While Aiden and Cole are completely comfortable with it and Xander can gravitate towards it sometimes, Ronan is always with people, one way or another.

At first, I thought it was because he loved partying so much, but it's probably something more.

To find him willingly alone is a first. He always makes up dramatic fights with Aiden and Xander when they pick their girlfriends over him. The fact that he kicked them out to stare at his screen is new.

He types something and my phone vibrates. I check it with a lump in my throat.

Ronan: You know, I hate being alone. It's when the demons come back and want to rage and burn the whole fucking place down.

I swallow, staring between his text and his face.

Demons.

For some reason, I suspected he had them, but I never thought they were real, I thought maybe I was projecting myself on him. Turns out, his demons are real; he just hides them so well you'd never even presume they're there.

I doubt the others know about their existence.

Sucking in a breath, I type back.

Teal: I stay alone because that's how I can control my demons. People bring them out.

As soon as I hit Send, I stare back at him. A smile tilts his lips and scrunches his beautiful face—his *stupid* beautiful face that I can't stop dreaming of.

He straightens in his seat then types.

Ronan: We're opposites that way. But hey, luckily there's some shit people say about opposites attracting.

Ronan: That's you and me by the way, not you and some other fucker.

Instead of continuing the dance over the phone, I quietly drop my backpack and phone on the floor and walk up to him.

He's still staring at his phone when I stand in front of him, blocking his view. His eyes slide from the phone to me and stay on me.

The more he looks at my face, the harder it becomes to breathe. It's like he's confiscating my air, my sanity, and all my better judgment.

He's confiscating things and feelings he has no right to.

"Whoa, this shit is good if it makes me see what I want." He twirls the joint. "I need to add to my stash from that Liverpudlian, stat."

"I'm really here," I murmur.

"You're not answering the text." He waves the phone. "Can I make you do that while you're standing here?"

I grab his phone and yank it from his fingers.

"Not on my phone, on yours...or your original image's, or whatever."

"I'm actually here Ronan. It's not an image."

He stares blankly for a second then without warning, he grabs my wrist and pulls me down. An excited yelp leaves my lips as I end up on his warm, hard lap.

He palms my cheek with the other hand and then pinches.

"Ow." I wince. "What was that for?"

"You're real."

"That's what I was saying."

"You're here."

"Obviously."

"Why are you here?" He narrows his eyes. "Did you have some sort of rendezvous with Captain?"

"You sent me a text saying you were here alone, remember?"

"So you're here for me?" He says it with such wonder, as if he doesn't believe it.

"Don't expect me to say it."

"You're so fucking infuriating—do you know that?"

"You kind of told me that in long clingy texts." I was supposed to scold him or something, but I sound happy even to my own ears.

I don't even remember the last time I was happy, or if happiness means just sitting on someone's lap and having them palm your cheek.

No, not someone. *Him*. Ronan.

His lips tilt in a smirk. "You still came."

I scoff.

"Now, *belle*, it's time for your confessions."

"My confessions?"

"Don't think I forgot about it. What did you do wrong?"

As he speaks, he strokes the skin of my wrist and runs his other thumb near my lip, but not close enough to touch it.

"I don't know," I murmur.

"Of course you do. You just don't want to say it. You have to, *belle*."

"What if I don't want to?"

"Then we'll just keep circling in an endless vicious cycle. I'm as fucked up as you are."

"Fine. It's about Agnus and how I refused to let go when you told me to."

"Why didn't you?"

I bite my lower lip and try to stare away, but he brings me back with a firm grip on my chin that has my thighs tightening.

"Why, Teal?" He has a way of speaking with a command in his tone that turns me to putty in his hands.

This is so wrong.

And yet so right.

"I wanted to see your reaction, okay?"

"You wanted to see my reaction. I like that."

"Well, I didn't. Your reaction sucked."

A wolfish grin curves his lips as he brings me nearer until his breath tickles my skin, hot and close, so damn close my toes curl—which they never do.

When he speaks, it's in low murmurs. "What did you want as a reaction? A hard fuck? A redo of fucking your mouth?"

My chest tightens in that way that's only possible around him, but I manage to keep my neutral tone. "Something that doesn't have to do with how everyone gets a share."

His grin widens at the way I mimicked him. "Jealous, *belle?*"

"Not as jealous as you are of Agnus. After all, he's my type. You're not."

He growls deep in his throat. "Don't bring up that fucker's name again. I'm not above murder. I mean it. I'm even consulting with Lars about ways to hide it."

That somehow makes me smile, but I quickly mask it. "No other girls either. I'm not above murder. I mean it."

"You're fucking crazy—of course you're not."

That makes my shoulders drop. I've been called crazy, a freak, and Satan's spawn more times than I could count, but for some reason, I don't want Ronan to label me that way.

"You think I'm crazy?" My voice is barely above a whisper, and I hate it.

"I don't think it. *I know it.*" This time he does run his

finger over my lips as if he's smearing my lipstick, just like that first time he touched me in the library. "And I want every last bit of your craziness."

My breathing hitches, my heartbeat bursting out of control. If those words are a way to get under my skin, they're working.

They're working so well.

He releases my wrist and removes my jacket, and then his fingers unbutton my shirt. I remain still, afraid a single move will be a mistake and I'll lose the connection rippling in the air between us.

But then his hips thrust into me from below, and I moan at the crude contact. Since I'm wearing the uniform skirt, his bulge brushes straight against my pulsating core.

He does it again, and this time, I grab both his shoulders for balance.

"Stay still," he orders.

My body goes stiff, but it's so difficult with the way he's dry-humping me. Just the friction over the clothes is enough to turn my thighs into a trembling mess.

While I'm trying to remain in place, he's already gotten rid of my shirt and bra and is holding both my breasts in his hands.

The moment he runs the tips of his thumbs over the tight buds, I gasp, my head almost falling over his shoulder.

"I see you're still sensitive here," he muses while continuing his double assault, twirling my nipples and thrusting into me over the clothes.

It'd be impossible to stay in place even if I wanted to.

His mouth finds my nipple and sucks on it, hard.

Oh. God.

I ride his bulge, unable to remain still. His sucking intensifies and so does my up and down movement against his erection.

He rotates his tongue against my nipple. Once, twice…

"Oh…Ronan…if you do that, I…oooh." I come hard against his mouth, against his clothed cock. He didn't even need to touch my pussy.

"Who's your type now?" He gives me an arrogant grin I'm not even able to react to. I'm busy trying to contain the last burst of pleasure swirling through me.

Ronan skilfully unhooks my skirt and drags my wet underwear down my shaking legs then throws them amongst the rest of my clothes on the ground. "You're my little whore now, aren't you, *belle*?"

"I'm not a whore." I try to argue, but my voice is too breathy, too lust-filled.

"You're my whore. Only mine."

He stands up abruptly and I fall down on the sofa, my mind filled with jumbled thoughts. "What—"

My words are cut off when he gets rid of his trousers and boxer briefs in record time and then his shirt follows.

I gawk, like an idiot. I couldn't stop gawking even if I wanted to.

Ronan is beautiful like a god, an immortal, a legend. I was never one of those girls who stopped and stared at abs. Hell, I saw his abs in his million pictures posted on Instagram, and I never thought of them as beautiful like I do now.

Maybe because now, something other than his physical beauty is visible to me.

I can see his scars, not like the ones on my knees, but the scars hidden underneath that six-pack and that charming smile. The scars no one sees but are known of by him, the scars he hides from by being with people.

After all, the most painful scars are the invisible ones.

I'm still studying him, getting my fill of him, but he doesn't even allow me that. He yanks me down on the sofa, the leather creaking, and looms over me, kicking my legs apart with his strong knee.

They do part. Of their own volition, they just…part.

I've never liked missionary sex, never liked looking at their blurred faces, but now? God, now, if he flips me over and takes me doggy style like I always demand, I might start crying.

I place a palm on his cheek and kiss him. I kiss him so hard I'm almost sure I'm sucking his soul out in the process. Ronan grunts in my mouth as he kisses me back with all his intensity.

He reaches between us and wraps a condom on his cock.

"I won't take it easy on you, *belle*. I won't speak love words in French in your ear or make love to you. I'm going to fuck you and hurt you and you're going to love every second of it."

His mouth goes back to mine as he thrusts inside me in one ruthless go.

I grip his back for balance as the air is knocked out of my lungs.

Oh. God.

This force is nothing like I've felt before. Ronan picks up his pace and fucks me hard and dirty.

Like he said it would, it hurts. He's big and he doesn't finish fast.

No.

He goes on and on. He fucks like he wants to hurt me, like he wants to engrave himself under my skin so he's the only thing I feel, the only one I smell and taste.

And he is.

My senses are overwhelmed by his spicy scent, by the low growls he emits as he drives his cock deep inside me over and over again.

It's like he's punishing me for everything that's happened over the last couple of days. He's making me delirious with both pleasure and pain. A sob echoes in the silence, and I soon realise it's my own.

He's owning me body and soul, and I have no way to stop

it or to put it on pause. All I can do is ride it, let him take me, float with me.

And it's the most freeing sensation I've had in my entire life.

Do I even want to stop this? What if, all those times I've been thinking about belonging, I've been approaching it the wrong way? What if this—this overwhelming pounding—is all I've been waiting for?

"Oh, Ronan…"

"You don't get to come yet." He bites the lobe of my ear and I shriek. "You get to feel this, feel us, so the next time you say I'm not your type, you'll think about this exact fucking moment of me owning every inch of you."

My nails dig into his back as I gasp for air and find the potent smell of him, of us, mingling and intensifying and taking me to newer heights.

When the wave hits me, it's different from the orgasms he's wrenched out of me thus far. This one beats under my skin before attacking me out of nowhere.

I'm falling hard and fast, and the only abyss is Ronan.

Just Ronan.

It's the best abyss I didn't know I needed.

He isn't finished. Not even close. He keeps powering into me over and over as if he'll never be done with me.

As if he can fuck me until eternity.

His thrusts turn longer and faster and more painful. They're so painful; it's delicious and a turn-on.

I've never been this aroused in my life. It's like he touches me and I'm a goner.

I'm shattered.

I'm empowered.

He reaches a hand between us and flicks my clit. "Now fall again with me."

I do.

I just do.

I come at the same time his back turns stiff and his thrusts come to an abrupt halt.

"Mine. Only fucking mine," he growls before he claims my lips in an animalistic kiss.

TWENTY-TWO

Ronan

Greed is just that—greed.

You never get enough no matter how much you get. You never stop, as if all your brakes have disappeared.

It's being submerged and finding no way out.

It's being asleep with the girl you never thought you wanted anywhere near you, let alone wrapped all around you.

Teal's lids closed soon after the second—or was it the third?—round. The second, definitely the second. I like to believe I'm above necrophilia, so let's leave it at the second.

Although my boundaries do seem to blur when this girl is involved.

Her hair partially covers her face as she rests her head on my chest and her fingers splay on my abdomen—her tiny, black fingernails.

With her long lashes fluttering on her cheeks, she appears younger, vulnerable, nothing like the Teal everyone knows—and is secretly envious of.

Secretly, because everyone wants to be as unaffected as she is, as confident as she is, but they never actually reach her level. In their cases, it's either an image or forced. She does it so well because she really doesn't care about societal standards.

Her care extends to a few people—Ethan, Knox, Elsa, and that fucking Agnus—and she doesn't even show it that much.

I trace a finger over her cheek and brush the black hair from her face to get a better view of her and commit her to memory.

No idea why there's this need to box her up somewhere, maybe reach inside her and have first viewing rights to what lurks in her pretty head.

I've always hated other people's secrets, but hers are that forbidden fruit I can't ignore, whose temptation I can't resist.

I want to claw into Teal's skin, and not only physically—I want to invade her head and see past it, inside it, everywhere in it.

Fucked up? Probably, but that's how I become around this girl.

That's what the great Ronan Astor is reduced to.

Even my dick, Ron Astor the Second, agrees with any idea that involves being inside her.

I haven't been flaccid since she showed up in front of me and I thought she was a ghost, a vision, or anything that would keep me company.

Like a good creep, I spend most of the night watching her sleeping face. Ron Astor the Second wouldn't have let me sleep anyway. The fucker is more than awake, as if he's high on Viagra.

I inhale her in, letting my lungs expand with everything about her. It's weird how she doesn't have those certain scents like other girls. She doesn't smell of Chanel or Dior. She doesn't even use any fruity or flowery soaps or shampoos. There's only this faint lime fragrance that comes off her, and it's not noticeable enough to be considered a perfume. It's almost as if she's trying hard to go undetected.

But she's not. Not even close.

The scent that invades my nose is more than lime and more her. A bit unhinged, a bit innocent, a bit…secretive.

Teal is the closest thing I've seen to fog. She's there, but when you touch her, it's almost as if she doesn't exist.

She mumbles something in her sleep, and I stroke her hair, my fingers getting lost between the silky strands. It's like they can never get dishevelled.

I wonder how she'd feel waking up to an orgasm. After all, she's slept for long enough.

It's not fair that she gets to sleep while Ron Astor the Second and I suffer in silence.

One way to find out.

I shuffle a little, and the leather sofa creaks in protest. I reach between us and twist her nipples. A mumble escapes her lip as my hand falls down and I rub her clit in tiny circles.

Unlike what I expected, she doesn't buck against my hand and remains completely still, her eyes shut tight and her brows furrowing. I think it's because of the pleasure she's trying to contain, but then she whispers unintelligible words. Another mewl falls from her mouth and it soon turns into a sob.

The sound is so haunted and raw it hits me straight in the chest.

"P-please..." she sobs quietly. "I-I'm sorry...so sorry...M-Mum...Mumm...I'm sorry...please."

I remove my hand as if I've been hit with a bat.

What in the actual fuck?

Teal's eyes snap open, and for a second, they appear like obsidian black holes. They're filled with tears, but there's nothing there, a blank, deep hole.

It's the first time I've seen her cry, and it's the most haunting scene I've ever witnessed. It's almost as if she's not feeling her own tears, as if she's not here.

As if she doesn't exist.

Or maybe she exists, but it's in a different dimension with different people and a different state of mind.

"Teal?" I call her name when she doesn't show any sign of recognising her surroundings.

She hasn't blinked in long seconds, her gaze still a void with no life inside.

I grip her hair a bit tighter. "Look at me, Teal."

Slowly, too slowly, her eyes slide back to me. The glint seeps into them, but it's almost as if she's not seeing anything.

It takes her a few seconds to somehow come out of whatever trance she's been in.

"R-Ronan?"

"Yeah."

"What happened…?" Her gaze gets lost between us as if she's trying to conjure up a memory.

Please tell me she didn't completely forget about last night; if that's the case, Ron Astor the Second and I will go bury ourselves six feet under.

"Oh…" She sits up and tucks her hair behind her ear, which I'm starting to think is her only nervous tick—or at least the only one she can't hide. "I don't usually fall asleep…" She trails off and peeks at me from underneath her lashes. "Did I say or do something?"

I lie through my teeth. "No."

Teal isn't the type who opens up if you confront her. If anything, I think she's the type who hides. If I bring down her walls, she won't only build them back up, she'll also make sure they're made of impenetrable steel this time.

"I think you just had a nightmare." I motion at her face.

She places her fingers under her eyes, and when she realises there are tears, she quickly wipes them with the backs of her hands. "Th-That's weird. I'm sorry."

"What are you apologising to me about?" If anything, I should be the one apologising. I triggered that somehow.

I pull my jacket from the armrest and wrap it around her shoulders. They're still trembling, and no matter how much she tries to hide her reaction, she's spooked and shaken. I'm a fucker, but I'm going to use this chance to draw her out.

Sorry, Ron Astor the Second, you need to wait for your turn.

Mum used to tell me that in order to get close to others, you need to offer a piece of yourself in return. That idea never appealed to me, so I built Ronan, the king with a popularity crown and a harem of girls. It seemed easier and Ron Astor the Second agreed, so it was win-win.

But now, that fucker and I both agree that the others aren't an option anymore, and it's not only because of the pact Teal and I made. I honestly have no interest in anyone else but her. It's a first in my life, and that's why I know it's special.

I've had non-special before. It was fun, but it was lonely. It always felt lonely afterwards.

With Teal, it's anything but.

I place my arm around her shoulders and pull her into me. She starts to protest, but I force her into the curve of my body, and she eventually gives up her futile fight.

We're sitting on the sofa and she's almost straddling my lap without actually doing so.

I trace shapes on her skin with my finger. "Do you remember your nightmare?"

She shakes her head against my shoulder. It's a lie. Her expression is sobering up, which means she's slowly but surely rebuilding her walls.

Not this time.

"I remember my nightmares." I smile. "In fact, it's only one, reoccurring over and over again, sometimes in the same night."

"What is it?" she asks.

"If I tell you, are you going to tell me about your nightmares?"

She swallows and I expect her to refuse, to wear her armour and hide behind her walls, but her head bobs up and down in a nod.

I plaster a smile on my face as I speak. "My nightmare starts in a dark, long street. I'm the only person there, and I'm a child. It's a bit haunting, a bit too silent, a bit too dark. I run down that street over and over again like a mouse trapped in a maze. I always end up on the same street with the same darkness and the same loneliness. I call for my parents, but neither of them answers. I don't stop running or calling them, though. I say, 'Mother. Father. I'm here. You forgot me here.' They never come. I only wake up when one person comes."

"Who?" she whispers, her voice almost spooked.

"Lars." I grin, chasing away the remnants of those images. "He's the one who wakes me every morning. I always ignore my alarms."

She glares up at me. "Stop doing that."

"Doing what?"

"Smiling while you're saying painful things. You shouldn't be smiling about that."

"Well, some philosopher Cole reads about says you can fight pain with smiles."

"You can't. You're only camouflaging it, and sooner or later it'll come back and bite you." Her teeth sink into her bottom lip. "I don't like it when you put a mask on in front of me, Ronan. In fact, I hate it, okay?"

"Okay."

"Okay?"

"Yeah, okay—what do you want? Some sort of a contract?" I tease.

She huffs. "You don't have to be a smartarse."

"Your turn, *belle*."

A long sigh slips through her lips. "My nightmares also start like yours."

"Like mine?"

"In the dark. It's always so black. Everything is." She stops and doesn't seem to plan on going on.

"And?"

"It's just that, dark. I can't move or speak, and sometimes, I wish I couldn't feel either. If I didn't, it'd just go away, you know?"

"But it never goes away."

"It never does," she murmurs in reply, even though it wasn't a question.

We share something, a feeling, a trauma. It's there in the way she shakes but tries to smother it, the way she bites her lower lip so she doesn't blurt it out.

One day she will, and one day, I'll be there to hear it all.

"Does your nightmare have something to do with how you like hurting me?" she asks, her huge eyes staring up at me as if I hold the answers to the world's problems in the palm of my hands.

I never thought I would want someone to look at me like that until her.

"What makes you think that?" I ask.

"You said you won't make love to me, won't whisper French words as you do with the other girls."

I raise an eyebrow. "You want me to whisper French words to you?"

"That's not the point." Her cheeks flush. "Just answer my question. Does it have something to do with your reoccurring nightmare?"

"Maybe." I pause. "Do you like being hurt because of your nightmare?"

She juts her chin. "Maybe."

The stubborn damn girl.

Time for a change of tactic. I grip her by the arm and stand up as I flip her to her stomach. An excited squeal leaves her lips as she stares back at me over her shoulder. "W-What are you doing?"

"Bad things, *trésor*."

"R-Ronan, don't."

"Don't what, *mon petit cœur adoré?*"

Her breathing hitches as her eyes widen until they nearly fill her tiny face. I place a hand under her stomach and pull her up so she's on her knees.

"Didn't you want me to speak French to you, *belle?*"

"Not like this," she murmurs, even though she doesn't make a move to fight me.

"Not like what? This?" I run my hard dick up and down her wetness, and a shiver goes through her entire body.

"Ronan…"

"I don't have another condom, but you're on the shot, aren't you? It was in that club resume." I grab her by the hip and slam inside her in one go.

We groan at the same time as we join. There's something about owning Teal, about being with her.

Greed. Fucking greed.

When it's combined with lust, there's absolutely no stopping it.

"Jesus," she grunts.

"I told you—not him. *Me.*" I lean over and grab a handful of her hair to pull her by it. The angle must be uncomfortable, but if she feels it, she's not saying anything. I run my tongue over her ear then bite. "You want French, *belle?* You think I'm in the right state of mind to think in French when I'm fucking you?"

She moans as she clenches around me. I fuck her fast and dirty like she's my salvation, like she's the only one I can have before the end of the fucking world.

Maybe she's right. Maybe it's because of the nightmare. Otherwise, why the fuck would I want to keep her when I've never wanted to keep anyone?

At that thought, my pace turns ferocious, animalistic even. I pound into her until she falls apart, screaming, then she bites her lip so hard blood coats her pearly white teeth.

I angle her head and kiss it. I taste the metal of her blood as I power into her with all my might.

Someone appears in my peripheral vision. I'm sideways to the door while she's facing away, still coming down from her high.

Cole.

He stands by the door, holding a book. He leans against the doorframe, crossing his feet at the ankles. Usually, if he's in one of his voyeurism phases, I'll tell him to fuck off. I don't. Instead, I let Teal fall to the sofa and throw the jacket over her back and arse to hide her nudity.

There's no way in fuck I'll let him see her naked, but that doesn't mean he won't see who she belongs to.

I grab her hip under the jacket and thrust into her a few more times, long and hard, and then empty inside her like I've never done before.

And it's not only because of the lack of a condom. I lied—I have condoms, plural. I never go out without them and I shove them in my fucker friends' lockers to prevent any teen pregnancy drama, but the idea of putting a barrier between me and Teal again sounded like a tragedy.

Off you go, condoms. This is our official goodbye.

"Nice show." Cole raises an eyebrow.

Teal gasps as she shrinks into herself, pulling the jacket all around her.

I remain completely naked as I stand up and glare at him. Cole always had a voyeurism kink—amongst others.

"Carry on." He pauses. "Or should I have applauded first?"

From behind me, I can make out Teal pulling on her clothes and haphazardly putting them on.

Fuck. Did she figure out I did it on purpose? Not that I should care. Both she and Cole need to know their places.

As in, no one will take her away from me anymore.

A few seconds later, she emerges from behind me in her

skirt and closed jacket and carries the rest of her clothes in a ball.

"I'll drive you," I say.

She cuts me a glare so harsh it's like a knife. "Screw you."

And with that, she grabs her bag and doesn't spare Cole a glance as she storms out of the Meet Up.

I remain standing there, ignoring Cole's smirk and my state of nakedness. All I can think about is the last look she gave me: anger mingled with disappointment.

Merde.

TWENTY-THREE

Teal

Later that day, I join Elsa and Kim for a girls' time.

In the past, I didn't know what girls' time meant. After all, Knox and Agnus and Dad have always been my entourage. Now that Elsa joined us, it's become more...well, interesting.

My foster sister isn't exactly the girly type, not like her best friend Kim who's sporting killer green hair that matches the colour of her eyes. Whenever they gather, they talk a little about their lives and a lot about Aiden and Xander and sex. Usually, those conversations don't bother me. I used to watch their blushing faces and wonder what they're being so embarrassed about.

After Ronan, I kind of figured it out. The mere thought of what he did to my body rises heat up my cheeks. I still feel him inside me with every step I take, and I hate that my only thought is how much I want to repeat it all over again.

If he didn't bloody ruin it.

As soon as we get into the small coffee shop and order, I excuse myself to the bathroom as Kim shows Elsa pictures of her little brother, Kirian, and they both swoon over him. If Aiden were here, he would've been jealous of that kid. No kidding. Hell, if Xander didn't already consider Kirian a little brother, he might have been jealous, too.

After finishing in the bathroom, I come out, staring at my phone. No texts.

I told myself I won't check for them, but I'm like a junkie. I can't stop waiting for something from him. Not that I would forgive him that easily for what he did, but still. Ronan not sending anything is suspicious as hell.

My feet come to a halt in front of the bathroom. Silver stands there, staring at her phone and touching a dainty butterfly necklace surrounding her pale throat. A soft smile grazes her lips. It's almost innocent—which is the last adjective I would've used to describe Silver. It's true that she's some sort of a bombshell, but she always came with an edge.

She has the most beautiful smile that she showcases on social media, usually with her powerhouse parents or stepmom or her father's PR team. Even Ronan used to post many pictures with her, half-hugging her or both smiling at the camera. He usually captioned it with: *Beautiful People.* The arrogant prick.

When I was stalking his Instagram, which goes back to years, I noticed that when he was around fifteen, he often posted pictures with the other three horsemen, Levi King—Aiden's older cousin—and Silver. She was the only girl amongst the five of them.

Then, little by little, she started to disappear from their pictures. Especially this year.

Upon noticing me, Silver drops her hand from her necklace and just like that, her expression hardens. All smiles and innocence vanish into thin air.

She stares at my shirt on which is written, *Nerd? I prefer the term 'more intelligent than you.'*

Her icy stare slides back to my face. "Teal."

"Silver."

She waltzes closer until she can stare down at me. Stupid tall people and their legs that go for miles. "I still haven't forgiven you for the other day."

"Neither have I."

"But I might."

"Not interested."

"Just…" she trails off, wetting her lips. That's the first nervous gesture I've ever seen from her. "Tell me how Kim is doing."

"Why don't you ask her yourself?" From what Kim mentioned before, she used to be close friends with Silver, but they fell apart when they were pre-teens and since then, Silver turned into a tormentor instead of a friend. However, neither Elsa nor Kim witnessed the other facet of Silver. Besides, after Kim was discharged from the hospital, Silver showed up, apologised to her and left.

Since we met at the club, Silver has been asking me about Kim's state regularly.

"She'll just curse me," she murmurs.

"That's because you haven't been there for her when she needed you the most."

"I know that. Just tell me how she's doing." She swallows as if chasing away a horrendous image. "Is she coping?"

"Yeah. She's doing better."

Her lips pull in a smile, before she clears her throat. "Okay, thank you."

"You can't keep asking about her behind her back this way, Silver. You have to face her one day."

"One day. Not today." She pauses. "Don't tell her I asked."

"Whatever."

She flips her hair. "And stay away from Cole."

"*You* stay away from Ronan."

We go our separate ways at the bathroom's exit. She leaves the small coffee shop without sparing a glance at Elsa and Kim. Perhaps it's because her parents are politicians, but from what I've seen, Silver is a master of disguising her emotions.

When I settle back at the table, two pairs of eyes almost

dig holes in my face. I take a sip of my orange juice and meet Elsa and Kim's incredulous gazes. "What?"

"What was that all about?" Elsa hisses. "Silver?"

"Yeah, Teal." Kim huffs. "Why were you talking to Silver?"

Because of you. I lift a shoulder instead.

"She's a bitch, Teal." Elsa grips her hot chocolate tight.

"I can be a bitch, too." I slurp from my juice.

"No, you're not." Kim rubs my arm. "You're so cool. You're just different."

I suppress a smile. This is why Kim and Elsa are special—they don't only see the façade but they take time to notice what's behind it.

"Besides." Elsa smiles in a sly way. "You're with Ronan so he'll eventually rub off on you."

My heart does that tightening thing whenever his name is mentioned. I pretend the juice is my only focus. "He doesn't matter."

"You think I haven't noticed the way you look at him when he's not paying attention?" Elsa sighs. "It's like you want to engrave yourself on his skin."

"I do not."

"Yeah, you do." Kim pokes my shoulder. "He's the same, you know. He looks at you like you're the greatest and most fascinating riddle of all."

He does?

How come I never noticed that?

Elsa winks at me. "I say you changed your views about love. It's not a bunch of chemical reactions anymore, right?"

"It is. All dopamine and neurotransmitters. It's all delusional." Even as I say the words, I don't believe any of them.

TWENTY-FOUR

Teal

Being addicted to something is the worst thing that can happen to anyone. It's like your entire life is based on that high.

While I always wanted to get rid of the trance mode, I never slipped into addiction. I never let anything become the centre of my life.

Not even my pain.

I got around it, fought it, and eventually, I made friends with it. That was the only way for me to survive.

What I never thought about was becoming addicted to someone rather than something.

Since I left the Meet Up over the weekend, all I've been thinking about is *him*. My unwanted addiction.

Fucking Ronan.

Around him I become this junkie in need of one more hit, one more smile.

One more touch.

If you asked me what I'm addicted to when it comes to Ronan, I wouldn't have an answer.

It could be his voice with the slight rumble, his symmetrical face that somehow became a piece of art in my mind. Perhaps it's his smiles—the genuine ones—or his clingy nature that for some insane reason comes across as adorable rather than creepy.

Or maybe, just maybe, it's the care he showcases discreetly.

Around him, I'm levitating before I realise it. I'm smiling like it's the most natural thing to do.

It isn't.

It shouldn't be.

I tell myself I'm only in his house because of Charlotte, but soon after I said my hello, I told her I'd be bringing up tea, even though she said Lars would do it.

I pass by Ronan's room and linger there for a second too long—or maybe ten seconds; I don't know.

God. I'm starting to be like one of those idiotic hormonal teenagers I thought I was above. Turns out I'm not—far from it.

Damn it.

Fine, I'll pretend I'm cool with what happened at the Meet Up. After all, the reason I left was stupid. I was overacting and being a fool and…fuck, I've been stalking his Instagram all weekend, waiting for him to post a picture with any other girl so I could pounce on him.

He didn't.

He posted two pictures. One was of him and Xander half-naked, wearing shades and lounging by the latter's pool.

The caption said: *He hates me for waking him up, but I'm happy to have* mon fréro *back.*

That put a smile on my face. Ronan always seemed to get along with Xander more than Cole and Aiden. Something tells me Xander is also more tolerant of Ronan's personality than the other two.

The second picture was of Ronan making a face behind an oblivious Cole, who was reading from a book.

The caption said: *Nerd.*

That's it.

He didn't send me a text or call or anything. Okay, maybe the way I left wasn't encouraging, but come on, this is Ronan. I expected a text that same night.

I kept staring at my phone through all of dinner until Knox made fun of me.

Then, he skipped this morning. Ronan is known to sleep in, but there are no parties he'd lose sleep over.

One thing led to another, and the next thing I know, I'm at his house.

Very tactful, Teal.

Well, since I'm already here, I might as well go with it.

I push open his bedroom door, and the sound of voices coming from the inside stops me in my tracks.

"Edric isn't pleased," says an older voice with a posh accent. It's not as posh as the earl of the house, but close.

He stands by the window. Ronan sits on the pane with a huge grin plastered on his face.

"I'm afraid my father's pleasure is none of my business." Ronan releases a long mocking breath. "Phew."

"You always had an attitude that doesn't suit your parents," the man says. His voice is familiar, I suppose because he's Edric's brother—the one who returned from Australia to help with the company.

From my position, I can only see the back of Eduard Astor. He's wearing a hideous dark red suit and brown, leather shoes.

"I know, right?" Ronan's grin widens. I can almost feel the force behind it and how he's trying to keep his muscles in place.

"Some might even suspect you take after me." Eduard's voice turns sinister, smooth. "Wouldn't that be the irony?"

"Fuck. You." Ronan stands so he's toe to toe with his uncle, but the smile doesn't leave his face.

"Language." I can hear the smirk in Eduard's voice. "You're an earl's heir."

"And you're an earl's brother. Act like one and stop fucking around or I swear—"

"What?" Eduard urges. "Finish what you started, nephew. Your noble blood says as such, right? As far as everyone knows, of course."

Ronan continues staring at him as if he wants to run a pole through his chest and snatch it from the back. The hate is so tangible I can almost feel it crawl on my hands and wrap its meaty fingers around my throat.

In this moment, I want to grab Eduard and bash his head against the wall—or better yet, throw him out the window and watch as his body splinters to pieces.

Ronan doesn't do hate; he does rivalry and he does spite, but hate always felt beneath his status, his name, and his entire aura. The fact that his fists are clenching and he's stopping himself from punching his uncle means something.

"Watch it, *Uncle.*" Ronan snarls the last word, enunciating it, as if wanting Eduard to feel it.

"Run your mouth and I'll run mine, my dear nephew. Remember Charlotte…" Eduard clutches Ronan's shoulder and smooths invisible wrinkles off his shirt. "Poor, soft Charlotte. Breakable, depressed Charlotte."

I lean over to get a better view of Ronan then a hand clasps my arm. I yelp, but the sound is muffled by a gloved hand wrapping around my mouth.

Lars.

He drags me away from Ronan's doorway, opens another door down the hall, and ushers me inside the room. He does a sweep of his surroundings before following me and closing the door.

Lars is the head butler of the estate and a character straight out of a period drama. Though Ronan likes to say he's his accomplice in murder plots, I don't believe that's the case. All the guy cares about is order, cleanliness, discipline, and tea.

Lots of tea.

He knows everyone's taste in that.

Dad has only been here a few times, but Lars already knows he prefers black tea over anything else.

Oh, and he brings me dark chocolate whenever I visit Charlotte, so I am always thankful for that.

While his expression never betrays his feelings, I've somehow gotten the idea he doesn't approve of me. He's like Charlotte's substitute in being my mother-in-law.

"What are you doing?" I fold my arms over my chest, going straight into a defensive mode, as if he didn't just catch me eavesdropping on his master.

"That's what I'm supposed to ask, Miss. What were *you* doing?"

"Passing by."

His expression remains neutral. "Didn't seem like passing by to me."

"Don't beat around the bush, Lars. If you have something to say it, say it."

He remains silent for so long I start to notice the grandfather clock ticking behind me. If he's doing this to unnerve me, it's starting to work.

"Don't tell the madam about whatever you heard." He pauses. "However, if you feel inclined to tell his lordship, I'll pretend I know nothing."

"But why?"

"What do you mean by why?"

"Why tell Edric but not Charlotte?"

"It's his lordship to you, young lady."

"Stop with the title bollocks. What's going on, Lars?"

He tips his nose up as if he's the aristocrat in the house. "If you haven't figured it out yourself, why should I tell you?"

"Seriously?"

"Seriously. Perhaps I was right—perhaps you don't deserve the young lord."

"What?" I scoff. "I don't *deserve* him?"

"You haven't proven you do, now have you?"

I open my mouth, but I'm incredulous so nothing comes out.

"That's what I thought." He heads towards the door. "Your tea will be up in fifteen minutes. Actually, make that thirty—and no chocolate for you."

I flip off the door as it closes behind him. The fucking snob.

Though he's a snob who obviously knows about whatever is going on between Ronan and Eduard, and he wants me to tell Edric.

I lean against the smooth surface of the table. From what I gathered, Eduard seems to be holding something over Ronan's head, and it has to do with Charlotte. He also mentioned something about Ronan's origins.

It has to do with Charlotte.

I gasp. *No.* It can't be.

I storm out of the room, not knowing where I want to go. No, actually, I do, and it's not back to Charlotte's room, that's for certain.

I want to make sure Ronan is fine, make sure he's not raging or bottling everything up inside. Even those who have a problem recognising emotions know when they hit.

At the top of the stairs, a presence halts my plan—a presence I wished to never see in this house.

I wish it were only occupied by Ronan and Charlotte. Even Lars snobbishness would've been fine.

Anyone but him.

A cold sweat breaks out on my forehead, and it takes everything in me not to fidget or run or dig a hole and disappear in it.

It takes all my willpower to stand in place as he strides towards me.

Edric is a big man, even bigger than his son, and because of his title, his presence seems to suffocate everything in its vicinity.

He stops in front of me, and a small smile pulls at his thin lips. "Teal, it's lovely seeing you."

I can't say the same.

The information I just learnt—the fact that he's probably not Ronan's biological father—should delight me, because it's this man's downfall. A week ago, it probably would've.

Now, it doesn't.

Now, all I think about is Ronan's pain.

Just how and when the hell did I start recognising his pain when I've been doing everything in my power to ignore mine?

Even now, my feet are urging me to go to him, to hug him.

Wait...

Hug him?

What the hell, Teal?

"Mr Astor."

"Edric is just fine, and don't let Lars tell you 'It's his lordship to you.' He tends to do that a lot."

I smile because I think that's what's expected in response to his dry humour.

"Listen, Teal." His smile slips, and I don't like what I see on his features. I don't like it at all.

In fact, I hate it.

I loathe it.

I wish there was an option to return his smile.

A man like Edric doesn't get to show the shadow of pain or sorrow. He doesn't get to be a human when he stole humanity from other people.

"I wanted to say I'm thankful for the time you spend with Charlotte, and even the text messages and the articles you send her. She looks forward to them every day and shows them to me with a big smile on her face. Your care means a lot to me."

I'm at a loss for words, unsure why he's telling me this. Besides, I didn't do it for him.

"Once again, thank you." His hard, stern expression returns. "I apologise if my son has done anything to disrespect you. He'll grow up...eventually."

"He's grown up," I say before I can stop myself.

"Excuse me?"

"Your son is grown up. In fact, he might have been grown for a long time and you just haven't noticed it."

He pauses, fingering his tie before he drops his hand to his side. "What makes you say that?"

It's my turn to pause. Could it be that Edric knows?

No. It can't be possible. He's so proud, so sure of himself, so aristocratic and pragmatic.

"Nothing. I'll go see Ronan." I turn and leave before he can question me anymore. If I spend one more minute in his vicinity, I might lose control over my mouth. As Knox says, I have a problem with keeping my thoughts to myself.

I knock on Ronan's door, but there's no answer.

"I'm coming in." My cheeks heat as I push the door open.

I expect to find Ronan and Eduard and I think about the possibility of punching the latter.

But there's no one in the room.

"Ronan?" I call.

No answer.

I tiptoe to the bathroom, calling his name again, but there's nothing.

Maybe he's in the wardrobe? I fling the doors open and sigh in defeat.

What was I thinking? In the wardrobe, really?

I'm about to close it when I inhale his spicy scent. It does things to me now. I'm starting to notice it on other people when I'm in the supermarket or at school, and that's not all. I even stop and think—no, it's not quite Ronan, not quite as sexy or rough or warm.

That's the problem with him. He can be rough, can give me what I want, but he can also be warm, like how he hugged me to his side after that nightmare.

I let my fingers run through his tidied shirts and T-shirts. They're organised by colour, which has Lars' fingerprints all over it. I'm tempted to ruin them just to get on his nerves.

I'm still contemplating that idea when I see some pink lace sticking out of a drawer. I pull it out, and my jaw nearly hits the floor.

It's a bunny outfit. Scratch that, it's one of those stripper bunny costumes with ears and the string-like underwear.

Elsa and Kim always mention Ronan's bunny hooker fantasy. Hell, he brings it up every chance he gets, but I thought it was just that, a fantasy.

I never thought he took it to the next level by keeping the costume in his wardrobe.

A noise comes from the door and I shove the outfit back where I found it then exit before he can find me.

"Hey," I say lamely and then wince.

He's in black jeans and a white T-shirt, his muscles rippling at the biceps. He's smiling, but the tension I sensed from when he was talking to Eduard still rolls off him in waves.

"Lars mentioned you were here. He forgot the part where you were going through my wardrobe like a stage-one stalker."

"Shut up." I pretend to be offended. "Did Lars mention anything else?"

"Aside from the fact that you can get your tea yourself because he's PMSing and not serving you today, no." He pauses. "Nice shirt."

I blush.

I fucking blush.

And the problem is, I also blushed when I ordered this shirt over the weekend and when I snatched the package from Knox's fingers and when I put it on this morning.

I don't blush. Ever.

Just like I don't feel like hugging people, and yet I've been doing both of those things lately.

"It's not about you," I try to deflect.

"*Belle*, it says 'Talk French to Me'. If it's not about me, I don't know what is." He approaches me, still smiling, but this time, it's not forced or camouflaging pain.

I wonder how he does it, how he hides so much and can be this happy to see me.

"You haven't answered my texts, *trésor*."

"That's because you didn't send them."

"Of course I did." He brings out his phone then his brows furrow. "Ah, fuck. I sent them to the group chat. Those bastards won't let me live this down."

I chuckle; I can't help imagining their replies to Ronan's consecutive messages. Deep down, I allow myself a moment of relief. He didn't actually ignore me over the weekend.

"What are you laughing at? You like my misery?"

"No." I snort out laughter.

"Okay, I've been called a pussy in five hundred ways." He shoves his phone back in his pocket. "This is all your fault, *ma belle*. How are you going to make it up to me?"

"Why would I?" I fold my arms, no longer laughing. "I'm the one who's mad at you, remember?"

"I'm not apologising for that. Cole needed to know you belong to me so he'll keep his claws to himself. Not sorry."

"It's not that." My voice is so small, pathetic.

His brows furrow. "Then why the fuck did you walk out on me?"

"It's nothing."

"Teal," he warns, gripping my arm in a tight hold. "Don't make me use force."

"Aren't you already?"

"This is only a preview. My actual force includes not giving you an orgasm."

I narrow my eyes at him.

"Tell. Me," he insists. "Or Lars won't give you any more dark chocolate. I'm the one who sends them over, you know."

"You…are?"

"Of course. How would Lars know, genius?" He inches closer. "Now, tell me why you left."

"It's stupid, okay?"

"Let me be the judge of that."

"I…" I trail off, staring at an invisible point at my side. "I didn't want to have sex in that position. I wanted to look at you, and you didn't listen."

Silence stakes a claim in the room, and I chance a peek at him. Ronan watches with an intense focus that almost makes me squirm.

"Ronan…?"

"You wanted to look at me," he repeats, as if not believing the words.

It's not a question, but I nod anyway.

He pulls me to him by the arm he's holding and wraps me up in a tight embrace. The same embrace I wanted to give him after I listened to his conversation with his bastard uncle.

"You're fucking me up, Teal," he whispers against my head, his hot breaths tickling my hair.

"Not as much as you are me." There's so much vulnerability in my voice, so much surrender, and for some reason, I don't hate it.

"I'm glad you're here, my crazy but beautiful *belle*."

For the first time in my life, I wrap my arms around someone. I feel his heartbeat against my chest and his breaths in my hair and his arms squeezing me too tight.

I do the same.

My nails dig into the cloth of his shirt and sink in there, soaking in the warmth.

The belonging.

The care.

I never allowed myself addictions before, because addictions screw you up and mess with your logic and your head.

But as I hug Ronan, I know I have no choice in this addiction. It's the type you just surrender to. You fall into it and let yourself float.

So I do just that, confessing in a soft voice, "I'm glad you're here too, Ronan."

TWENTY-FIVE

Teal

For the following week, Ronan doesn't leave my side.

He's there in the morning to pick me up. He's there to drive me back home, and sometimes, he kicks everyone out of the Meet Up so we can spend the night.

Those nights and afternoons are my favourites. Not only does he bring each and every one of my fantasies to reality, he goes a step beyond. He chases me around the cottage and the lake, making me feel like I can escape him just to pounce on me then fuck me in all positions possible.

I never thought I'd crave sex with someone as much as I do with Ronan. It's not only about the joining of our bodies, but also about what leads to that. It's about the emotions he shows when he's owning my body.

I might not understand them that well—emotions, I mean—but I can see the meaning in the glint in his brown eyes. I can feel it in the way he touches me and hugs me like he wants to shield me from the world.

He's been having some sort of a battle against the world lately. He made it his job to announce I'm his fiancée all over RES, and he's been plotting to ruin Cole's books every day since the garden incident. It's strange to see Ronan act so territorial after he did everything to get rid of me.

In doing that, he's been slowly but surely carving himself a cosy place in my heart. At some point in my life, I honestly believed I didn't have a heart, or if I did, it only served its anatomical function.

But now, whenever Ronan is around, that organ goes in and out of sync. Everything he does moves me one way or another. It can be as small as smiling genuinely each time he sees me or how he keeps winking at me when we spend time with Charlotte. Or perhaps it's how he brings me a bar of dark chocolate every day as if it's become his ritual.

We spend entire nights texting back and forth. When I don't answer within thirty seconds, he sends me a long dramatic text that basically says to answer him.

Ronan is still Ronan with his goofy attitude and tendency to turn every serious situation into a joke, but now I realise it's part of his defence mechanism. It comes naturally to him, though, and he basks in being the centre of attention.

Unlike me.

Elsa says even though Ronan and I are different, we have chemistry. No idea what that means, but it's probably something along the lines of how he can't keep his hands off me. Truth be told, I can't stay away from him either.

I'm that addict now, and if I don't see him for a day, something feels so utterly wrong.

Knox says Ronan is changing me for the better, but my brother doesn't know the internal battle I've been fighting because of that change.

On one hand, when I'm with Ronan, I forget about everything else, but on another hand, those other thoughts barge in uninvited whenever I'm alone.

I'm not alone now, though.

Ronan has an arm around my waist as he leads me through the crowded streets of London. I don't like crowds—there are so many people and obstacles—but with him, they kind of disappear.

All that remains is his warmth close to mine. His scent. His closeness.

Just him.

Crowds and people disappear when he's around.

"Hey, Ronan?"

He grins down at me, showing me his straight, blinding smile. "What's up, *belle?*"

I try not to get caught in his orbit, though it seems to be an epic fail most of the time. "How come you never asked me to have a threesome?"

He raises a perfect brow. "You want a threesome?"

"No."

"Then why are you asking about it?"

"You always ran after Elsa and Kim to have a threesome with you." And I might feel left out because I was never included. What? He really talked about it all the time before.

"Jealous?"

"Hmph. Maybe I'll have a threesome with two men, too. Maybe Cole and Agnus, we'll never know."

"Teal…" he warns.

"What? You're not the only one who gets to think about threesomes with other people." And yes, hurting him back is my defence mechanism against whatever is burning in my chest right now.

"The threesome with Kim and Elsa was my way to egg on Aiden and Xander. That's all. Besides, I have no interest in threesomes anymore."

"You don't?"

"Nah. You're the only one I want and I don't care for sharing." He narrows his eyes. "That goes for you, too, mmkay?"

I remain silent, but only because I'm suppressing a smile.

Ronan pokes my cheek. "Mmkay?"

"Fine." Not that I ever had an interest to begin with.

"There, much better. The thought of you with any other man makes me want to plan mass murder with the aid of Lars' little black book."

This time, I can't resist the grin that plasters on my skin. I like the idea that Ronan, who never acted possessive over anyone is this way with me. I probably shouldn't, but I do.

"You like that, don't you, *belle*?"

"No."

"Uh-huh."

"Are you done parading me around?" I deflect.

While I enjoy his company, I want to do it alone, without other people's interference.

He waggles his brows. "I'll never be done parading you around, *belle*."

"I promised Charlotte I'd spend time with her."

"I come first. Besides, Lars is there until we get back."

For some reason, it feels as if Ronan doesn't want to stay in his house for very long. I know it's not because of Charlotte, or even Edric. He might act aloof around his father, but I've seen the way he looks at him—like a son looking up to his dad. It's the same expression Knox has when Dad is around.

The invisible connection between Ronan and Edric always made me uncomfortable in my own skin.

I hate it.

I loathe it.

I wish I could destroy it.

"Lars isn't my biggest fan," I say instead.

"He's no one's biggest fan." He points at his chest. "Except for *moi*."

"Arrogant much?"

"One of us has to be. Imagine we're at one of the adult parties and you're silent or thinking about escaping. I have to be the one who keeps the atmosphere up."

"Wouldn't people think you were with a boring fiancée?"

"Fuck people. They're not the ones who sleep with you every night."

My cheeks turn hot, but I manage to say, "You don't sleep with me every night."

"I can change that."

"Ronan." I eye our surroundings in case anyone heard.

"What? We're engaged. That means I'll end up marrying you and you'll sleep with me every night, no exceptions."

Something in my chest falls. The reality of the situation I've been ignoring crashes down on me in one go.

There'll be no marriage.

That's not the reason for this engagement.

Someone slams into my arm, and I startle. An electric current shoots through my limbs. My breaths shorten and my legs become unable to carry me.

The attack comes on so fast, without any warning. It could be because I was lost in my head or because I was too at peace with my surroundings.

I shouldn't have been.

My environment has always been the enemy.

I was trapped in that unknown and I couldn't do anything about it and —

Warm hands wrap around my cheeks, wrenching me back from those memories.

"Hey…" Ronan's voice softens as he makes me face him.

My gaze slowly slides up his chest and to his deep brown eyes. There's something calming about them, like the lullaby I never had.

"You're okay," he continues. "You're going to be okay."

"How do you know that?" I murmur. "How can you be so sure about it?"

"I'm only sure about one thing, and it's you, Teal. I have no doubt you'll get through this. Do you know why?"

Something stings my eyes, and I refuse to believe it's tears. "Why?"

"Because you're the strongest person I know."

I don't allow myself to think about my next action.

I rise up on my tiptoes and seal my lips to his. I kiss him as deeply as he's touching me.

Fuck people.

He's the only one who's visible in the crowd.

Even if things between us started for the wrong reasons.

TWENTY-SIX

Ronan

"**A**re you going to reply or should I show up and fuck up your peace?" Cole's bored voice recites the text I was supposed to send to Teal two weeks ago but ended up sending in my fucker friends' group chat.

"I never thought I would say this"—Aiden clutches my shoulder—"but I'm proud of you."

"Answer…please?" Cole reads on. He's sitting on the sofa, leaning on a hand and clutching his phone.

Aiden releases me with distaste. "I won't get behind that, so no, not proud of you."

"Fuck you." I motion at Cole. "And you." Then I point behind me at Xan, who's going through his texts. "And you too."

"What?" the latter protests. "I haven't said anything."

"You were about to, so that's a fuck you in advance."

I throw my weight next to Cole. We're having a small gathering at the Meet Up after the game. The other players are either drinking or trying to convince girls to shag them.

Loud music thumps from the walls. It would've been better in my house—just saying.

But, oh well. Not only would the mighty Earl Edric rip me a new one, Mum would be disappointed, and I would never do that.

Parties at the Meet Up can be fun, except you don't find places to shag and stuff. Not that I'm interested in that—or maybe I am; depends on whether or not Teal shows up.

I've been watching the entrance like a fucking creep for the past hour or so. She was at the game with Elsa and Kim earlier. Kim has forgotten all about me now that Xander is back. She used to call my name, but now his repulsive number nineteen is all she cares about.

Teal was more interested in her phone than me—I know because every time I raised my head, she was engrossed in that fucking thing. Next time, that phone and I are having a word.

I can't believe I'm jealous of a phone.

Wait. Jealous? No. I don't do jealousy. The feeling is beneath me and would never exist in my vocabulary—especially not for Teal.

My phone vibrates and I pull it out faster than a junkie in need of his next pill. The name of the sender on the screen makes me grip the phone harder.

It's definitely not the text I've been waiting for.

Eduard: Edric says he'll have a family gathering to announce something. Do you have any idea what it is?

I don't, and even if I did, that fucker wouldn't get anything from me.

Dear old Dad has been acting a bit weird lately. I thought the time he spends with Mum is because he has a control freak diploma from the eighteenth century, but Lars has been saying annoying shit lately.

"Pay attention."

"Young lord, you are being blinded by that girl and losing focus."

"Did I mention that you should pay attention?"

When I told him to be more specific or to fuck off, he chose the latter, huffing like a damsel in distress.

Fucking Lars. I'm going to corner him one of these days or steal his little black book and have a look.

What does he want me to pay attention to? His lordship being a control freak or Mum calling him her love when he's actually her tormentor?

And Lars is wrong—I'm not blinded by Teal. I stare at my phone after making Eduard's message disappear. Why the fuck isn't she texting me?

"Green is on her way." Xan grins like an idiot.

"Elsa, too." Aiden takes a drink of his soda. He never drinks, like ever. He and Cole say it diminishes their logic, and they're the type of fuckers who need all their neurons to plot chaos.

"Teal?" Cole asks.

"No clue. I'm not the clingy type." I grin. "I do know Silver is somewhere upstairs though."

She's not. I haven't seen her tonight, but egging him on is my favourite pastime. People pay money for this type of entertainment.

Cole's gaze slides from his book to me then back as if I don't exist, but if I managed to draw his attention from his book, it means this shit is working.

"Not the clingy type? I beg to differ." Xander scrolls through his phone then flashes one of the texts they weren't supposed to see in a million years.

Ronan: Remember when I said you always have to answer my texts? Well, maybe I haven't said those exact words, but they're out there now so you might as well do it. Call me. I want to hear your voice.

I release a long sigh. "Okay, what do I have to do for you to erase those texts from your phones?"

"I can't be bought, Astor." Aiden takes another sip of his drink.

"You mean after the stunt of burning my book?" Cole appears to be contemplative. "How about…never?"

Vindictive fucker.

"Are you kidding?" Xan laughs. "I'm already making these into framed prints and keeping them for future reference."

My best option, for now, is to steal their phones and flush them down the toilet. That is if they don't keep shit in the cloud. Whoever invented that—I hate you.

Elsa and Kim come in, both wearing jeans and tank tops. I stop breathing, holding it in for long seconds before I let it go.

I feel her before even seeing her. She's in the middle, wearing a long black T-shirt-like dress that stops under her knees. The writing for today is 'If karma doesn't hit you, I fucking will.'

She's bloody crazy, and her crazy is becoming my kink. I shouldn't care about kink—or think about it—but Teal is turning everything against me.

In a good way.

In the best way imaginable.

Her hair is loose as usual, making her face appear smaller and her frame tinier. Her white trainers stop at her ankles.

Her black eyes aren't smothered with that dark makeup she usually hides behind. She's a bit demure today, appearing more compliant, and for some reason, that makes me apprehensive.

All disasters start with a change. Like that night.

I shake my head, pushing that idea away.

Her gaze roams around the room, and it takes her exactly three seconds to find me. The moment her eyes lock onto mine, it's like the entire world has hushed into the background. There are no sounds, no colours, and no scents.

There's only her, the girl with odd preferences and a fucking attitude.

But she's also the girl who deeply cares but doesn't know how to show it. The girl who keeps checking on Mum and asking me about her favourites because she wants her happy.

The girl who turns into a compliant submissive in bed but is a tigress outside of it.

I'm about to go to her. I don't know what I'll do, probably kidnap her to somewhere no one can find us or interrupt us.

Before I can move, some loser from the rugby team intercepts her. Elsa and Kim are already by Aiden and Xan's sides, kissing like they're in a low-budget porn.

But I'm not focused on them.

My entire focus is on the fucker who just cut off my eye contact with Teal.

He's taller than her, so I can't get a clear view of her expression.

A black halo swirls around my head, refusing to evaporate.

I stride in their direction and barge straight between them. He—David, I think his name is—steps back as if startled.

I grin. "May I help you, David?"

"No, I was just asking Teal about an assignment."

"This doesn't look like class, does it?"

Teal tries to elbow my side, but I keep out of her reach and then grab her hand in mine.

David appears flustered, but he holds his ground. The sorry fuck. Why are we even inviting rugby blokes to our parties?

"I was just—"

"Leaving," I cut him off.

"No. That's not—"

"In case you haven't noticed, Teal is taken." I smile. "In fact, she's someone's fiancée—*mine*. So stay away from her."

Instead of shutting up and screwing off, he continues speaking. "I think that's up to her to decide."

I tug Teal to me, place a hand on her cheek, and slam my lips to hers in one ruthless kiss that makes her gasp. I take the chance and claim her tongue, tasting her as I've never done before. I can feel the attention everyone at the party is giving us, and I let them watch the show; I let them know who she belongs to.

Jealous? Me? No, not at all.

I don't wait for David or anyone else to get into our bubble. The moment my lips leave hers, I drag her behind me and out of the Meet Up. The music and the voices fade more and more the further we stride away. We're in the car park when she yanks her hand from mine.

"I can't keep up," she pants.

"We have to do something about your short legs." I face her.

She folds her arms over her generous tits. "Maybe we should do something about the caveman scenes. Have you been taking pointers from Aiden or something?"

I scoff. "Come on, *belle*. I'm the type who gives lessons, not the other way around."

"Yeah, right." She tucks her hair behind her ear, and even in the dim light coming from the cottage, I can make out the reddening of her cheeks.

"You like it." I grin. I step up to her and she stares at me with wide eyes, frozen in the moment. "You like how I go caveman for you, how I staked a claim on you in public and marked you as mine."

"I don't know what you're talking about."

"And yet, you're not looking me in the eye."

"I am." Her gaze slides to mine then shifts after a fraction of a second.

I grab her by the chin and run my finger down her swollen bottom lip. "Admit it."

"You're a bastard."

"We've already established that."

She throws her hands out to the sides. "Now what?"

"Now, we're out of here."

"But…to where?"

"The sky's our limit, *belle*. I'll start by fucking you, and then I'll end the night by fucking you again. The in-between probably includes that, too, but I'm open to suggestions."

She smiles a little. "You still have the stamina after today's game? You were running for ninety minutes straight, and the way you went back to defence when one of your back liners didn't do their job? Your manager should've subbed him out, but no, they saw you were playing their position along with yours, so they were like, okay, we can keep him. Going back and forth must've exhausted you, and let's not talk about the assists you made for Xander's favours. I get it, he's coming back after long absence, but why do he and Aiden get all the limelight while your effort is chalked up to assists? It's not fair, and the way Cole thinks he's a better midfielder than you…" She trails off as my grin widens more with every word out of her mouth. "I was rambling, wasn't I?"

"No, continue. We're at the part where Cole thinks he's better than me, which is obviously blasphemy."

"Shut up." If possible, her cheeks redden some more. My Teal doesn't usually blush, but when she does, it's like the world has turned red. She's real even when she's embarrassed.

"I thought you weren't watching me," I say. "You were all over your phone as if you were having some sort of an affair—not that I said anything to anyone, because my fucker friends would think I'm clingy. Did I mention they're calling me a pussy because of you?"

"Yeah, you kind of did."

"You're making it up to me."

I thread my fingers in hers and drag her towards my car. With the whole party scene, there are too many vehicles here. It takes precious minutes to find mine.

"Wait." Teal tugs on my hand.

"No waiting. Ron Astor the Second needs his dose."

She laughs, and the sound is so rare and feather-like I can't resist stopping and facing her.

"What?" I suppress my own smile. Seeing her face radiate is contagious.

"Don't tell me that's the name of your dick?"

"Could be. Why? You have a problem with it? I'm open to suggestions, but he only answers to that name. In my defence, I named him when I was thirteen and straight out of a family history class."

She bursts out laughing, hiding her mouth with the back of her hand.

"What is it, *belle*?" I feign offence. "Speak now or forever hold your peace."

A thump comes from our right, and both of us pause.

"That's what I asked you to wait for," Teal whispers, her laughter vanishing. "There's a weird sound coming from that car."

"*Belle*, this is posh London. We don't have serial killers amongst us…" I trail off when the sound comes again, and this time, I recognise from which car it is coming.

A black Jeep.

Cole's.

Oh, fucking fuck. What did he do now?

"We should take a look," Teal says.

"That's probably not a good idea."

"What do you mean it's not a good idea?" Teal's cheeks redden, and this time it's far different than embarrassment. It's anger—no, rage in its purest form.

"It means we shouldn't get involved." Cole's shit is Cole's shit. Besides, I might have an idea of what's going on in that car, and it has more to do with kink activity rather than sociopathic.

But he had to bring it here, seriously?

That's a new level even for him.

"Shouldn't get involved?" Teal's voice rises. "Someone might need help in there. Someone might be screaming at the top of their lungs, but no one is hearing them. They need a voice, but they get nothing. It's because of people like you that they get nothing, the people who say they shouldn't get involved, who say they shouldn't step up to help someone in need or—"

"Hey." I wrap both palms around her face, trying to cool her down.

She's skipping over words and appears to be on the verge of a breakdown. It's one of the rare times Teal shows what's inside her, shows what she has hidden underneath the aloof persona and the 'fuck the world' exterior.

"It's going to be okay," I murmur against her forehead. "You're going to be okay. I'm here for you."

A sob catches in her throat like when she was coming down from that nightmare. Her nails dig into my Elites' jacket as she draws in measured breaths, trying to compose herself and control her state.

"Can we take a look?" she murmurs against my chest.

"Sure." Fuck Cole. I would do anything for that pleading in her voice, especially with the way she's holding on to me.

I'm about to head to the car when Cole strides out of the Meet Up. He watches us for a second, probably wondering why we're near his car.

I glare at him from over Teal's head. "There's a sound coming from over there, Captain."

He must recognise the accusation in my tone.

"It's my mother's dog." He smiles at us, appearing like a prim and proper gentleman. "I have to get it back to her."

His mother's dog? Come on, he could've come up with a better excuse.

Still, I go with it and grin at Teal. "See? I told you it's nothing."

"Don't trap dogs," she tells Cole. "They don't like it."

"This particular one does." His lips move into a sadistic smirk. It's so brief I wouldn't have noticed it if I weren't throwing metaphorical daggers at his face.

I pull out my keys and throw them in Teal's hand. "Wait for me in the car, *belle*. I need a word with Captain."

She disappears around a tree in the car's direction. The thump comes again, but Cole pretends as if it didn't happen as he runs his fingers over his book.

"You needed a word with me?" he asks, as if this is an everyday occurrence.

"Your mother's dog is throwing a fit."

"He can…wait."

"Funny, I don't remember your mum owning a dog."

"It's new. My pet."

"Fuck, Captain. You're sick."

"Are we going down that road, Ronan? Because I have a few witnesses who might say the same about you."

I flip him off then turn to leave. They're not kids, and it's none of my fucking business.

"Does Aiden know?" I ask over my shoulder. Cole is still standing where I left him, watching me closely.

Like a good kid with serial killer tendencies, he never does anything when others are around.

Never.

It's his techniques that allow him to get away with murder—figuratively. If there's literal shit, I don't want to be involved.

"Why should he?" he shoots back.

"I don't know, Captain, maybe because your decisions have no impact on the grown-ups' decisions. If Jonathan King and your dear stepdad decide things will go otherwise, they will."

He remains calm, but his book tilts a little, which means he's gripping it hard.

"Don't kill anyone." I grin. "I mean it. I don't want to be interviewed as the killer's best friend. They will ask if I saw the signs, and then I'll have to say I burnt your book. Do you see the pattern there?"

"No."

"Neither do I." I wave without turning around. "Don't kill. Save that shit for your thirties."

After I disappear from his vicinity, any thought of him vanishes.

Time for my Teal.

I meant it earlier—there'll be a lot of sessions for Ron Astor the Second. Okay, fine. Maybe I shouldn't have named him in front of her, but I kind of lose control of my tongue when I'm with her—in different ways.

My phone vibrates. Eduard. Fucking again.

Eduard: If you know something and you're not telling me, I might be inclined to think you don't respect our deal, dear little nephew. It's very unfortunate.

Fuck him and his fake posh behaviour and all of his existence, basically.

There was a moment in time where his existence was the reason I continued mine. Mum used to read me books about a witch who cast a spell on a prince and made him lose his memory, and with that, he forgot all about the princess he loved.

I told her I wished I could find the witch. She frowned, and I realised I'd said the wrong thing. It was a curse; I wasn't supposed to wish to erase my memories, so I told her it was because I wanted to find her over and over again.

Mum was my princess. She was the reason I wanted that curse, because I thought if I forgot, I wouldn't have those nightmares that made her stay up all night beside me.

I turn my phone off and climb into the driver's seat, trying to regulate my breathing.

"Surprise." Teal's tentative voice wrenches my attention towards her.

She's sitting in the passenger seat and has taken off the T-shirt dress. She's now wearing the bunny outfit I keep in my wardrobe because I was plotting to have Kimberly wear it a long time ago.

The one-piece outfit moulds to her body, bringing attention to her cleavage, which is pushing against the material. Her thighs are bare, the thin strip of fabric glued to her pussy.

I always told the others I had this fantasy, and I did watch it on porn—don't judge—but now that it's real and Teal is wearing it, something in my chest fucking snaps.

It's not a good snap.

My mood darkens and my heart beats so loud it's the only thing I can hear in my ears.

"Oh, wait. I forgot." She reaches into her bag, brings out bunny ears, and places them on her head. "Now it's complete."

Now it's complete.

Now, it's fucking complete.

Her face flashes back and forth as if it's a ghost. Terror like I've only felt once in my life plays in my head over and over like a distorted film.

Manic laughter, drunk people, dark, so fucking dark and alone.

So alone.

Mother.

Father.

Help me.

"R-Ronan?"

"Remove it."

"W-What?"

I grab her by the arm and rip the thing off her.

Her yelp and my groans fill the space, but all I can hear is that small child's quiet sobs.

Help.

Help me.

TWENTY-SEVEN

Teal

The bunny outfit goes to shreds around my body, and for a second too long, I'm so stunned I can't react.

I can't react when the bunny ears break in two.

I can't react when the cloth is ripped, revealing my breasts and my stomach and pooling around my waist.

The only thing I can look at is Ronan's face, the way it's blackening and nearly spiralling out of control.

It's too similar to my phases.

It's like one of those times where everything feels like too much—the world, the people, even the fucking air.

It's too strong, too potent, and you can't escape it no matter how much you try.

I run, but it follows.

I sleep, but it perches over me like a constant weight.

People say it's just a phase and that it'll eventually go away.

It doesn't.

You breathe it in the air, drink it with water, and taste it with food.

It doesn't only become a part of you—it is you. If you somehow managed to remove it, you wouldn't recognise yourself anymore.

It's not a fucking phase. It's a state of being.

And sometimes, it acts out.

Sometimes, you can't control it even with carefully developed coping mechanisms.

I never let anyone see me when it's about to come out. I run and hide.

I purge.

The moment I feel it coming close, I just leave.

The only people who've seen me at my lowest are Knox and Ronan.

And now, I'm seeing him at his lowest, too.

The fact that I could be the cause of this creates a black hole in my chest.

What have I done?

The only reason I did this was because he always said it's his fantasy. He begged Kim to wear it, and I was secretly green with envy whenever he asked that of her, and not me.

Today, I wanted it as a gift after his win. I never meant for it to turn into this.

His fingers stop at my sides. Both his hands grip me, his fingers digging into my flesh as he lowers his head, breathing harshly.

Damn it.

It's the guilt. It's catching up to him, and that shit fucks you up.

I know because even now, I feel it. Even now, I feel those hands digging their way into my skin.

"R-Ronan..." My voice trembles, and I hate myself for it.

I hate that I can't be a solid rock for him like he was for me that night at the Meet Up and every night he spent with me, pretending he didn't witness my nightmares.

He just held me and whispered soothing words into the top of my head until I fell back asleep.

Why am I so broken that I can't do that? Why does it sound like I'm the one who's asking for help instead of offering it?

"Stay like this," he says quietly, so quietly, I suspect I heard him right.

"But…"

"But what?" His head is still lowered, and I hate that too. I hate that I can't get lost in his rich brown eyes and have them invade me, own me. They can even shred me apart, as long as they look at me.

"I hate this," I confess.

"Hate what?"

"Not looking at you. The fact you're not looking at me."

I make a bold move then, something I've never done before. I hop over him so I'm straddling his lap, my knees on either side of his seat, and I fumble with his belt.

"What are you doing, *ma belle?*" There's a slight amusement in his tone, and I nearly jump to the ceiling because of it.

"I was promised Ron Astor the Second, and I still haven't seen him yet," I joke.

"Does that mean you only want me for my dick?"

"Of course. You thought it was you?"

"That sounds as if I'm your whore."

"You are, just like I'm yours." I finally manage to free him of his boxers after so much stupid fumbling. He doesn't even attempt to help me, the dickhead.

"You're mine, huh?" He grips me by the hip as his other hand clutches my jaw.

This time, he's the one who's making me stare at him, and I wouldn't have it any other way.

As long as he looks at me, I pathetically feel like maybe everything will be okay. No, maybe not pathetically, but magically. So…magically.

I never believed in magic, but I also never believed in feelings or in people. Now, I believe in Ronan.

Maybe it's because I now know he's probably not Edric's son and his origins aren't what I thought.

But would that have made a difference?

It's Ronan.

He didn't ask for permission when he invaded my life, and he certainly won't be asking for it now.

My thighs shake when he brings me down on his dick, sheathing himself whole inside me. My eyes roll to the back of my head as he fills me to the brim.

Oh. God.

"Fuck, *belle*. You feel so good and tight and fucking right." With my breasts in his face, his breaths tickle my sensitive skin when he speaks.

I'm about to thrust them more, demanding attention, but Ronan doesn't need that. His mouth latches onto a nipple, making me moan then whimper as he runs his tongue over it. He pounds with his hips from the bottom, driving into me deep but slow. It's like he wants to feel me, to engrave me in his memory.

And that, the fact that he's memorising me instead of the usual rough pounding, flutters my heart.

It's a strange type of sensation, something that makes my own hips jerk in reaction.

My fingers dig into the material of his jacket as I go up and down his length with a pace that matches his.

He releases my nipple with a pop and stares up at me with that gleam in his eyes—the gleam I lost a few minutes ago, the gleam that comes from pain and trauma. Deep-seated trauma.

I seal my mouth to his.

His lips claim mine in a raw passionate kiss that robs me of breaths, thoughts, and logic. It's almost as if I never existed until this moment.

When I'm joined with him this way in all senses of the word, it's as if nothing else is here with us.

No broken parts, no nightmares, no wars to wage.

But that's a lie, isn't it?

I can pretend it'll never happen, but it will.

I can pretend I won't hurt him, but I will.

Sooner or later, it will come to pass.

It *fucking* will.

That thought makes me hug him closer and kiss him harder and faster, committing him to memory, taking him all with me.

For the first time in my life, I have doubts. I've plotted this for so long, but now, those doubts won't leave me alone.

"Thank you for existing, *ma belle*," he whispers against my mouth, and I come then.

I fall willingly, knowing there's nothing that will hold me.

But I'm wrong, there is something—or rather someone.

Ronan's hands surround me like a vice as he pounds into me some more before warmth fills my walls then drips between my thighs.

Oh God.

He grabs my nape with a strong palm and drags me closer so he rests his forehead against mine. We're breathing each other's air, but it almost feels like it's not enough—like I'll never get enough.

And that's dangerous.

No—it's more than dangerous. In my case, it's fucking deadly.

He's an Astor. So what if he could be Eduard's son, not Edric's? He's still an Astor.

And the problem is, the more time I spend with him, the more that fact blurs. Everything blurs, and he's the only thing remaining.

Ronan.

Just Ronan.

My chest squeezes at the thought. I don't want him to be just Ronan. He *can't* be just Ronan.

What have I done?

This is what happens when you're addicted. You don't realise the heights of your addiction until it's too late, until it's the only thing flowing in your veins and you can't get rid of it unless you fucking bleed out.

I can't bleed out.

I've bled out before.

Now, it's his turn, not mine.

I push off Ronan and scramble to the passenger seat. My sweaty stiff fingers fumble for my dress and then pull it over my head, ignoring the remnants of the stupid bunny outfit.

Just a few breaths. Just a few. If I do that, I'll be able to control whatever jumbled mess is going through me. I'll ignore the feelings and everything that comes with them.

"What are you doing?" Ronan tucks himself in, appearing nonchalant, but his jaw ticks.

"Nothing."

"Don't give me that. You're putting up your walls. Why the fuck are you putting up your walls, Teal?"

God. Damn. It.

How could I be so careless as to allow him to recognise that?

Even Knox doesn't notice it as much anymore. I've perfected it. I've become a pro at it.

This is wrong. This can't go on.

"I'll give you what you want." I face him with a slight smile.

"What I want?"

"I'll talk to Edric and end it."

"End it," he repeats, as if he's getting a feel for the words.

"Yes. Isn't that what you always wanted? For the engagement to end?"

"Fuck that, Teal."

"Well, isn't it? You threatened me about it before."

"The keyword being before. Have I threatened you with it in recent memory?"

"In that case, I'm the one who wants to end it." After all, the reason I wanted this is because of Dad, and he signed a binding contract with Edric a few days ago.

I've been on the verge of doing it myself since then, but I always kept coming back to Ronan for more.

One more time, I told myself. *Just one more night in his arms.*

I should've known better. That's how all addicts act.

"You want to what?" he snaps.

"It was a phase anyway." I nearly slap my mouth after I say the word phase.

It's not a phase. *Nothing* is a phase.

I loathe that word.

"It's not a fucking phase and you know it." His face tightens. "You just felt it, and now you're running away from it."

"Just like you're running away from all your problems with all the partying and drinking and drugs?" I lash out. That's what I do when attacked, I attack back, and I'm venomous, like a fucking deadly snake who can never stop. "What did you think all the parties would do, huh? That maybe at the end of the night, you'd be a better person, you'd actually look at yourself in the mirror and have a genuine smile? Those people will never be you. They'll never feel what you feel or speak the language you want to speak. They don't care, Ronan. No one does, so how about you stop taking refuge in useless people? Or better yet, how about you stop trying to make me one of those people? I'm not and I never will be."

My breaths are harsh after my outburst.

In my attempt to come out from under the microscope, I went too far, and now I have no way to stop it.

I have no way to take it back.

I tuck a strand of hair behind my ear with a trembling hand then I let it drop to my lap.

He's not talking. Why isn't he talking?

If he lashes out at me. If he tells me I hide from people for the same reasons, I'll take it. I'll swallow the knife with its blood.

I'll do anything as long as he says something.

I steal a peek through my lashes. Ronan is watching me closely, but his expression is blank, non-existent even.

"Do you know why I take refuge in people?" he asks quietly.

I shake my head. I don't.

"I'm not interested." If I know his pain, it'll gut me to the point of no return.

"Too bad, because you're going to listen, Teal. You're going to listen to the story of a boy who hates himself so much he needs other people in order to exist."

TWENTY-EIGHT

Ronan

My mother used to tell me a lot of folk stories. She had a grandmother in the countryside of southern France and she would gather her, my aunt, and their cousins around a bonfire and tell them stories about magic, but also about the devils that come out of the flames.

In return, Mum told me about her grandmother's stories. She even used to wear the costumes and have us try them on to live out the characters.

And by us, I mean Mum and me.

Dad would give us that look—a bit of amusement, a lot of snobbishness—but Mum always managed to drag him in and have him watch us make fools out of ourselves.

Mum, Dad, and me—and Lars serving drinks while silently judging.

We used to be a happy family.

We used to be a family—full stop.

The crack happened when I was eight. It was Halloween. I loved Halloween. It meant shopping with Mum and picking costumes after thinking about it for months.

I was supposed to be a vampire that year because Mum had fallen in love with some film named *Dracula* that she wouldn't let me watch. She was supposed to be the fairy princess Dracula was about to save. I remember Dad being grumpy because he wanted to do the saving, not me.

At that time, I didn't understand what he meant. All I knew was that I got to dress up and play around the house with Mum.

Since I was a special kid from a special family, Mum and Dad said I didn't get to act like the others in public, so we always had our costume parties at home with only Dad and Lars as the audience.

It was fine with me. I didn't want anyone to find Mum beautiful and decide to take her away like in the novels with half-naked men that Mum hid from me. I took a peek once, but I didn't understand much except that Mum read them a lot when she stayed in bed all day.

That year, the Halloween celebration was cancelled—or rather, our private Halloween was.

Dad said he was taking Mum to a party. I begged him not to go, and if he had to, to please take me with him.

"No," he snapped. "You'll stay here and that's final, Ronan."

"But I want to go with you." I tugged on my Dracula cape and stomped my foot.

"Ronan, *mon chou*." Mum crouched in front of me and patted my cape. "Your uncle Eduard will come and take you to a party. You like parties, don't you?"

"I like the parties with you more."

Tears shone in her eyes. "*Mon ange*."

"Come on, Charlotte." Dad glared at me. "Stop being a brat, Ronan."

"Don't be harsh on him, *mon amour*." She ran her soft fingers over my hair. "Be a good boy for Mummy and I promise we'll have all the parties you want."

"Charlotte." Dad grabbed her by the arm and took her.

Just like that.

I remember running after them to the door before Dad snapped at me one more time to stay inside. Mum got into the car with tears in her eyes. She was still wearing her princess dress and her skin was pale. I thought she wasn't supposed to wear costumes outside.

Then I was sitting on the sofa, sipping from the juice Lars prepared for me and deciding maybe I hated Halloween after all.

Or maybe I hated Halloween when Mum and Dad weren't in it.

Or maybe I hated Dad because he ruined our costume party and took Mum to another party for grown-ups.

That was when Uncle Eduard came. He was drunk; I could tell by the shrill laughter and the way he smelled like 'John's cheap liquor', as Lars called it.

He was wearing a green suit and had a clown mask in his hand. When he approached me, he slurred. "Happy Halloween, little nephew. Look at you all scary."

"I'm Dracula today." I puffed out my chest.

"Ooh, I'm scared. Come on, I'm already late." He extended his hand to me, and I took it.

Uncle Eduard didn't come by often. Dad always yelled at him and called him useless and said he spent a lot of his money. Besides, Uncle Eduard always looked like a clown, even without the mask. He has a nose that's nothing like Dad's and mine. Mum calls them beautiful. She's never called Uncle Ed's nose beautiful.

Lars intercepted us at the entrance and stopped to look Uncle Eduard up and down then smiled at me. "Would you rather go to bed early, Ronan?"

"No. I want to show off my costume."

"You heard the kid, Lars. Get out of the fucking way."

"Language, sir."

"Oh, fuck you and your sir, Lars." Uncle Ed dragged me behind him, loosening his tie. "Even the fucking servant thinks he can tell me what to do. You'll see, Edric. You'll fucking see."

"Mum says those are bad words," I whispered.

"They are, aren't they? Charlotte is such a good woman, so, so good. Edric always got good things. Even his wife and son belong in a museum." He smiled at me, but it was fake. Even at that age, I knew there was something wrong with that smile.

Uncle Eduard ushered me into a van. I thought it was cool at the time. It was as big as a bus and there were lights and we had a screen between us and the driver. The windows were tinted like in Dad's car so I could see the people but the people couldn't see me.

How cool is that? I thought.

I must've spent so long staring at the lights because Uncle Ed asked me if I liked them. I said yes. He was drinking from a blue sparkling bottle.

"What is that, Uncle?"

"This, my dear nephew, is how I remain sane despite all the shit your dad puts me through." He loosened his tie again. "Fucking Australia. He's basically sending me to exile."

"What does exile mean?" I sat on the bench across from Uncle, my feet dangling in the air.

"It means your father hates me."

"He said he doesn't. He only wants you to do better."

"Fuck it. You sound like him even this young."

"Where are we going, Uncle?"

"My friend's party. Everyone will be wearing costumes like you." He abandoned his chair and offered me the sparkling drink. "You want to try it?"

"Is it alcohol?"

"No, it's juice. Sparkling juice." Uncle Ed grinned. "It makes you stronger so you can protect your mother. Don't you want to protect your mother?"

"Of course I do." I puffed up my chest and took the drink. Mum and Dad said I shouldn't take anything from strangers, but this wasn't a stranger; it was Uncle Ed.

The first sip made my face scrunch up. "Eww, it tastes bad."

"You're a coward then." Uncle shook his head.

"I'm not a coward." I took one more sip and closed my nose like I did whenever Lars made me drink milk.

I hate milk.

Maybe this was like milk but for juice.

The more I drank from it, the closer Uncle got to me. Soon enough, he was hugging me, setting me on his lap.

I didn't know how it happened, but then, my cape was gone and my shirt was half-open and Uncle was feeling up my wiener.

Why would he want to do that? I always tugged on my wiener and even showed Mum. Dad told me not to do that in front of Mum and said my wiener is for me alone, said no one else should see it or touch it.

"What are you doing?" My voice was wonky, as if I were going to fall asleep.

"I'm not your real uncle, my beautiful boy." His voice was wrong, so wrong. I didn't like his voice and I didn't like that he was unbuttoning my Dracula trousers and touching my wiener.

"You're Dad's brother...my uncle." I held on to the glass of sparkling blue with stiff hands, thinking if I didn't, something bad would happen.

"Not a real one. That's why he thinks I'm disposable." He ran his tongue over my cheek, leaving a damp, disgusting trail.

"Eww. Stop it, Uncle."

He gripped me hard by my wiener over my trousers and I screamed. His other hand wrapped around my mouth, muffling my voice. "Listen, my beautiful boy. You'll let your uncle take care of you, massage you, and you'll keep your fucking mouth shut. If you say a word about this to your father, Charlotte will get sick and die. Do you know what death means, brat? It means you'll never see her again."

No. Mum will never die.

I didn't know if it was his words or the fact that I didn't like the way he touched me or how he took away my cape and ruined my costume, but something made me snap.

I bit his hand and threw the glass and the blue juice at his face. His hold on me faltered and I fell to the floor.

"Mum will never die!" I still spoke strangely, but I managed to slide open the car's door with shaking fingers.

"Jesus Christ," Uncle cursed. "Stop the car."

I didn't wait for him to say the words—I jumped. I remember rolling once then hitting a pole. I remember his head peeking out then him muttering, "Fucking bastard. Enjoy the cold."

And then he left me in the middle of a deserted street.

In the beginning, I couldn't even stand. It was the alcohol, or perhaps it was the slight pain in my side from when I hit the pole.

It was a lot more than that, though.

It was fear—worse than Halloween, worse than the costumes.

I needed Mum and Dad, and I didn't know how to find them.

They were at a party, and they'd sent me with Uncle Ed. I hated Uncle Ed. I was going to be happy when he went to Australia.

I remember holding on to a pole with stiff fingers and then walking slowly at first. I remember buttoning my Dracula shirt and trousers because Dad had said an Astor always had to look proper.

And then I ran. I ran fast and hard down the street, then I tripped and fell and then stood up again and ran. There were lots of trees on the side of that road, and they had faces, and their faces looked like the demons from Mum's stories.

I called out for her then. "Mother! Where are you, Mother?"

When she didn't answer, I called, "Father? Come find me."

He didn't answer either. I didn't stop limping and tripping and falling, but I couldn't cry.

There wasn't a single tear in my eyes.

An Astor doesn't cry. Dad's words were the only sound in my head.

I was a proper boy. A good boy. I couldn't cry.

So I called out for them again. "Mother! Father! Where are you? Come get me."

They didn't.

People wearing wolf masks scared me and I screamed, but I didn't cry.

I couldn't cry.

I knew I shouldn't.

That's when I saw them. Bunnies—or rather women wearing bunny costumes and giggling.

They had bunny ears and their pink bunny dresses were flying behind them as they laughed and giggled.

Suddenly, I didn't have the urge to not cry. I had the urge to run after them and catch them.

But the moment I rounded the corner, they were gone.

Lars found me soon after. He'd followed us because he was worried. I didn't tell him what had happened. I said I'd had a fight with Uncle Ed, and he just nodded.

Mum and Dad didn't come home that night or the night after. They had a Halloween party for three nights, and I didn't sleep once during that time.

All I could do was have nightmares about dark streets and a weight on my body and a bunny running down the street.

And Lars found me every time.

I didn't say anything to Dad because Uncle Ed was leaving anyway, and I hated myself. I hated Dad too for leaving me with him that night. I also didn't want Mum to know; it'd destroy her.

She trusted him with me, and he stabbed that trust. She'd

hate herself for not seeing the signs, and she'd suspect something else had happened.

Nothing did, though not for lack of trying on his part—he did attempt to corner me a few times when he visited.

I was Uncle Ed's forbidden fruit. The more I escaped him, the harder he tried to put his fucking hands on me, but I was smarter.

When I was a kid and couldn't defend myself, I hid behind Lars. I was always with Lars whenever he came to visit. Lars, who already suspected something, never ever left me alone. He made sure to have me in his sight all the time.

When I grew up, Uncle Eduard kept his hands to himself, as he should've, because I told him in no certain terms that I'd beat him the fuck up if he as much as puts his hands on me.

He always brought up my weakness for Mum. Whenever he felt like I would slip and tell Dad about his paedophile activities, Eduard reminded me of how much it would shatter my mum. How much it would make her already fragile mental state worse.

That was and is the only reason Eduard Astor still exists in my life.

I've borne the memory all this time. I can carry it until the very end. Mum doesn't need to know about this, and Dad certainly doesn't.

He abandoned me that night, and deep down, I never forgave him for it.

I pause after telling Teal the story. I left out the fact that the man who did that to me is my uncle and the part about the bunnies because I don't want her to be disgusted with me. I don't want her to think I'm sick for having a fantasy about bunnies when they're associated with the darkest night of my life.

"That's why I'm always with people," I say. "People allow me to think less about myself. When I was a child, I had this idea that having so many people around meant nothing like that would happen to me again, but in order to be with people, I had to be liked by people. That's the reason behind that image and the parties and the sex. I didn't shag girls because I wanted to, but because I needed the company. I needed to not sleep alone. I needed to wake up in the morning and find many people in my house because that meant I wasn't alone and nothing bad would happen to me."

Two streams of tears fall down Teal's cheeks. She's been holding them in for so long while I've been telling her that memory, but now, it's like she has reached the saturation level and can't keep it in anymore.

"Here's the thing, *belle*." My voice drops. "Since you came into my life, I don't need people anymore. I just need you."

I sound like a sappy fuck, but I don't care. I'm not allowing her to walk away from this. It might have started wrong, but she's grown to be the most beautiful thing I've ever laid eyes on.

"How can you make me cry when I can't cry for myself?" More tears soak her cheeks, but she doesn't attempt to wipe them, as if it's freeing in some way.

"We're so alike." She sniffles. "It's scary."

I smile tentatively. "Does that mean you've changed your mind?"

"No, Ronan. It means I need to stay away from you so I don't destroy us both."

TWENTY-NINE

Teal

People say actual craziness isn't noticeable. It seeps under the surface and eats at you piece by bloody piece. It creeps up on you like a vampire to blood or a predator to prey.

But I do. I feel it.

I wouldn't call it craziness, but it's something abnormal.

It's what stops me from laughing out of courtesy when everyone else does. They recognise the societal norms; I don't. Even Knox does. He's way better at blending in than me, and it's probably why the therapist liked working with him, but never with me.

I heard her tell Agnus I'm a well. She said there's a lot of digging that needs to be done, and I'm not allowing her to do that.

I'm an anomaly even with the people who treat crazy, and I've always taken pride in that.

I looked in the mirror and liked my scowling face. People react differently to trauma. There are those who lean on their closest family and friends. There are those who fight so they can smile again. And there are those who close in on themselves and eventually spiral out of control.

Then there's me.

I never spiralled out of control; I didn't drink, do drugs, or even try weed or smoking. I was always a good girl, but with the worst facial expression.

I didn't allow myself to smile, and eventually, I didn't know how to smile. What right did I have to laugh when I never made peace with myself?

What right do I have to exist as if nothing happened?

There's a girl I left behind, a small child no older than seven who screamed for help and I didn't hear her—or rather, I couldn't. That girl, the seven-year-old me, wants retribution.

No—she demands it. And I have to give it to her, even if a sacrifice has to be made.

I walk down the hall to Dad's office, determination bubbling in my veins.

When Ronan confessed his trauma to me a few days ago, I couldn't breathe properly.

I still can't.

Every time I think about him, I have this ball the size of my head clogging my breathing. I can't stop dreaming about a small child running alone in the streets with no place to go and no one to ask for help.

And then, the face of that child wasn't Ronan's. It was mine. It was the girl who stopped smiling because someone confiscated that smile and refused to give it back.

I unlock my phone and stare at the texts he's sent since that night at the Meet Up.

Ronan: When someone pours their heart out to you, the least you can do is not leave.

Ronan: Aside from the tidbits I told Xan, you're the first person I've told the entire story to. Now, I'm feeling rejected, and I'm tempted to find you and punish you.

Ronan: I wish you trusted me enough to let me see you.

Then his last text came today.

Ronan: Why the fuck do I have no pride when it comes to you?

Probably the same reason I have no walls when it comes to him. After that therapist called me a well, I started to believe it. I started to think no one could understand me or dig deeper into me, and that's why I strengthened those walls.

Until *he* came along.

I've never felt as open and as in danger as I do with him. I always thought people aside from my family would eventually leave. Not Ronan.

Never Ronan.

He barged in so easily it's as if the well never existed.

And that can't go on.

For his sake, not mine.

He'll eventually hate me, so I might as well do it now rather than later.

I knock on Dad's office door.

"Come in." His reply is curt.

I push the door and step inside, inhaling a deep breath. Dad and Agnus are sitting across from each other in the lounge area. Both their jackets are discarded and they have the cuffs of their shirts rolled up. Dad doesn't have his tie on, but Agnus still does, and he generally looks in a less dishevelled state. They each have their tablets in hand, which means they're exchanging data.

"Am I interrupting?" I ask.

Dad's face eases with a smile. "You can never interrupt me. Come here, Teal."

I sit by his side, in the spot Dad pats.

Agnus starts to stand up. "I'll be downstairs if you need anything."

"You don't have to leave," I tell him. "I want to talk to you both."

Agnus settles back down. Now, as I look at him, I realise whatever I felt for him in the past was fleeting. He's been there for me and Knox our entire lives, and that gratitude has lived with me for as long as I can remember, but that's it.

That's all.

The only consuming feelings I've ever had are for this boy who can make me laugh when I didn't even know that I could.

Dad slides the tablet on the table. "Is something wrong?"

"No...well, maybe."

"Does it have to do with the fact that you skipped school for two days?" Dad asks.

Why did I think he was too busy to notice that? This is Dad. At some point, he felt my pain before I could notice it myself.

"Dad, promise you won't hate me?"

"That's off the table—not even if you killed someone."

Agnus raises a brow. "We can always cover your tracks."

Dad gives him a look.

"What?" Agnus lifts a shoulder. "I can help her get away with murder."

"Don't put ideas into her head..." Dad focuses on me. "This doesn't have anything to do with murder, right?"

"No." *Yet.*

"So what is it about?" Dad asks.

"I know I told you I want to be engaged to Ronan, but can I change my mind?"

"Of course." Dad doesn't even miss a beat. "As I said, I would never make you do something you don't want to."

I release a long breath, feeling some of the weight vanishing off my chest, only to have it replaced by a different type of weight.

"Why?" Agnus' quiet voice drifts into the air.

"Why?" I repeat.

"You were so hell-bent on being engaged to that kid, but now you've changed your mind. It's not that I didn't think you had an ulterior motive, but I doubt it's only because of the partnership between us and Edric's company."

"Agnus." Dad shakes his head, but it's more out of resignation than anything else.

"She asked for this, and now she's ending it." Agnus' attention doesn't waver from me. "This isn't a children's game, Teal."

"I know that." *More than anyone.*

"I'll support you through whatever decision you make." Dad takes my hand in his, and the warmth touches me deep inside. "But I thought you were getting along with Ronan? Elsa and Knox talk about it all the time, even when you try to quiet them."

I bite my lower lip. "Dad...have you ever felt like you need to let someone go for their sake?"

Silence fills the office for a second and I almost think he won't answer, but then he says, "I have. It was Elsa's mother. I should've sent her to a psych ward, for her sake."

"But he didn't," Agnus says in a detached, stone-cold tone. "He didn't follow his head, and that mistake not only cost him nine years of his life, but also of his children's lives."

"Lovely reminder, Agnus." Dad's voice is hard with disapproval.

"It wouldn't have happened if you'd listened to me," Agnus continues in the same tone, scrolling through his tablet.

"And you won't let me live it down for a lifetime, will you?" Dad asks.

"Probably not." Agnus lifts his head and his emotionless eyes trap me in their merciless hold. "If there's anything you need to learn from him, it's that you should never follow your heart, Teal. That thing is untrustworthy and will land you in trouble and bring regrets."

"Don't listen to him. He's old and pragmatic, and did I mention he's been single for life?" Dad brings my attention back to his kind eyes. "I admit I made a mistake with Abigail, but it's because of her that I have Elsa, you, and Knox. I would never regret that fact."

I smile at that.

For a long time, I believed Dad only took us in because of

guilt, but that was never the case. He could've sent us into the system—or even thrown us back out on the streets.

He didn't.

"Think about it," Dad continues. "And if you believe your decision is final, I'll be happy to oblige."

I nod, even though my decision is already cemented and is screaming loud and clear in my head. "Can I ask something else?"

"Of course."

"I know Knox and I told you we'd never ask about Mum or where she is, but I think I'm ready. I want to know."

Dad and Agnus exchange a look before the latter goes back to staring at his tablet.

"What?" I ask.

"Your mother is no more, Teal," Dad says in a sympathetic tone. "She died that same year you ran away. I was searching for her to have her give up her parental rights when I learnt she died of an overdose."

Oh.

I remain still, unsure what to feel. No, I know what I feel.

Nothing.

I just learnt my mother and only biological parent—the only one I know of—is dead, and all I keep thinking about is how she doesn't have to pay.

She left without paying.

She died as if she didn't do anything wrong.

My nails dig into my lap until I register the sting on my flesh.

Now, her accomplice will pay for both of them.

Dad pats my shoulder. "Are you okay?"

I nod. "I don't know why, but I think I kind of suspected it."

"One less piece of scum in the world," Agnus says without lifting his head from his tablet.

"That's insensitive," Dad tells him.

"The woman abused her own children—that's what's insensitive," Agnus says in his usual cool tone.

"Agnus," Dad warns.

"He's right," I say, not wanting them to fight because of this. It's not like I wanted to find her for a noble cause, or like I wanted the engagement with Ronan for the reasons I made everyone believe.

I'm the worst scum.

I guess that's what happens when you're born the daughter of a whore.

After wishing them a great rest of the night, I leave Agnus and Dad's office. I come to a screeching halt at the door. Knox stands there, feet crossed at the ankles as he leans against the wall. It's then I realise I didn't close the door earlier and my brother probably heard the whole thing.

I make sure to shut the door this time before I speak. "How much did you hear?"

"I already knew about Mum."

"Y-You did?"

"I wish I was detached like you." There's pain in his voice, and I recognise it without struggling to. Knox's pain was the only pain I could feel—until Ronan.

"Knox…"

"I searched for her when we were in Birmingham and—wait for it—I went back to that brothel, when I was maybe fifteen. When they told me she overdosed and died, do you know what I did?"

I approach him slowly, shaking my head.

"I cried so hard I thought I would never stop crying." He laughs, rubbing the back of his nape, but it's forced. "Pathetic, isn't it, T?"

"No. She was our only family."

"She was the whore who let those fuckers in while we were sleeping and—"

I slam a hand on his mouth, cutting him off. I don't want to hear it. I'm so close to reliving it, and that's never good.

He removes my hand gently. "Point is, we're each other's family. Dad and Agnus are our family. I shouldn't have cried for that whore, and that's when I realised I wasn't crying for her. I was merely mourning our childhood and how abnormally we grew up because of her. It's okay to cry, T. It purges more than those runs."

"Thank you, Knox. I needed that today."

"Happy freedom day." He grins.

On this day eleven years ago, Knox and I broke the chains. We ran and never looked back.

We were kids, but we earned our freedom. We saw an out, so we took it. If we'd stayed there, I would've become like my mum and Knox would've probably killed himself or gotten into drugs and overdosed like a certain mother.

We've always saved ourselves, and that will continue.

He glares at me. "For the record, tell anyone I cried and I'll murder you."

"Depends on how you act."

"I won't be your bitch, sis." He switches to his overdramatic tone. "Remember, I came out first."

"Which means you cried first, right?"

"You little bugger." He puts me in a headlock, and I stare up at him with a smile.

He softens almost immediately, letting me go as awe fills his features. "You're...smiling."

"You're one of the few who gets to see it, so engrave it somewhere."

"Ronan is rubbing off on you, isn't he?"

"It's not about him."

"Yeah, right, could've fooled me." He raises an eyebrow. "I was going to kick him out of our lives until I saw you with him. You've never been at ease with someone like you are with

Ronan. Not even with me—and I hate it, by the way. I'm supposed to be your favourite."

"You are." My chest aches, but I mutter, "I'm breaking it off with him."

"Why?"

Ugh. Why do he and Agnus have to ask that question? Would it be the end of the world if they didn't know?

"Can't you see it? Ronan and I couldn't be any more opposite."

Lie. We share more than the world will ever know, but I'm not telling Knox that.

"And yet you make it work. He's been asking about you every time he sees me. He's not doing well, T."

"What do you mean?"

"I don't know. He's distracted at practice and hasn't been throwing his usual jokes."

He'll move on. Ronan is the strongest, most admirable person I know.

He called me strong, but he's way stronger than me.

I hid and shunned people. He slammed straight into them.

And then into me.

And now, we're here.

And we shouldn't be here.

After saying goodnight, I retreat to my room and slide down the door after I close it.

Something burns in my chest, and it…God, it hurts.

It hurts so much knowing what I'll do to him. That's why I've been delaying it, trying to talk my brain out of it.

Maybe I can live without revenge.

Maybe…

The little girl with black hair and soulless eyes appears in front of me. Silent tears fall down her cheeks, but she's not speaking. She's not doing anything.

She just stands there in her torn collar and dirty dress.

Help me.

Save me.

Free me.

She doesn't have to say the words for me to feel them. She's always been there; she's the constant shadow on my shoulder.

And now, I have to get justice, for her.

For *me*.

You know what? I'm done hiding and running away from the inevitable. Agnus will get me the supplies if I ask him to.

I retrieve my phone and call the number I should've dialled sooner.

"Hello," I say. "Can we meet tomorrow?"

After he confirms, I pull out a piece of paper and pour my heart onto it in one go.

This is my legacy.

My goodbye.

THIRTY

Ronan

When the great Earl Edric Astor says he's having a family meeting, everyone must drop to their knees and listen. Well, not exactly, but something like that.

So we're all here in the dining room. And by we, I mean, Mum, Eduard the fucker, Lars—because we've basically adopted him—and yours truly.

Mum sits at the head chair, or more like Dad sat her on it while he stands behind her. She's wearing a beige dress that makes her appear paler, or maybe she's been paler than usual.

Lars, like any adopted child, doesn't want to tell me why Mum's cold has been going on longer than ever. He's after the parents' favour.

But he still stands beside me, not taking a seat. It's like he's expecting an order of tea and wouldn't want to miss it when it arrives.

Eduard is across from me, throwing a glance my way now and again. He's wearing a purple suit that makes him look like a clown.

I shake my head at that image.

He keeps touching his tie, which means he's nervous as fuck. He probably thinks I talked to Dad or something. I play a dick card and let him think that.

Be nervous, Ed.

I hope you stay nervous until the end of your miserable life.

I retrieve my phone discreetly under the table. There are text messages from my friends. I changed the group chat's name to The Four Fuckers, like we're four musketeers. Xan said there are only three musketeers and Cole just changed the name back to The Fuckers.

He has no imagination.

I try to pretend I'm interested in their texts, but I'm not, so I go straight to Teal's messages.

Nothing.

Empty.

Nada.

She hasn't acknowledged my existence since that night. Okay, so maybe throwing my childhood trauma on her all at once wasn't my brightest moment.

And okay, admitting I have no pride when it comes to her is frowned upon in Ron Astor the Second's playbook, but she's not any girl.

She's Teal.

I can't fight the need to be with her every waking moment. I want to hold her, and maybe if I do so tightly enough, she'll eventually open up to me, too.

Maybe she'll feel safe enough to tell me why she puts up walls after we have sex or when she sleeps in my arms.

It can't be the depravity—she loves that as much as I do. It's a game we play, and it's a damn good one at that. I hope to hell it's not the performance, because Ron Astor the Second and his legendary size would take a rope to his neck, and that'd be a fucking tragedy.

Maybe I need to kidnap Knox and torture the answers out of him.

Or not.

Kidnapping and torturing your future brother-in-law is frowned upon in 99% of cultures.

Besides, I want her to be the one who tells me, not him.

But if she thinks she can run away from me by skipping school, she must not know me.

I'm an Astor. We don't stop.

My great-great-grandfather brought his wife from Africa. When his family didn't agree, he kind of gave them the middle finger and married her anyway. Or rather, he pestered her until she agreed to marry him.

I'm that type of Astor.

He camped out all the way in Africa—I'm lucky I just need to camp out in front of the Steel household.

"Ronan."

I lift my head from my phone at Dad's voice, realising I've been staring at the lack of texts for way too long.

"No phones," Lars whispers. "How hard is it to follow that simple instruction, young lord?"

I glare at him and he feigns nonchalance, staring at Dad.

I grin, sliding the phone in my pocket. "Please, proceed. I apologise for my inadequate behaviour."

Dad must sense the sarcasm in my overly posh tone, but he brushes it off. "We're here because your mother and I need you to know a few things."

"Another trip?" I scoff. "Oh, wait—is it the Maldives this time?"

"*Mon chou…*" Mum's eyes fall downwards, and I wish I could somehow stab myself in the balls. The jab was supposed to be at Dad, not her. He's the one who's always whisking her off somewhere.

"Ronan," Dad scolds.

I stand up. "I'm not interested in your destinations, Dad. Lars needs the details."

"Don't you need the dates, though?" Dad snaps back. "So you can throw your endless parties."

"Lars…" I stare at him incredulously. "You bloody traitor."

"Language," Dad scolds. "And I'm speaking to you, not Lars. You really thought something could go on under my roof and I would know nothing about it?"

Yes, Dad. It already fucking happened.

It takes everything in me not to stare at Eduard. I'm trying to erase him from existence.

"What are you trying to prove with all those parties, Ronan? The drinking? The weed? The alcohol?" Dad's voice turns more lethal with every word. "Do you think you're a kid?"

"Not anymore," I say, and this time, my eyes slide to Eduard. He squirms in his seat, smoothing out his tie.

"Take it easy, Edric." He smiles, as if trying to alleviate the tension.

Fuck him.

And fuck Dad.

And even Lars, the fucking traitor.

"Stop it." Mum's voice turns brittle. "Please."

In a second, Dad is by her side, grabbing her by the shoulder.

I turn to leave. I have no time for family drama, and if I spend one more second in the same room as Eduard the fucker, I'll jam a knife in his throat, and once again, murder is frowned upon in 99% of cultures.

"*Mon chou*, don't go," Mum pleads.

"I'll speak to you later, Mother."

"There's no later." Dad's booming voice stops me in my tracks. "She's dying."

I whirl around so fast I'm surprised I don't fall on my face. The words he said echo like doom in the asphyxiating silence.

I see them in a different light now.

Dad placing his hands on my mother's shoulders...her pale face and the tears gathering in her eyes...Lars staring at me with sorrow...

He knew.

He fucking knew.

"What did you just say?" I whisper.

"Your mother has uterine cancer, and she has always suffered from immunodeficiency disorder. The cancer relapsed a year ago, and the surgeries failed."

"What do you mean they've failed? And why am I just learning about this now?"

"It was me." Mum stands up and nearly drops back down. Fuck. When did she become this weak? Why haven't I noticed that she usually only speaks to me while sitting or in her bed?

I run to her and force her to sit down then kneel by her side.

She strokes my hair back. "I asked your father and Lars not to tell you. You were my miracle, *mon chou*. When I first married your father, the doctor told me I couldn't have kids because of my immunodeficiency disorder. Four years after, I found out I was pregnant and begged your father to let me bring you into the world. Nine months later, you came along, and I was the happiest woman alive. You gave me the privilege of being a mother. The moment the nurse put you in my arms, I cried like a baby while you smiled. It's weird, isn't it?"

Her voice catches, and something in my throat does, too. "The cancer started when you were around eight and we thought we got rid of it back then, but it came back last year. That's why we've been going on those trips, *mon chou*. You're so young and lively, and I didn't want to put this burden on you."

"Burden?" My voice breaks. "What are you talking about? You're my mother."

"It's because I'm your mother that I have to protect you." A tear falls down her cheek. "But I can't disappear from your life anymore. I hate it more than anything in the world."

"You won't." I stare at Dad, who's watching us with furrowed brows.

"We have results to pick up next week," he says.

"That's good news, right?" I stare between them, and the silence nearly suffocates me.

"The doctors said I only have a 15% chance of survival, and I failed on a 50% chance before, so we don't have much hope."

"But...but there's chemotherapy and—"

"No," Mum cuts me off. "I'm not doing chemo again."

"She's refusing that." Dad's forehead scrunches.

"And you're agreeing?" I snap.

"Chemo will only keep me away from you, and then I will die in pain without seeing your face." She cups my cheek. "I don't want that."

"I won't leave your side." I grab her hands harder. "Don't do this, Mother. You can't leave me. I'm your miracle, remember?"

"It's because you're my miracle that I want to spend whatever time I have left with you..." She trails off, a sob catching in her throat. "Please, I'm begging you and Edric to not take this away from me."

She brushes a trembling kiss on my temple, and her tears drop onto my cheeks as she stands up and starts to leave the room. I try to help her, but Dad holds me back with an arm on my shoulder.

Instead, he motions at Lars to follow her.

"She feels weak when she can't walk on her own," Dad tells me after she disappears. "The therapist says to be there for her without making her feel weak."

"How could you not tell me this?" I throw all my anger and frustration on my father. "How could you keep me in the dark about something as important as this?"

"You heard her. She wanted it this way."

"Or maybe you made her believe she wanted it. After all, the decisions are always yours and everyone else has to follow."

"Ronan, I understand this is hard for you —"

"Hard." I laugh. "Try something stronger than fucking hard."

"Edric, I'll just…" Eduard motions at the entrance.

The fuck.

I forgot he was here all along.

"No, wait." Dad motions at him. "I need to discuss business decisions with you. Stay the night."

"Business decisions," I scoff. "With dear Uncle Ed."

"Maybe you need to cool your head, Ronan," Dad says.

"Fucking maybe."

I throw one last glare at Eduard before I storm out of the dining room. I go straight to my parents' bedroom, but Lars stops me before I go in, telling me Mum needs rest.

I tell him we're not speaking until he dies then I go to my room, open my laptop, and search everything about my mum's condition. Then I stop and catch my breath, because sometimes, as I read about the effects and the shit she went through, I feel like there's no air in the room.

I spend an entire night like that, researching then staring at the ceiling, thinking I'll lose my mum then going back to researching again.

In the early morning, I go to Lars and tell him we're calling a truce so he can tell me all he knows. Apparently, on that nightmare night, Mum and Dad didn't leave me because of a Halloween party, but because Mum had intense pain, and as soon as they got to the hospital, she was admitted and diagnosed.

All the overseas trips were to a private clinic where Mum had to stay with her regular doctor.

The reason they came back after the last surgery is because Mum couldn't take staying in the hospital anymore and wanted to be with me.

Her depression has been reduced since they returned, which her doctor says is a good sign, but they won't know anything until the test results come out.

"Not telling you was entirely her ladyship's choice," Lars

tells me after he's done with his retelling. "Don't blame your father for it. He's suffering as much as her. Why do you think he has that scoundrel taking care of business? It's so he can devote all his attention to your mother."

I point a finger at him. "Truce over. We're not on speaking terms."

"Tea?" He offers me a cup.

"Not speaking, Lars." I leave his kitchen, and just like that, I find myself in front of her room again.

I place a hand on the door, and for a second, I feel like that kid who called her name and got no reply in return.

I can live in a world where I'm protecting Mum by burying the truth inside, but how can I live in a world where she doesn't exist?

I have no idea how long I stand there, breathing harshly, feeling as if I'm about to combust.

It's long enough that I slide down to the floor in front of the door with my back to the doorframe. It's long enough that I relive all the stories she used to tell me when I was a child.

They all had happy endings, because she has always been a romantic at heart.

She always loved too much, cared too much, so why the fuck is this happening to her?

Charlotte Astor is one of the good ones. She does charity. She gives and gives and takes nothing in return. She loves and cares, so why the fuck did cancer choose her? Why didn't it hit a lowlife like Ed?

Or even me?

I pull out my phone and go straight to my conversation with Teal. There's no new text.

It doesn't matter. I can call her, visit her.

Fuck my pride.

I need her like I've never needed anything before. I just need to hug her, and that's it.

A hug.

I call her, but she doesn't pick up.

If she's grown attached to clingy texts then that's what she'll get.

"Sir." Lars's shadow falls on me.

"We're still not talking."

"Sir."

"And I don't want fucking tea."

"Ronan," he says sharply.

"What?" I snap, finally looking up at him.

He holds out a folded piece of cream-coloured paper.

"I don't know where my father is. Sorry—*his lordship*."

"He went out for an early-morning meeting." Lars thrusts the letter in my face. "This came for you."

For me? Who the fuck sends letters anymore?

"Who is it from?" I ask.

"Miss Teal." Lars raises an eyebrow. "She left with his lordship."

Teal sent me a letter then went somewhere with Dad? Why would she do that?

Ah, fuck.

She's not thinking about ending the engagement, is she?

I open the letter, and my heart nearly stops beating.

THIRTY-ONE

Teal

Ronan,

I've never written a letter in my life, but you broke my patterns for everything, so what does adding writing a letter to the mix matter? Right?

I'm trying to throw a joke in there, but that probably didn't come through. As you know, I'm kind of socially awkward.

You said in your text you wished I trusted you enough to let you see my pain. It's not that I don't trust you, because I do. It's weird, but if you stood at the bottom of a cliff, I would fall over with my eyes closed. Do you know why? Because I know you'd catch me.

I know you'd never let me hit the ground or rock bottom or any of that.

The reason I couldn't come forward as you did isn't that I don't trust you; it's that I don't trust myself.

I'm a fraud, Ronan. I didn't get engaged to you because of Dad's company, although that did play a part. I got engaged to you for other reasons, and all of them have to do with the pain I refuse to let others see.

Pain is weakness, and I hate thinking about or reliving the last time I was weak.

But now, I will, because I hope by the time you finish

reading this letter, you'll be able to understand that not all people deal with pain the same way.

You came out. I hid.

For me, the pain started when I was born as a prostitute's daughter. Knox and I begged to go to school, but she barely let us. All our mum cared about was drugs and money to get those drugs.

She opened her legs for anyone as long as she got her next shot of heroin. She didn't care that we heard everything or that we hid so we never got in the way of the men who left her room.

Over time, she got clients who weren't interested in her cunt, but in seeing her children naked.

Or rather one client.

He came in the dark when we were asleep and made us strip. When Knox cried, she hit him and said either we do as instructed or we wouldn't go to school.

So we did.

We removed our clothes and stood in the dark as that man was making those sounds of masturbation.

Of course, I was clueless to that fact back then. I was so naive that I told Knox maybe he was in pain. My brother told me to shut up because he understood what was going on before I could. His innocence was stolen away before mine.

Then, that client disappeared, and that was that. I thought it was all over.

It wasn't.

One night, I was asleep and I felt something wet and hot on my clothes.

In the morning, I went crying to Mum, begging her to help me. She just washed me and told me to stay still and not cry. If I cried, she'd throw me and Knox out for that man to take with him.

I stopped crying that day.

I haven't cried since.

The second night, his filth was all over my bare skin.

Then it was on my face.

I didn't ever speak during those nights. I stayed still until he finished. I stayed still until I felt his hot liquid, because that meant it was over.

Knox found me one night when the man was sneaking over to where I slept. He hit him on the head, took me by the hand, and we ran.

We didn't stop running in the streets.

We were running so neither Mum nor that man nor the people who worked with her could find us.

I didn't cry, though, not even when Elsa's mother trapped us in her basement. At least she didn't touch us, and when she did, it was once when she cut our knees so we resembled her son.

At least, in that basement, we were away from Mum and that man.

But you know what? I might have been away, but I was never far.

The man and his hot liquid kind of lived with me. I dreamt about it, had nightmares about it, and in every one of them, I couldn't move.

I stayed completely still, just like Mum ordered me to.

All I could think about was his voice when he spoke to Mum and gave her money.

I always peeked out of my room, trying to see his face. Mum smiled like the fucking druggie she was whenever she saw him. He was an important man and he didn't speak like the people in Birmingham. He spoke like an actor.

After Ethan took me and Knox in, I made it my mission to find that man from my nightmares. The man who perched on my chest every time I slept.

I searched for him everywhere, but I was too clueless and too young; I didn't know what I was doing.

I also had no idea what I would tell him if I found him. All I knew was that I needed to see him, and when I did, I'd figure out what I would tell him.

I did find him.

And I did know what I wanted to tell him.

Only it wasn't words. The moment I saw him, I knew exactly what I'd do to him.

I'd kill him.

It was that simple.

He held me a prisoner all my life. I couldn't break free, not even with the therapists or in a family setting or anything.

I never told this to anyone, but you might as well be the first to know it. The little girl who was violated over and over again never left me. Her shadow is currently perching on my shoulder, telling me to set her free, and I know I won't be able to do that unless I kill him.

That girl cries all the time, her eyes hollow and haunting, but I can't even cry. She can't speak, but I can. She can't help herself, but I will.

It's my duty. It's why I grew up. Why I ran. Why I exist.

It was so simple.

But then you came along, and I thought maybe I could exist for something else. Maybe I could be with you and let you in.

I want to.

You don't know how much I want to, Ronan. I've never felt as alive as when I'm with you. I never woke up and felt happiness until I realised you were by my side.

You're the only one who gave another meaning to my life aside from revenge. You set me on fire, and you didn't run away from the ashes. You kissed me and didn't want to leave me.

I don't deserve that.

You're the light despite the darkness. You're the hope despite the black dots. You're strong despite the weakness.

You didn't let that man take your life. I let him take mine.

The thing is, we met under the wrong circumstances, Ronan.

I didn't approach you for you. I approached you for your family name.

I approached you because you're the son of the man I decided to kill.

Your father took my life, and now I'm taking his.

I feel so sorry for you and Charlotte and even Lars, but I can't live in a world where scum like Edric Astor exists.

I know you will never forgive me, but I hope you find it in you to understand me.

What I feel for you is more than love. It's something overpowering, but also empowering. It's believing I can be normal even when I don't know what normal is. It's smiling and laughing out loud without even realising it.

I wish we'd met under different circumstances and with different names.

I wish I could wake up to your face every day.

If there's a next life, let's meet there, okay?

Goodbye,
Teal

THIRTY-TWO

Teal

I t's so easy.

The whole process went off without a hitch. I had to stop and stare in my rear-view mirror a few times, expecting to find police cars following us.

There aren't.

The trip to the forest takes me less than fifteen minutes. There were almost no cars on the way, no people roaming around this early morning, and I make sure to use deserted routes.

No one has witnessed the man beside me, his eyes closed and his entire body slack. If they did, they'd think he was asleep and I'm just taking him on a drive.

I *am* taking him on a drive—just not where he's supposed to go.

When I called Edric for a meeting, I told him it was urgent and about Ronan. He immediately agreed.

Then, I drove to his mansion in Knox's Range Rover—I left him a note about it and kind of suggested he get a new car.

After I gave Lars the letter I wrote to Ronan, there was a small voice that told me I should turn around and leave—just go somewhere, anywhere. I don't have to do this or anything that followed.

But the little girl on my shoulder is still crying. She can't stop, and neither can I.

So, I asked Edric if he was okay with joining me in my car because I didn't want to talk about it in his house. Once again, he didn't suspect anything as he slid into the passenger seat.

The moment he looked down to click the seatbelt into place, I jammed the needle I'd already prepared in his neck, and not just any jamming—I did it intravenously.

Since I decided to kill him, I've been arranging my dominos one by one. I knew how I'd kill him and how I'd get there. I've been watching videos about intravenous injections and practising on dolls. I learnt it so thoroughly I could do it with my eyes closed.

My medicine of choice is rocuronium because it's paralysing, fast, and long-lasting. It's also prescription only, but when I asked Agnus if he could find a way to get it, he brought me two bottles the next day, no questions asked. That's what I love about Agnus—his ability to understand. He only said to call him, not Dad, if I do something.

I'm not calling anyone.

The drug took effect on Edric within a minute. I still remember the confused expression on his face after the sting of the needle as he slowly turned around.

He didn't understand what had happened.

He didn't understand that I'm capable of doing that to him.

I haven't looked at his face since then. I still don't.

All I've done is drive.

At one point, I'm too light-headed; it's kind of alarming. It's like I can't feel my face or my limbs or anything.

With the dose I gave him, I have around twenty to thirty minutes until he regains complete consciousness. Sure, I could've found a poison, injected him with it, and ended it there.

But that's too peaceful, too easy.

Besides, he needs to know the sins he's paying for.

His limbs start twitching and so do his lids. It's a knee-jerk reaction that means the drug is slowly starting to wear off. I have another needle at the ready so when he meets his end, he won't be able to move a muscle.

Like me.

Like the little girl crying on my shoulder.

He'll die unable to do any fucking thing about it, just like I couldn't.

This isn't revenge. This is fucking karma.

I slam on the brakes right at the top of a hill. The early morning lights are visible in the distance. Today, the clouds are so thick and grey, as if in mourning.

Taking a deep breath, I face him.

His eyes are open, but he can't turn around to look at me. He just stares ahead like a zombie with his brains sticking out.

"You're going to die, Edric," I say in a neutral tone, knowing the effects of the drug are fading and he can hear me even if he can't move. "It's a nightmare to want to move but not have the ability to, isn't it?" I continue. "That's how I felt every time you walked into my room and jerked off to my body. That's how I stayed when your semen coated my skin."

He makes an unintelligible sound, but all he manages to get out is drool that trickles down his chin. I couldn't begin to think what he means by that—not that it matters. This time, it's all about me, not him.

"I screamed in my head, too, just like I'm sure you're doing right now. But you know what happens when you scream and there's no sound? You kind of stop screaming, stop making yourself noticeable, and soon enough, you stop existing. You want to purge it somehow, but you can't cry or talk or even breathe. That's how I've lived for the past eleven years, like a shadow of myself, a ghost of what I should've been.

"I was so numb, I slept with countless men as soon as I could. I lost my virginity at thirteen just so I could get rid of the numbness and prove I'm not a freak, prove I can feel, but no matter how much sex I had, the numbness never left. It's there, in every fucking moment, in every waking second, and even in sleep. Until…Ronan."

My voice breaks and I clear my throat so he doesn't hear it. "That's another reason why I hate you. You didn't just steal my childhood—you also took away Ronan. Why did he have to be your son? Why is the only person who makes sense your fucking heir? Do you know what the ironic part is? While you were engrossed in your paedophile activities with me, your own son got molested."

The sounds he's making increase in volume, his mumbled words successive but still unintelligible. The seatbelt holds him in place, so he couldn't move a muscle even if he tried to.

"Right." I laugh without humour. "You don't know that because you're not only a fucked-up human being but also a horrible father. Yes, Edric, Ronan was molested during that Halloween night he dressed up as Dracula and you left him alone. That's why he's so overly joyful sometimes. It's his defence mechanism when the memories become too much, just like it's my defence mechanism to run, to prove I actually exist."

His fingers twitch, and he almost lifts a hand but it soon falls limp by his side.

"*Nooooo…*" he slurs, the sound almost haunting.

"Yes," I say. "And now, I have to erase you off the face of the earth. You know, my original plan was to kill you then walk away, travel, and live the life you robbed me of. But I can't do that anymore. Do you know why?"

He makes another noise, and this time, I place the needle near his throat. That makes him pause his attempts to move.

"Because I can't live in a world where Ronan hates me. I can't be out there after killing his father and knowing the pain

I caused him." A tear slides down my cheek then, and I taste salt.

I pause, my eyes widening.

A tear.

My first tear for myself in over a decade.

Edric stares at me, too, as if feeling my pain and how the reality of things is slashing me from the inside out and I have no way to stop it.

Only he doesn't feel. He's a monster.

"Why did it have to be you? Just why?"

He doesn't answer.

He can't.

"It's the end, Edric. It ends how it started." I hit the accelerator. "See you in hell."

I can't live in a world where Ronan hates me, so it's only fair I pay for my sins in this life.

Where Edric goes, I'll go.

Maybe there, I'll be free.

Maybe there, I'll think of a life where Ronan and I were meant to be together.

I'm sorry, Ronan. I'm so sorry.

THIRTY-THREE

Ronan

*F*uck.

Fucking, fuck.

Okay, maybe if I could get that word out of my immediate thoughts, I could actually think straight and function.

Fuck!

I jump to my feet and storm to the kitchen, crumpling the letter Teal left me in my fingers and shoving it in my pocket. I couldn't get her words out of my head even if I tried. There's this constant sound that won't end or stop.

The weeping of a small girl.

My breathing deepens at the thought of what happened to her and the way her voice, her tears, and her feelings were stolen.

It wasn't only her innocence; it was her life essence. No wonder she built walls and forts and did everything possible to stay away.

I'm nothing in comparison. I had my parents, even if they were absentee. She had no one. Her only parent was a monster.

And now, she thinks my father is also a monster.

He's not.

Edric and I might have some issues—okay, a lot, and all of

them have to do with his stiff personality and the way he stole Mum away from me—but he's not a paedophile.

He's not sick.

Besides, he was too busy with Mum during the time frame Teal described. He didn't go to Birmingham, and he never spent ten minutes away from Mum.

I know, because I hated him at the time. I hated how he wouldn't let me stay in Mum's room. I always thought he was controlling her, but it turns out he was only respecting her wish.

However, I do know who went to Birmingham on Dad's behalf. I know who took care of the business and used the Astor name as he saw fit.

He sits on the counter in the kitchen. He hasn't left, of course. If Dad says he wants to have a word with him and there's a possible new business venture, Eduard the fucker mopes around like a dog waiting for a bone.

Lars notices me first and cuts off his one-sided glare to-wards Eduard. The latter is nose-deep in his English scones and bacon.

Lars has never hidden the fact that he doesn't like Eduard, but since he never actually confirmed what happened that night, he couldn't be Dad's informant. Not to mention the fact that I would've fucking murdered him if he'd spilt my secret to Dad without my knowledge.

He already has fewer brownie points for hiding Mum's sickness.

Eduard lifts his head from his plate and maintains eye con-tact. Soon enough, a glint shines in his bland green eyes and his giddiness comes out to play.

He's always acted that way around me, as if I'm a puppy he lost and he wants it back at any price.

For a second, there's this urge to grab the kitchen knife and jam it straight into his eyes and poke them the fuck out.

Or his intestine.

This fucker didn't only ruin my life, he also destroyed Teal's. I might have been ready to forget about me for my parents' sakes, but Teal is another story altogether.

Teal will be the reason for his fucking demise.

"Morning, dear nephew—"

I jam my fist straight into his nose. He shrieks and tumbles from the chair, causing the plate to clatter on the counter.

Before he can get his footing back, I punch him again. He wails, clutching his bleeding nose. "What the fuck is wrong with you—"

I shut him up with another fist to his face. "That's for me." *Punch.* "For every fucking time I felt disgusting in my own skin." *Punch.* "For betraying my parents' trust." *Punch.* "For all the times I had those nightmares and thought the world was an empty hole like that night."

He's on the ground by the time I'm finished with him. He splutters on his own blood, and it drips from his nose and mouth, mixing with his spit and pooling on the marble ground. "R-Ronan…" He chokes on his words. "It was a long time ago. I haven't done it since then. I-I promise."

"How about the little girl in Birmingham?" My voice is cold, so cold I sound almost like Dad. "Remember her?"

"W-What?" Eduard is on all fours like the fucking animal he is, so when he stares up at me with confused eyes and blood marring his features, I almost believe he doesn't remember.

I almost believe he didn't do it.

But the thing about Eduard is, he's a fucking liar. He's perfected it so well, going unnoticed in a crowd. He's the monster you never see until he's squeezing you between his claws, ready to rip you apart.

It could be because I'd already seen his monster image, but Eduard hasn't fooled me since that night.

There's this sick spark in his eyes as if he's living the

violation all over again, enjoying it, finding gratification in the memory.

And for that reason alone, I'm so close to jamming a knife in his fucking heart—that is, if he had one.

"Birmingham, Eduard. Fucking Birmingham." I kick his stomach, making him topple over. When he tries to get up, I kick him again until a crunch of bones echoes in the air.

He wails, "Lars, you fucking idiot, stop him."

In a second, Lars appears by my side, and I'm ready to punch him too if he so much as tries to get in my way.

Lars, however, has his neutral, snobby expression on as he gives me a napkin. "You got filthy blood on your hands, young lord."

"L-Lars!" Eduard shrieks then it ends on an *oomph* when I kick him in the ribs.

"This was long overdue." Lars steps aside. "I'm here if you need any assistance."

"O-Okay, okay! Stop!" Eduard crawls away from me, hiding behind a chair like a small kid with issues. "The only ones I touched in Birmingham were fucking whores. They didn't matter."

"Whores?" I repeat. "In what universe are children considered *whores?*"

"Their mother was selling them. Besides, I didn't have intercourse or force that kid to touch me like with the others. She had it easy—why the fuck are you bitching about it? I didn't kidnap and rape her." He scoffs. "I'm a proper gentleman."

I lift the chair and bring it down on his head, making it splinter into pieces. He falls limp on the ground, blood oozing from a wound in his nape.

I'm breathing so harshly I can't even make out what I've done.

Is he dead?

Did I kill him?

The moment he spoke about her like that, I couldn't stop myself. There was an urge and then there was only one course of action.

Lars kneels beside him, checking his neck with his white gloves. "He just passed out. His pulse is steady."

My jaw clenches, and for a moment, I have the urge to finish him off once and for all, but before I can do that, Teal needs to know the truth.

She has the wrong brother. Dad was never a criminal, even if he housed one.

I call her, but she doesn't pick up. *Not again. Fuck.*

I curse under my breath, but then my phone vibrates.

Knox.

I've never answered so quickly in my life. "Do you know where Teal went?"

"No." He sounds agitated. "But she took my car and left me this fucking note saying she loves me and she's sorry. Teal doesn't say that, mate. Besides, Agnus just told me he gave her some paralysing drug."

That fucker.

"She was acting weird last night," he continues. "I shouldn't have left her alone."

"Okay, okay, we'll find her." I pace the length of the kitchen. "Any ideas where she could be?"

"No, but I have a GPS tracker on my car, or rather Dad does so he can locate me whenever he wants. I'll send you the signal—it's closer to you."

Thank God.

"What do you plan to do with him? His blood is messing up my kitchen," Lars asks after I hang up on Knox. He's glaring down at Eduard as if he's mentally sharpening the best knife in his collection so he can drive it into his chest.

"Do you have a rope?" I ask.

He smiles. "Of course, sir."

I hope I'm not too late.

Don't do it, Teal. Don't make this mistake.

THIRTY-FOUR

Teal

My fingers hover on the engine's button.

I can't.

No, I can.

This is what I've lived all my life for. This is my mission in life, the reason I exist.

The shadow of the girl on my shoulder is begging me to go on, to step harder on the accelerator. I need to go, I need to—

"Char...lotte... Ronan..." Edric mumbles from beside me. His foot kicks forward but soon falls down.

"Shut up." I release the steering wheel and grasp the needle. "You don't get to play the victim game with me. You don't get to use Charlotte or Ronan."

He's staring at me, but there's no fear or franticness in his eyes as I expected. He's not even pretending to have any acceptance. If anything, he appears sad, mortified, even.

"...w-write s-something to h-her..."

"Why would you get to say your goodbyes? Knox and I didn't. We couldn't. We had to run away so you would never come near me again."

"N-No...not me..."

"You won't even admit to it?" My voice rises. "The curtains have fallen, Edric. There's no one to save you."

Or me.

I've already picked my path. I don't get to change my mind.

A banging sounds on the door and I startle. *Shit.* No one is supposed to come this far out.

I hit the ignition and spring into action.

"Teal!" Ronan's voice comes through the window, muffled but strong.

My shoulder blades snap together.

What is he doing here? How did he find me? He's not supposed to find me.

Don't look at him.

Don't you dare look at him.

I slowly close my eyes. If I look at him, I won't be able to go through with this.

If I look at him, I'll be tempted to abandon everything and run into his arms, but that will only destroy me in the long run.

"Teal!" He bangs on the window. "Open up."

I don't.

I won't.

"*Ma belle*...please look at me." His voice softens, and something inside me breaks. It breaks at his nickname for me and the way he's calling me his beauty.

Tears stream down my cheeks. I couldn't stop them even if I wanted to. I held them hostage for so long, and now they're breaking out.

I hit the button, and the lowering sound of the window echoes in the silence of the morning. However, I don't look at him. I feel like if I do, I'll break down in sobs, and I can't have that.

"Teal," Ronan coaxes. "Can you shut off the engine?"

"No." My voice trembles around the word.

"Hey...I know the amount of pain you're in. I won't pretend I understand it all, but I understand some. However, you're making a huge mistake, Teal. It's not my father."

This time I do look at him, my veins nearly popping out of my neck with tension.

How dare he say it's a mistake?

Just because it's his father doesn't mean he didn't do it.

I regret lifting my head immediately. Ronan is holding up a half-conscious Eduard, his face nearly unrecognisable. Blood drips down his temples, his chin, and his ugly red suit.

"It was this fucker." Ronan's jaw clenches. "He's the only paedophile in our family."

My jaw drops open as Ronan tells me the story of how his uncle used to go to Birmingham and how Charlotte was sick at the time so Edric never left her side, not even for a minute.

I can't concentrate. For a second too long, I'm just staring ahead as the pieces fall together.

That's why Eduard seemed familiar when he was talking to Ronan in his room that day…the tenor of his voice, his back. I gasp as the rest of Ronan's words register.

The only paedophile in our family.

He's the man who molested Ronan, isn't he?

Why had I thought the secret was that Eduard was Ronan's biological father? He couldn't be; the similarities between Edric and Ronan are undeniable. I was only trying any method possible to stop relating the source of my pain to the source of my happiness.

My gaze bounces between Eduard and Edric, whose eyes are rimmed with tears. He figured it out, too.

I kill the engine. My own eyes won't stop fucking leaking, and I don't have the will to wipe the tears away.

"E-Edric…" Eduard begs. "Stop your son's madness."

My skin prickles with all the emotions I've been directing at the wrong person.

This arsehole has been hiding in plain sight all this time. I've been plotting Edric's demise when he didn't do a thing.

God, what have I done?

"I-I'm g-going to k-kill you, Eduard," Edric manages to get out past a clenched jaw.

His brother's face pales at that. The realisation of what he's done sets in. He knows, he just knows his fate at Edric's hands will be worse than anything else that could be done to him.

"Edric…you believe this nonsense?" Eduard's voice shakes. It literally shakes.

"Kill. You," Edric mutters.

"I was abused too," Eduard pleads, that tremor still there. "I-I…my first stepfather used to do things to me, Edric. Your father saved me. You think I want to be this way? You think I like it?"

"But you acted on it." Ronan shakes him as if he's a sack of potatoes. "Does being traumatised give you the right to traumatise others?"

"I'll make you regret the day you were born." Edric's voice is clearer now, the drug's effect barely noticeable. "I'll shun you, break you until you choose to put a bullet in your head."

"Edric…" Eduard's voice catches. "You can't do that. I'm your only brother."

"I have no brother."

That sets Eduard off.

His features contort, and with the blood, it looks as if someone smeared it all over his face and he's now transforming into a monster.

Or rather, he's revealing the monster that's been inside him all along.

"If you want someone to blame, blame your pretty little child." His gaze slides to Ronan and he grins. "You were the forbidden fruit I could never have because of that fucking Lars, so do you know what I did, my dear nephew?"

"Shut up," Ronan commands while gritting his teeth.

"No, it's truth time, so let's do it." He laughs, showing his bloodied mouth. "I've fantasised about your entire body, about your little hands and small penis. I jerked off to your picture more times than I could count, my lovely little nephew. So when I couldn't have you, I found other little hands who resembled yours, and I made sure I could mark their skin. They didn't bite and hit like you, so I did it for them. They cried, though— except for this one." He motions at me but never takes his attention off Ronan. "I remember her—of course I do. She was one of the quiet ones, the ones who didn't speak a word. I didn't tarnish you, my little boy. Aren't I a good uncle?"

"You fucking—"

Eduard cuts Ronan off. "If you want to blame someone, blame yourself. You're the reason for all their trauma. If you had let me touch you, I wouldn't have ruined other children. You're to blame Ronan—only you. When you're holding your beautiful fiancée, I want you to remember I came all over her cunt because I couldn't have you."

Ronan growls and drags Eduard to the cliff. I'm opening the door and running after him before I even realise it.

He holds his uncle by the collar on the edge. "Say goodbye, Eduard."

"You're going to kill me and then what?" Eduard laughs like an insane man out of a psych ward. "Can you live with the fact that you're behind all those children's misery?"

"Shut the fuck up," Ronan roars.

"It's you, my little nephew. It's all because of you."

"It's not." My voice is thick with emotions as I stop a small distance away, afraid of triggering Ronan if I get closer. "It's not you, Ronan. It's him. You're not responsible for his choices and his actions. You're the victim, he's the assailant."

Ronan breathes harshly, his chest rising and falling so fast I'm afraid something will happen to him.

"It's not you," I repeat, inching towards him.

My arm finds his and he lets me touch him. He doesn't flinch or shove me away.

A warmth expands in my chest as I slowly stand beside him, my heart beating loud and fast.

Ronan's fingers start to uncurl from around Eduard's, and I release a slow breath. It's not that I'm worried about that bastard; I just won't allow Ronan to become a murderer because of him.

I'm good with becoming one, but Ronan can't. He's prim and proper and…light. He's my light, and I won't let any darkness wrench him away from me.

The door of the car opens, and Edric slowly pulls himself out.

The slight disturbance of the scene distracts me for a second too long.

It's enough for everything to end.

It's enough for my world to be flipped upside down.

"You know what? If I can't have you, why should anyone?" Eduard throws his tied hands around Ronan's neck from behind. "Till death do us part, my little nephew."

And then he pulls Ronan with him over the cliff.

THIRTY-FIVE

Edric

Being born with a title brings responsibilities.

I was raised to believe in two things. One, the Astor name. Two, not showing emotions in order to uphold the Astor name.

My life has been ruled by strict traditions and expectations. My father was considered a disgrace for marrying a commoner after my mother died.

I thought he was brave.

But I knew I wouldn't be forgiven such a mistake. Two generations in row would kill the respect we'd gathered for years.

That's why I married into status. I was lucky enough that the woman I wed wasn't the woman my father originally had planned for me.

What Charlotte doesn't know is, I saw her first at one of Father's banquets. She was this cheerful soul who made me feel something other than the constant pressure of duty.

I'm the one who put it in Father's head to arrange a marriage with her father, but since she had an elder sister, I was to marry her. I found a solution, a way around that once I noticed Céline's abnormal interest in her father's car. I approached her with a smile and encouraged her to follow her heart.

I didn't have any doubt of failure, because Céline was

adventurous, romantic, and very much in love. I only took that step knowing full well she'd agree. She did just that and eloped.

As a result of my carefully laid-out plan, I ended up with Charlotte.

At first, she hated me and thought I was too proud and arrogant—her words, not mine—and she didn't quit reminding me of that fact. However, I didn't give up, and eventually, my beautiful wife took the time to pause her judgmental opinions and stopped to see me. When she did, I finally had her.

Charlotte is the reason for my happiness. She's the one person who's able to make me think less about duty and more about life.

She is life.

Or rather, the centre of mine.

When the doctor said her health might not allow her to birth any children, I went against my family's rules about procreation and told her I didn't need them. Her health and life were more important to me than any foolish need to keep the Astor name alive.

When she became pregnant, she begged me to keep the baby. She said she wanted to give us both a miracle.

And she did. That's how Ronan came to life.

Our first meeting with him was through a smile. I've never felt more proud than I did at the moment when I met my beautiful boy.

He and Charlotte are my life—even though I'm admittedly bad at showing it. I leaned on Charlotte's emotive nature to get to him. I'm too stiff while she's too out there, so her emotions reached him better.

However, I used to feel Ronan and I were connected, even though I didn't talk much. He'd snuggle up to me and come tell me about all the dragons he killed in his video games. He'd ask me for things and complain that Lars was making him drink milk.

Then he stopped.

Just like that, my son stopped coming to me. He stopped talking to me about his dragons and his drinks and his friends.

He never stopped with Charlotte, though. I chalked that up to the fact that he always felt closer to her, and while it stung, I left him to his own devices.

Charlotte's health took up all my time and attention, and I neglected Ronan because of it. I thought he was a grown-up and that he preferred Lars anyway. After all, Ronan talked to him more than he ever talked to me.

My wife told me he respected me as a father and I could get close to him if I tried, but I brushed her off. Perhaps I was scared he'd close himself off to me like I'd closed myself off to Father when he brought me a stepmother and a stepbrother only a year after my mother's death.

I know how it feels to have a strained relationship with your father, and I didn't want to repeat it with my son.

Before I knew it, Ronan was as tall as me and also as proud as me. He never divulged his true feelings and deflected all my questions.

After I heard Teal in the car, everything else fell into place. I recalled how Ronan wouldn't join me for lunches when Eduard was around, but he'd stay if Charlotte was there. He was subtle about it, making sure no one noticed his discomfort. He laughed and joked as usual, but now I know he was proving he was okay.

He has been doing that since he was a boy. My son has been pretending he was fine since he was eight.

That was around the time he stopped coming to me.

I always thought the parties and the weed were to prove something, but I presumed it was his way to get out of the pressure. I never thought it was because I'd opened my house and my business to my son's rapist.

Not only my son's, but many other children's.

Eduard has always been a bit irresponsible, but he worked hard when I told him to. He looked up to me, and he did as I ordered. He always had women hanging off his arm, but I should've known from the way he showed them off as prizes that they could be camouflage.

Eduard and Ronan are similar in hiding, in pretending, but I of all people shouldn't have missed it.

I can blame it on my preoccupation with Charlotte's illness, but that doesn't, under any circumstances, forgive the fact that I let my son down.

He needed his father, and I didn't give him one.

He needed Eduard away, and I brought him back in.

He needed someone to listen, and I wasn't there.

If Charlotte finds out about this, she'll sink so low in depression and there will be no saving her.

Like me, she'll think she let her miracle down. She'll blame herself for not seeing it sooner and will think she's a horrible mother. She's not. She was just sick. She's sacrificing what's possibly her last chance at treatment to be with Ronan because, as she told me, she can't die without giving him the happiest memories.

Charlotte won't know. I'll be the one to fix it.

I'll fix everything.

Starting with the mess Eduard left behind.

Maybe then, my miracle will forgive me.

THIRTY-SIX

Teal

I don't remember how long I sit in the hospital chair, but it's long enough that I cry.

It's long enough that I don't stop crying.

Knox caught up to us in the forest and held me all the way here, but I didn't stop crying, not even after Dad, Agnus, and Elsa followed.

I cry like a baby. I cry like I'm just learning what it means to cry.

We've been sitting here for what seems like an eternity. The waiting time goes on and on like doom brewing in the distance.

The guys follow. Aiden, Xander, and Cole are standing near the corner, their heads bowed. They haven't said a word to each other, as if afraid that will break whatever trance has fallen over the waiting area.

Lars comes by, too, his brows furrowed and his snobbish expression gone. It's worry, I realise. He's worried.

I don't know why that makes me sob harder. If Lars, who hardly shows any emotions, recognises how bad it is, this is turning awful.

"It's going to be okay, T." Knox hugs me to his side. "Come on, sis, stop crying."

"I can't." I hiccough.

My head hurts from the unrelenting tears. The moment I get a small bit of relief, I think of Ronan and a new wave hits me.

It's as simple as that.

I don't think of Eduard or what I did to Edric or about myself, my life, or any of those things.

I only think about him.

"W-What if I lose him, Knox?" I speak through my tears. "What was I thinking? What did I do?"

"Hey, that fucker lessened his fall, okay?" Knox says. "Ronan was breathing when the medics got him out. He's going to be okay."

"But what if he isn't? What if…what if…" God, I can't even say the words. I don't want to think about them, but they're the only things engraved in my head.

The shadow on my shoulder is no longer there. The little girl disappeared the moment Eduard fell off that cliff, but there are other things here on her behalf. Things like gloomy thoughts and black smoke.

"Teal?" Edric's voice drifts from the corner. "Come in. You can see him."

I jerk up to a standing position, my heart beating in and out of sync in my chest. I jog to the room then stop in front of Ronan's father, gulping my salty tears. "E-Edric, I'm so sorry for…"

"No worries." He smiles. "If anything, I'm the one who should be sorry towards you. I should've seen it sooner."

I shake my head, not having words to say.

"We'll talk later." He motions at the room. "Go in."

I push the door open and tiptoe inside as if I'm going through a crime scene—and I might as well be.

The image of when Eduard pulled Ronan with him keeps flashing before my eyes. I reached a hand out for him, but all I could catch was thin air.

At that moment, time stopped and I wished I could turn it back and not do what I'd done. I wished I had investigated Edric's actions before I plotted his demise.

But most of all, I wished I had chosen Ronan. I wished I'd taken him away and started anew with him.

The first thing that greets me in the room is the strong light. Soon after, it's the bruises on Ronan's half-naked chest and the cast wrapped around his arm.

His beautiful face has some blue bruises. The sight of him makes me hiccough as I approach him with unsteady steps. I couldn't stop the flow of tears even if I tried.

"Why do you look beautiful even when you cry, *belle?*" he teases in a husky voice.

I drop beside him on the bed, sniffling and trying to get my feelings in check. I fail miserably and end up blabbering. "I'm sorry. I'm so sorry, I didn't mean to hurt your father or make you go through this. I was selfish and you got hurt and I…I…"

"Hey." He cradles my hand in his good one. "It's not your fault, Teal. Besides, I'll be as good as new tomorrow. I'll only lose use of my left hand for a few weeks, so you kind of have to do everything for me."

"Anything." I nod frantically.

He grins. "*Anything?*"

I nod again.

His grin falls, but he strokes the back of my hand. "Let's start with you not leaving my side ever again."

"You…" I swallow the lump in my throat. "You still want me?"

"Still? Did I ever stop?" He brings my hand to his mouth and brushes his dry lips against the skin. "I'll never stop wanting you, *belle*. You're made for me."

"You're made for me too." I wrap my arms around his neck, my tears wetting his skin. "I love you, Ronan. I love you as I've never loved anyone before."

He lowers his voice. "Even after what Eduard the fucker said?"

I pull back to stare at him. "I told you, his words don't matter, okay? You do."

His sensual lips move in a heart-breaking smile. "I do?"

"Of course."

"Don't you dare leave me, Teal, or I'll pull an Astor move on you."

"An Astor move?"

"Yeah, it involves chasing you to the end of the world, and that's kind of not fun." He grins. "For you, not me."

"Now I'm intrigued."

"Why am I not surprised?" He tugs me to him and plants a soft kiss on my nose. "I love you, Teal. Now and always."

Now and always.

EPILOGUE 1

Teal

One year later

There's something about seeing the world through different lenses.

Before, it was blurry. Now, there's sense to it, a clarity I wasn't able to feel before.

There's something called happiness, and there's something called joy.

For my whole life, I never actually understood what happiness meant and why people would crave to be happy. It felt like a high that would just eventually wear off.

That is, until Ronan became a constant in my life. He's happiness incarnate.

He's a high that will never wear off.

After we graduated, we spent the summer travelling. Just that, travelling, from one country to another and from one city to the next.

We were free souls discovering the world and people and cultures. He called me a nerd whenever I asked about museums, and I called him a gigolo whenever he wanted to go to the trendiest bar.

Ronan will be Ronan no matter what happens. Fun and

parties are in his soul. Whenever anyone needs a party thrown, he'll be at the front of the line planning his next 'epic' event. The last was Aiden and Elsa's marriage. He was so extra in his speech, acting salty because he wasn't the best man.

Since then, he's been bribing Xander to be chosen as the best man, threatening to delete them all from his chat.

He won't.

What he doesn't tell them is that the horsemen saved him from his head several times in the past. They weren't there just for the parties, like most other people; they were there for him, and Ronan would never forget that.

To say we're both over Eduard would be a lie. Sometimes, it feels as if he's still the shadow looming over our lives, even after his death.

Ronan and I still have the nightmares, but they're sparse and far in between. We go to joint therapy now, and it's the best therapy I've had in my life.

When it gets to be too much, I just say it. However, it usually doesn't, because I know I have my family, and most of all, I have *him*.

Ronan.

The moment he strokes my hair off my face or kisses me, I usually climb on his body and demand he fucks me.

Of course, he obliges, and he makes it dreamier every time, rougher, harder. Ronan has never treated me as if I'm a delicate flower, and I love him the most for it. Even when he fucks me slow, it's to make me feel him—feel us—not because he's afraid of touching me.

Ronan and I are never afraid of touching each other. If anything, it's what brings us closer and makes us calmer.

We started with a touch. The first time he did it in RES's library, I kind of fell under his spell and he fell under mine.

Today, I have a surprise for him.

We came to his parents' house for dinner. Charlotte is

finally out of the danger zone. Those couple of months after Eduard's death were complete hell.

Edric had to make his brother's death seem like an accident, and Charlotte's illness was taking its toll on him and Ronan. I held my fiancé's hand through it all until the results came out and the doctor said the last surgery had been a success.

She had to do a lot of recovery therapy, and Edric didn't leave her side through it all. Ronan didn't either.

One of my favourite memories about that time was when Edric asked Ronan for forgiveness for not seeing Eduard's actions, and Ronan said he was sorry he hadn't seen his mum's illness.

Edric and Ronan grew so close during Charlotte's recovery journey. I think seeing them together by her side helped her mental state more than any doctor would tell them.

Ronan and I were supposed to leave after dinner, but he said he needed to grab something from his room.

He's been taking a long time, so I might as well ask him now.

"Lars." I grin when I see him coming out of Ronan's room. "How do I look?"

I pull on my white T-shirt, on which is written 'Belle'.

I'm also wearing a black tulle skirt, a leather jacket, and boots—comfy, as usual.

"That's the second time you've asked me that question tonight, Miss Teal."

"Stop being such a snob, and it's only Teal," I tease.

Lars and I have grown close over time. He wouldn't admit it, but he always has a dark chocolate bar ready for me then he whines about how I keep stealing them.

"You look beautiful." He lifts his chin. "And stop eating the chocolate no one offers you."

I make a face as he strides down the hall then I go into the room.

Okay, this is it.

It's not like it needs to be traditional or something—not that I care about that anyway.

"Hey, Ronan, when are we getting married…?"

I trail off when I find him in the middle of removing his trousers in front of a bed filled with baskets of dark chocolate.

"Fuck, *belle*, you weren't supposed to come in yet."

I grin. "Don't stop on my account."

His hands remain on his belt. "Lars said dark chocolate is the best bribe I could use with you."

"Lars wasn't wrong."

"Wait." His hand leaves his belt, and I nearly reach over to put it back.

Ronan is so beautiful, sometimes I stay up just to stare at him.

It's not only his physical beauty, though; it's also his soul that speaks to me and wrenches me out of my own soul.

He's the calm after the storm.

He's the light after the darkness.

He's everything.

"Go back." He narrows his eyes. "Did I hear something about marriage?"

"Yeah. I thought…you know…we'd make things official?" Otherwise I'll start punching every girl who looks at him at uni.

He still attracts attention like a magnet. I thought that would be over after RES, but nope, his popularity knows no limits. I need to stake my claim before anyone tries to take him away.

It's not that I'm threatened or anything, but I'm as greedy about Ronan as he is about me. That will probably never change.

People say we're too young to get married, but it's not about age for me. I've decided Ronan is the only human being

I'll spend the rest of my life with. It's a cemented fact. So why delay it?

"Hey." He appears offended. "I was planning a night out to ask you. This is not fair."

"You wanted to ask me?"

"I wanted to marry you before that fucker Aiden married Elsa, but you always say all the grandiose stuff is stupid, so I figured I'd wait."

My heart skips a beat as I stand on my tiptoes, wrap my arms around his neck, and seal a kiss to his cheek. "It isn't stupid when you're involved, Ronan."

His grin widens. "One to nil, Xander."

I laugh. "So does this mean you'll marry me?"

"Of course I'm marrying you, and you didn't ask first—I did."

"We'll agree to disagree, your lordship," I tease. "What did you have in mind with the chocolate?"

"A few things." His eyes shine with mischief.

"Like what?"

"Like this." His lips meet mine, and then we're falling on the bed.

If this is my life going forward, I'm so ready for it.

EPILOGUE 2

Ronan

Five years later

"**W**hat did I say about interrupting me, *belle?*" I grunt in her ear as I flatten her against the table.

"I don't know…" she moans, her legs opening wide.

She sauntered into my office and demanded I fuck her. She does that a lot, not that I'm complaining.

The best thing about being bosses in both our families' companies is the fact that we get to mix business with pleasure.

"You don't know?" I pound into her hard as she releases those deep-throated moans.

Her fingers grip the edge of the table as if it's a lifeline. I don't stop or slow down. I fuck her hard and fast and out of control, just like we both like it.

"Are you going to take it out on me later?" she whimpers.

Holding her by the hip, I push her short hair aside, baring her nape, and I lean over to whisper in her ear. "You bet, *belle.*"

She comes then.

My wife is a glutton for punishment and for promises of it. Knowing tonight will be even harder than right now makes her hotter and wetter and even more compliant.

This is only her appetiser. I power into her for a few more seconds before I follow right after.

We're both breathing heavily as I fall over her, my clothes covering her sorry excuse for a blouse.

She blindly reaches a hand up and digs her fingers into my hair, twisting her head so her lips can meet mine. There's nothing I love in the world more than kissing this woman and imprinting myself on her.

Since I first met Teal, she's always gotten under my skin. It started with irritation then hate, and then it turned into the most powerful feeling I could have for another human being.

She understands me even before I say anything. She holds me without me having to ask for it.

Teal has always struggled with feelings, but not with me—never with me. She was strong then, but now she's invincible.

Our childhoods will always be a part of who we are, but we're over that. We turned the page and started our own tale.

We work and travel. We have family dinners with Ethan and Knox and that fucker Agnus, who never ceases to remind me that he was Teal's type first.

My wife has told me I'm her only type now. Next time, I'm making her say it in front of that arsehole.

Mum and Dad are travelling—for tourism, not medical treatment—and they usually drag a grumpy Lars with them. He never fails to remind them that every hotel has awful service.

Teal and I also go to friends' gatherings, and I still throw parties Aiden usually doesn't appear at because he takes Elsa somewhere no one knows about. Fuck him, really. Xan and Cole do, and since we all work together in one way or another, we never actually broke apart after RES.

Teal straightens and pulls up her underwear while I button my trousers.

"I'll let you get back to it, *your lordship*." She fixes my tie, staring at me with that playful lust in her dark eyes. She then reaches over and wipes my lower lip with her thumb. "Lipstick."

"You know what, wife?" My voice is husky.

"What, husband?" She bites her lower lip.

"Fuck work. I prefer you." I push her against the edge of the table and she gasps, and when I lift her, her legs wrap around my waist in a vice-like hold.

"Have I mentioned today how much I love you, Ronan?"

"I must've forgotten."

"I love you," she whispers in my ear.

"Not more than I love you, *ma belle.*"

THE END

WHAT'S NEXT?

Thank you so much for reading *Vicious Prince*! If you liked it,
please leave a review.
Your support means the world to me.

If you're thirsty for more discussions with other readers of the
series, you can join Rina's Spoilers Room at
www.facebook.com/groups/RinaSpoilers

Next up is Cole's book, *Ruthless Empire*

ALSO BY RINA KENT

For more books by the author and a reading order, please visit:
www.rinakent.com/books

ABOUT THE AUTHOR

Rina Kent is a *USA Today*, international, and #1 Amazon bestselling author of everything enemies to lovers romance.

She's known to write unapologetic anti-heroes and villains because she often fell in love with men no one roots for. Her books are sprinkled with a touch of darkness, a pinch of angst, and an unhealthy dose of intensity.

She spends her private days in London laughing like an evil mastermind about adding mayhem to her expanding universe. When she's not writing, Rina travels, hikes, and spoils cats in a pure Cat Lady fashion.

Find Rina Below:
Website: www.rinakent.com

Neswsletter: www.subscribepage.com/rinakent

BookBub: www.bookbub.com/profile/rina-kent

Amazon: www.amazon.com/Rina-Kent/e/B07MM54G22

Goodreads: www.goodreads.com/author/show/18697906.
Rina_Kent

Instagram: www.instagram.com/author_rina

Facebook: www.facebook.com/rinaakent

Reader Group: www.facebook.com/groups/rinakent.club

Pinterest: www.pinterest.co.uk/AuthorRina/boards

Tiktok: www.tiktok.com/@rina.kent

Twitter: twitter.com/AuthorRina